PENGUIN BOOKS

THE SHOOTING PARTY

Isabel Colegate's other novels are *The Blackmailer* (1958),
A Man of Power (1960), *The Great Occasion* (1962), *Statues
in a Garden* (1964; Penguin, 1983), the Orlando trilogy
comprising *Orlando King* (1968), *Orlando at the Brazen
Threshold* (1971), *Agatha* (1973), *News from the City of the
Sun* (1979) and *A Glimpse of Sion's Glory* (1985). She is
married with three children and lives near Bath. For *The
Shooting Party* she received the W. H. Smith Annual
Literary Award for 1981.

THE SHOOTING PARTY

ISABEL COLEGATE

Penguin Books

PENGUIN BOOKS

Published by the Penguin Group
27 Wrights Lane, London W8 5TZ, England
Viking Penguin Inc., 40 West 23rd Street, New York, New York 10010, USA
Penguin Books Australia Ltd, Ringwood, Victoria, Australia
Penguin Books Canada Ltd, 2801 John Street, Markham, Ontario, Canada L3R 1B4
Penguin Books (NZ) Ltd, 182–190 Wairau Road, Auckland 10, New Zealand

Penguin Books Ltd, Registered Offices: Harmondsworth, Middlesex, England

First published by Hamish Hamilton 1980
Published in Penguin Books 1982
Reprinted 1982, 1985 (four times), 1986, 1987, 1988

Printed and bound in Great Britain by
Cox & Wyman Ltd, Reading

IT CAUSED a mild scandal at the time, but in most people's memories it was quite outshone by what succeeded it. You could see it as a drama all played out in a room lit by gas lamps; perhaps with flickering sidelights thrown by a log fire burning brightly at one side of the room, a big Edwardian drawing-room, full of furniture, tables crowded with knick-knacks and framed photographs, people sitting or standing in groups, conversing; and then a fierce electric light thrown back from a room beyond, the next room, into which no one has yet ventured, and this fierce retrospective light through the doorway makes the lamplit room seem shadowy, the flickering flames in the grate pallid, the circles of yellow light round the lamps opaque (a kind of tarnished gold) and the people, well, discernibly people, but people from a long time ago, our parents and grandparents made to seem like beings from a much remoter past, Charlemagne and his knights or the seven sleepers half roused from their thousand year sleep.

It was an error of judgment which resulted in a death. It took place in the autumn before the outbreak of what used to be known as the Great War.

*

The countryside of Oxfordshire includes some areas of flat meadowland, watered by slow winding rivers and abundantly wooded. A broad band of clay soil stretches from the Gloucestershire border near Lechlade across Oxfordshire as far as the Buckinghamshire border beyond Bicester. The River Thames flows eastward through this clay country and a few miles before it reaches Oxford, where it turns south, it runs for some distance

1

beside a belt of mixed woodland where it forms the boundary of Nettleby Park, an estate which belonged in 1913 to Sir Randolph Nettleby, Baronet, a country gentleman.

*

'Rooks and Wood Pigeons. I forget unless I've been away what a constant background murmur they keep up – that and the sound of horses' hooves on the gravel or in the stableyard, the smell of damp leaves and woodsmoke, the sound of bees. The house is full of insects coming in to lay their eggs or die or both; you see them on sunny days in front of all the windows on the south side of the house, bees and a few wasps and hundreds of tiny fruit flies. The servants are always opening and shutting windows and flapping at them with dusters. There are butterflies too, Red Admirals and Peacocks, perched on the window frames; and for that matter harvest mice coming in for the winter. "With a house full of people," Minnie says, "it is too much." I sometimes wish the mice and the flies would keep the people away. Minnie likes a house full, especially after a fortnight in Marienbad, which may or may not improve her liver but invariably increases her appetite for society. If they must come at least they can say they get some decent shooting. If I can do nothing else I can play the part of head gamekeeper.'

'You are always writing in that big black notebook, Grandpapa.'

'It's my Game Book. Well, part of it is my Game Book. Part of it is my thoughts. It's not a bad idea to get in the habit of writing down one's thoughts. It saves one having to bother anyone else with them.'

'I hate writing.'

'That is because you are not very good at it. Very few people like doing what they are not very good at.'

'I am very good at drawing.'

'Here is a piece of paper and a pencil. You can draw me a nice picture of a hare while I finish making up the records for the day.'

The child bent her head obediently over the paper and Sir Randolph turned to the other end of the notebook. 'Pheasants 612,' he wrote, 'Hares 12, Rabbits 22, Woodcock 2... Lord Hartlip, Mr Ormston, Mr Harry Stamp ("Stupid ass," he muttered) Count Rakassyi'. . . .

Rogers was there, the butler.

'Tea is in the drawing room, Sir Randolph.'

'Already? All down already are they? People seem to change their clothes quicker every day – do you suppose they've given up washing, Violet? What d'you think about that?'

'I believe Nanny would like Miss Violet in the nursery.'

'Off you go then. Let's see the picture first. Not got very far, has it? Only one line.'

'It's a very long line.'

'You need more than one line to make a hare.'

'My hairs are only one line.' She chose one carefully and pulled it out. 'Look.'

*

The park itself was very large in those days, nearly a thousand acres (about an eighth of the whole estate), surrounded by a wood and protected on the outerside by a wall, except where the river formed the boundary. The depth of the belt of trees varied; there were also small woods and clumps of trees within the park, some predominately of oak and ilex, others with Scots firs growing among the deciduous trees. Most of this planting had been done about a century before by Sir Randolph's grandfather, an early enthusiast for the then much less sophisticated sport of shooting game.

Also within the confines of the park was the Home Farm, which included some arable fields, and immediately outside the walls on two sides were fields of corn, turnips and clover. In the autumn the pheasants reared in the spring and early summer by Glass the gamekeeper fed on the stubble, a few partridges alongside them.

*

Darkness was falling by the time Glass reached his cottage, having seen to the temporary storage of the game which would later be distributed among the tenantry or Sir Randolph's local friends. Glass's wife had died five years ago and he lived alone with his only son, Dan.

He unhooked a piece of sacking from outside the back door

3

and dried the legs and underparts of his two retrievers. The bitch pushed herself forward to be dried first, groaning gently to show her appreciation as he rubbed her chest and stomach, and waving her feathery tail as she tried to lick his face. The less demonstrative Sam was easier to deal with. Glass led the way to their kennel, a brick building on the other side of the yard with iron railings in front of it and room for many more dogs than just Sam and Bess. He checked that Dan had put out their food bowls and given them a fresh supply of water, then locked their gate and went back to the cottage, pausing to run his muddy boots under the outside tap before going in.

Dan was standing in front of the kitchen stove in his stock-inged feet, eating a bun. With him was John Page's daughter Flo, wearing a woollen cloak and holding a basket.

'Mum said to tell you Dad's back is bad again. He'll not be able to beat for you tomorrow.'

'Darn it. That back of his. Can't Doctor West do anything for it? Is he off work too, then? Not much use in a sawmill with a bad back, I suppose. What's this then?'

'Mum sent them. Lardy cakes.'

'That's very nice. How many's Dan eaten then? Be a good girl, look in on Tom Harker on your way home and tell him I need him as a beater tomorrow starting at eight to beat the park clumps into Badger's Wood before the shooting starts. Will you remember that? Eight o'clock sharp, Batty Clump.'

'Tom Harker?' said Dan, shocked.

'There's no one else. I've a hundred men out tomorrow, nigh on. It's the biggest day.'

'You said you wouldn't have Tom Harker again, not after the last time you caught him.'

'Can't be helped. I don't like it. Why should I give him a free look at where the best game's to be had? But he knows what's he doing. I need a reliable stop if John's not with us.'

'I can do that.'

'You'll be the other end of the line. Besides, what if Sir Randolph wants you to load for him again, like he did today?'

'I wish he would. But Charlie'll be all right tomorrow. He only put his foot down a rabbit hole. Where any fool could have seen it.'

'Any fool doesn't see all you see, young Dan,' said his father.

Flo laughed admiringly; then heard her own laugh and thought it sounded silly, so stopped abruptly. But it was true that Dan was the most observant person she knew; he always had been. They were the same age, fourteen.

'He only poaches for the pot,' said Glass. 'At least I hope he does.'

*

The head-keeper's cottage was some little way away from the village, on the edge of the woods. It stood back from the road, beside a gate leading into the woods. There was a semi-circle of grass in front of it, where the cart-horses which pulled the long timber-waggons could turn or wait. An oak tree stood on the green, with a stone water-trough beneath it. Flo paused there, to light her lantern. She had not lit it before leaving the cottage because she knew that Dan would never have bothered with a lantern on a night like this. There was a moon, even though at the moment it was obscured by cloud, but Dan anyway knew his way around so well he hardly needed to see; he knew where he was by smell or sound, like an animal. Flo liked the lantern for the companionship of the flickering candle rather than for the light it shed. She knew her way almost as well as Dan; each tree that grew up from the hedge was familiar to her, each gateway, ditch and patch of copse between the keeper's cottage and the nasty little place – or so she considered it – where Tom Harker lived. It was a one-storied redbrick building, of which one end was an outhouse – pigsty or stable – and the other contained two rooms where Tom Harker and his mother had lived until the old lady died, ninety at least and not a tooth in her head, two years ago; since when Tom had lived there alone, his lengthy unexplained absences less frequent than when his mother had been alive. He was a thatcher by trade and had presumably wandered in search of work, or perhaps just from love of wandering – there was usually enough work on the estate. Rumour had it that he had a wife in another village, whom he had never brought home for fear of old Mrs Harker's temper, which was known to be fearsome. Some expected that after his mother's death the wife would be seen at last, and some thought that even her nonappearance was not necessarily conclusive – maybe after all these years she'd had enough of him.

However it was, he lived there alone, with a slinking, shadowy, thin collie bitch that had never been heard to bark (a poacher's dog if ever there was one, Glass thought). In spite of his elusiveness, and the fact that he was known to do a bit of poaching, he was looked on as a respectable man, a good son to his mother and a man of his word, kind to the children who stole apples from his three prolific old trees and – had they not all heard him say so a hundred times? – never in his life the worse for drink. Which was why when Flo, seeing no light at his window, first tapped at his door, then pushed it and looked into a dark room which smelt quite strongly of, for one thing, tobacco, but more than that something that seemed to her pretty well indistinguishable from the smell which came from the big holes on the hillside above the track which led through Badger's Wood, she knew it would be no good looking for him where she might have looked for any other man who was not at home at that time of day, which was to say in the pub; his oft-repeated views on the evils of alcohol were too well known for that. She could think of nowhere else where he might be found after dark, but there was a faint glow from the fireplace in his kitchen which seemed to indicate that he was at any rate in residence, so being a conscientious girl she waited. It was not a cold night and in view of the badger smell she thought she would prefer to wait outside. She put her lantern down on the doorstep and sat beside it, pulling her cloak round her with the hood right over her head so that all she saw when she looked out was the steady flame of the candle and the corner of Tom Harker's rainwater butt.

*

Tom had watched the shooting party going home, as the afternoon ended and a faint mist began to rise from the ground. He had climbed over the park wall into the beech wood, his collie scrambling over behind him, and had waited beside one of the trees, looking over the park towards the copse where the guns traditionally took their last stand on the second day of a three day shoot. Three of them were well within his view, the others beyond the trees of the copse. He remained unobtrusive because such was his habit; but had he been seen it was not likely that anyone would have objected – a big shoot in which well-known

6

sportsmen were taking part often attracted spectators, and he was in a position where there could have been no fear of his interfering with the sport.

He heard the beaters in the wood as they came through the undergrowth, occasionally whistling or calling out, tapping the tree-trunks and frightening the blackbirds who scattered with alarm calls through the bushes. Then the pheasants began to call. One or two must have flown out on the other side where he could not see them – 'Over!' he heard 'Over on the right!' – then shots, then a few more shots, and then suddenly they all seemed to break, hundreds of pheasants it seemed, flying out over the guns (beautifully presented, as usual, Tom noted, in grudging recognition of Glass's expertise), and all the guns seemed to be firing at once. He could see his three, each with two loaders, one to receive the empty gun, one to hand it back re-loaded, while the shooter himself never moved his gaze from the oncoming birds. A few birds seemed to be getting away over the man furthest away from Tom, but the two nearest him – they were Lord Hartlip and Lionel Stephens – were shooting with a speed and accuracy from which as a fellow sportsman he was unable to withhold his admiration. A smaller bird made a sudden appearance to one side of the wood, flying very fast. An easy swing from Lord Hartlip and it fell, a woodcock to add to his score. You wouldn't see better sport anywhere in England, Tom Harker thought, finding no difficulty in accommodating that notion in his mind along with his views about the stranglehold of the rich on the life-blood of the working man. The fusillade of shots coming to an end, he heard Glass's voice calling loudly 'All out, Sir Randolph,' and watched the men who had been shooting relax, strolling towards each other, hands in their pockets or lighting cigarettes, having handed their guns to their loaders to be carried home, while the dogs, encouraged by their handlers, hurried about their work of retrieving the fallen birds, and the game cart, drawn by the old cart-horse whose job this had been for nearly twenty years, drew near to receive its final burden of the day. The beaters in their distinguishing, long cream-coloured smocks emerged from the wood. He saw Glass talking to a group of them – giving them their instructions for tomorrow probably – while Sir Randolph walked over to join them, his odd, wide-brimmed old hat marking him out from the others.

7

What a long time they took to disperse, Tom thought. Didn't they want to get home to their tea? There were even one or two ladies with them, who having joined the party for lunch had stood with the guns afterwards and, unlike the rest of the wives, daughters or whatever they might be, had stuck it out until the end, perhaps because it was such a warm afternoon. After the early morning mist, the sun had shone all day – back at the house it had been a great day for flapping dusters at the insects – and Minnie had said at lunch, 'Really the autumn colours are better than ever this year,' and Sir Randolph had said, 'You say that every year,' looking at her plump slightly flushed face (she was wearing her new tweeds and was a good deal too hot) with that rather ironical, rather penetrating look which not everyone knew betokened affection. Minnie was a foolish woman in many ways and not everyone knew that in her husband's eyes her foolishness constituted a great part of her charm.

The ladies were walking up and down in front of the rows of dead birds, nearly all of which had by now been picked up and laid beside the road where they could be counted and admired. Groups of men, those who had been shooting as well as the beaters and gamekeepers, gathered and dispersed in front of the sacrifice thus displayed. Tom, who needed to know the coast was clear before pursuing his own affairs, shifted from one foot to another, waiting for them to get a move on.

Slowly the shooting brake, drawn by two black horses, was led forward from the shelter of the copse. It was a big black equipage, funereal in aspect – indeed Sir Randolph's mother, who had died in 1898, being herself ten years younger than the century, had been carried in her coffin to the churchyard by its means – with a raised seat in front and room for six people to sit facing each other behind. The ladies climbed in. There was more delay while politenesses were exchanged about which gentlemen should accompany them. At last, a full complement of passengers being found, they moved off down the drive towards the house, whose chimneys could be seen among the surrounding ornamental trees half a mile or so away.

The game waggon was then quickly loaded, and with its iron upper structure festooned with pairs of birds, hares swinging more heavily behind, it was laboriously turned and set off in the opposite direction towards Home Farm, followed by the smaller cart which carried spare cartridges and was drawn by a stout chestnut cob whose alternative employment was to pull the milk float. These were farm horses and were not stabled at the house. They passed quite close to where Tom was standing, the sound of their heavy feet clear in the still evening, the last light of which touched the polished brass of their headplates and on their heavy collars.

The four or five remaining members of the house party were now walking quite briskly back towards the house, the loaders and dog-handlers following them and about to turn off the main drive towards the back parts of the house, the kennels and gun rooms, while the rest of the beaters and gamekeepers dispersed in the general direction of the village. Tom waited until they were nearly all out of sight, and until the gold of the late afternoon had been succeeded by the soft pinkish-grey of the early dusk before he moved. The mist was now rising much more noticeably from the ground, still low but thickening, beginning to spread a layer of damp haze which in the morning would linger on the lower ground like spilt milk, while the sky above it became the pale clear blue of another late October day. Tom moved quietly round the outskirts of the park, keeping to the trees, until the ground began to slope down towards the thick belt of woodland which bordered the river. Here, at a gate which opened onto one of the wide grassy rides which at intervals had been cut through the wood towards the river and which tomorrow should see the most spectacular of the pheasant shooting, he stopped and fumbled in the capacious pockets of his long jacket. Here, while the men who had been busy all day were going home and Glass's normally unremitting supervision of his domain would be temporarily relaxed, was the place, with the bitch's help, to net a rabbit.

*

'Is the Israelite not among us?' murmured Sir Randolph, accepting a cup of tea.

He was leaning towards his daughter-in-law Ida, and spoke for her ear alone. Minnie, some way away from him behind the silver teapot and spirit kettle, was particularly fond of Sir Reuben.

'Such a dear man,' she said of him. Indeed she often addressed him so. 'My dear man,' she would say. 'My dear man, you really shouldn't,' as another costly trinket fell into her lap. He was nothing if not generous with his millions.

'Hush,' said Ida reprovingly. 'He fell into a bog and is having a mustard bath.'

'You don't say. A bog? There aren't any bogs.'

Minnie had heard him.

'He got his feet wet,' she said gently. 'Crossing a ditch. I persuaded him to let me send Hopkins along to him with a mustard bath. You know they can be so comforting.'

'Ah, well of course if a fellow will come out shooting inadequately shod.'

'He was not inadequately shod,' said Ida firmly. 'He was shod the same as everyone else. I particularly noticed.'

Ida was fond of her father-in-law but had come to regard it as her special function when she was staying at Nettleby – which was often, because her husband was in the diplomatic corps and usually abroad and it was agreed by everyone to be important that their four children should spend a proportion of their formative years in their grandparents' house – to see that he did not, as she would have said, 'get away with it' too often. Minnie seldom remonstrated with her husband; it was a feature of their marriage that neither, in spite of behaviour on both sides which must at various times have caused each of them surprise and probably pain, had ever been heard to criticise the other. Ida was a matter-of-fact sort of person who considered that Sir Randolph's eccentricities were too much indulged by his household. She had seen to it that her own husband had none; he would be an ambassador in no time. She had a direct gaze and rather protruding teeth in a large healthy face, looked Dutch and was, in fact, half-French on her mother's side; she spoke four languages fluently. Sir Randolph liked her in spite of her occasional sternness with him. 'No beauty,' he said of her, 'but a good sort. You don't want too many people about with imagination and all that rubbish.'

Imagination and all that rubbish did seem, though, to have afflicted some of her children. He was often surprised that such prosaic parents should have produced those four. He could see the eldest grandchild now across the tea table, nineteen-year-old Cicely, flirting with the Hungarian Rakassyi while Tommy Farmer, Roland Farmer's boy who had just got into the Grenadiers and was Cicely's contemporary, looked quite out of his depth. Marcus, her fifteen-year-old brother, sitting the other side of Tommy, ate up his tea undisturbed by conversational niceties. Cicely had inherited her mother's teeth but they appeared in a long delicate face and, combined with large shining brown eyes, a small but aquiline nose and a mass of fair hair tending always to escape from its confining pins, amounted to an effect of vibrant charm. She also had a breathless talkative manner, modelled to some extent, he suspected, on that of Aline Hartlip, to whom among other attributes it had certainly brought a great deal of social success. It was not perhaps exactly appropriate for a nineteen-year-old, and it did lend itself to the making of outrageous remarks.

'I have to cover my legs with powder, it's the only way,' she was now saying, 'And lie on my back with my feet in the air, and then my maid and I both have to pull as hard as we possibly can for hours and hours.'

Count Rakassyi looked concerned. 'Can it be worth this agony?'

'Oh yes, they look wonderful when they're on. I feel tremendously proud of myself in them. Tommy's seen them, haven't you, Tommy? My new hunting boots – yes you have, Tommy, how dare you pretend you haven't?'

But Sir Reuben was now joining them, making his way across the highly polished floor and the Persian rugs and round the little tables and the potted plants towards the tea table, apologising for his lateness.

'It was Hopkins, I know. She can be such a bully,' said Minnie, turning up the little flame under the silver kettle so that his tea shou d not be cold.

'She insisted absolutely that the cure could be effective only if I sat with my feet in this tub for half an hour and not a moment less.' Sir Reuben raised his shoulders and held out his hands, palms upwards, in a gesture of helplessness which also called to mind, as many of his gestures did, something ancient, Levantine, subtle and insinuating – an echo of a white market-place beneath a thousand-year-old sun. His head was large, his forehead high and domed, his nose of formidable size and boldly hooked, his eyes dark, turned slightly downwards at the outer corners, his mouth delicately shaped and sensitive, his chin firm. After all this his short stature was a surprise: had the nose and chin tended a little more to meet each other, he would have seemed a kind of Asiatic Mr Punch.

He said he had thought again today how perfect the Nettleby coverts were, as good in his opinion as Sandringham or Holkham, though on a smaller scale of course.

'We copied them,' said Sir Randolph. 'Straight copy.'

'Now that I didn't realise. How very interesting. How did it happen?'

Sir Reuben leant towards his host, his whole demeanour seeming to express a sympathy so profound as to be on a spiritual rather than a mundane plane. Sir Randolph, recounting the story of his grandfather's friendship with the first Lord Leicester, who nearly a hundred years ago was already planting his woods with sport in mind, thought again how hard it was to believe this man's fame as the most pitiless of negotiators in the Rand mining world, and responded again to the sympathetic attention, the quick apprehension and the strange sense of un-fathomable melancholy.

'Ah, Sandringham,' sighed Minnie. (They had gone on to discuss pheasant-rearing and the methods first used at Sandringham and copied at Nettleby.) 'We've been, of course, but only once. It's not the same.'

'How could it be?' Sir Reuben said, laying a hand on hers.

They sat in silence, smiling reminiscently, the two old favour-ites, while Sir Randolph forebore to mention what he might have mentioned, the fact that Minnie's enjoyment of the late King's approval, and his own consequent efforts to bring his sporting facilities up to the standard expected by his Royal guest, had all but bankrupted the estate.

'Didn't you use to take the kale in the morning?' Charles Farquhar was saying. 'I was sure I remembered taking the kale in the morning last time I was here.'

'There wasn't any kale last time you were here. It was January.'

Sir Randolph considered Charles Farquhar a person of no sig-nificance. He was a good shot, though hunting was his real en-thusiasm, and he gave one a good day's partridge shooting at his

12

place in Norfolk, so that Sir Randolph had no objection to asking him to stay every now and then, but saw no need to bother with him conversationally. Minnie had said he ought to be asked on this occasion because Aline Hartlip was coming.

'It is *de rigeur* to ask them together nowadays,' she had said.

Aline was a fairly demanding guest and if the presence of the handsome but stupid (in Sir Randolph's view) Charles Farquhar would keep her quiet so that her husband could concentrate on his shooting, Sir Randolph was perfectly happy to ask him. Gilbert Hartlip was one of the best shots in England, if not the best of all, and it was a pleasure to see him in action – sometimes a bit of an anxiety as well, for he had some of the star performer's temperament and could be very difficult if he thought he was not being given his due share of the best places. He also had a habit of allowing his loader to keep his personal score – Sir Randolph had seen him several times ask the man after a drive how many birds he had shot. Sir Randolph, although he knew this to be quite a common practice, privately considered it not sporting. He did not think shooting game should be competitive, although he supposed that if you had a reputation as great as Lord Hartlip's you were allowed to compete against yourself. He hoped that that was all that Gilbert was doing. On the other hand he had happened to hear this same loader asking Lionel Stephens' loader what his score was, and as Lionel Stephens had been shooting brilliantly all day it looked as if there might be a personal rivalry starting up; an uncomfortable thought.

He noticed that Lionel was looking calm and fit, unlike Gilbert Hartlip, who was pale – it was well known, though he did not like it to be referred to, that he suffered from bad headaches after shooting. Lionel was what you could call a fine figure of a man, and unlike Charles Farquhar he had a brain as well as a physique. He was not as tall, not really as massive as Bob Lilburn, to whose wife Olivia he was now talking; but Bob for all his heroic appearance was not half the athlete the other was. Had he not climbed the Matterhorn?

'Well, dawn you know,' he was saying, his boyish smile combining enthusiasm with modesty. 'Of course the dawn in the high Alps is a marvellous sight.'

'How I should love to see it,' said Olivia with glowing eyes.

That was real beauty, Sir Randolph thought. A beautiful

woman, a handsome man on either side; how proud of them he felt. Pity poor old Bob Lilburn was a bit of an ass, nice though he was.

'No,' said Aline Hartlip on his other side. 'There's absolutely nothing in it.'

'What do you mean?' She smiled at him, her thin clever face expressing her disbelief in his naïveté. 'Don't pretend you are not as interested as we all are. But I had a little talk last night and I can tell you there's nothing in it. In fact I honestly believe she didn't know what I was referring to.'

'Nor do I. Though I can guess it's some kind of wickedness.'

'It's not wicked to speculate, now is it? And one can't help doing that when one has what one has there, something of the highest quality – she is now isn't she? – allied to something that looks as if it's of the same quality but isn't, to which second person the first person has done her duty in the shape of a son and heir – and now there's a third person, also of the highest quality – I think, don't you? – and obviously enslaved. Of course one speculates. I can't think of anyone whose happiness I care more about. She's so utterly exceptional. Of course I have always been green with jealousy too because she's the supreme enchantress, don't you agree?'

'I knew it was wickedness of some kind. As for degrees of supremacy in the arts of enchantment you know quite well who wins those laurels. What a competitive pair you are, you and your husband.'

'Gilbert? Competitive? But he doesn't even join in the game!'

'I meant to refer to sport. In his case.'

'Oh, sport. Sport doesn't interest me at all. Except that of course one likes a man to be good at it.'

'In that case you could hardly have made a better choice of husband.'

'You would think so, wouldn't you? But d'you know something very odd was happening today. Did you notice?'

'Certainly not.'

'I mean that a certain person, and I won't say who because you know how one always hears one's own name, was shooting nearly as well as a certain other person. If not altogether as well. I mean it never happens. But never.'

'Then no doubt it wasn't happening today.'

'It was. It upset him terribly.'

'Oh nonsense. How can he be bothered with that? It isn't even as if the other is in the same league. He's not a famous shot like your husband. It's just that he's one of those all-round athletes who can't go wrong at any sport. He's not interested in trying to equal Gilbert.'

'Of course he is. Everyone wants to beat the champion.'

'Shooting is not a game. It's not a competitive thing. I can assure you you're quite wrong, Aline, that's not how our young friend's mind works.'

'Even with the madness of love running in his veins? To shine in front of her?'

'Your wickedness knows no bounds. In her eyes that would not make him shine.'

'In any woman's eyes it would. Why else do you think men do these things? That's so, isn't it, Charles? Men do deeds of valour to win the hearts of women, isn't that so? What other reason could there be?'

'None, my dear Aline, none,' said Charles Farquhar cheerfully.

'A deed of valour,' said Sir Randolph, determined that Aline should not see how much she had disturbed him, since that had presumably been her intention (had he not always thought her too thin? Emaciation in women was a sign of a malicious nature, he had always said so). 'A deed of valour for any man is to partner my dear wife at bridge. I did it once thirty years ago and I've never touched a card since. But I can see by the look in her eye that someone's going to have to do it. The bridge fever is upon her. We have one other expert I know. Now, who else?'

Sir Reuben Hergesheimer was an excellent bridge player. Both he and Minnie often played for very high stakes; there was no one else in the party who was in their class.

'Perhaps just a rubber or two would be rather nice,' said Minnie, quite as if she had not played bridge for an hour or two between tea and dinner most evenings for the past thirty-five years. (She had even sometimes played after dinner too though generally speaking that was when the gambling became serious and so was left to the men after the ladies had gone to bed.) 'Aline?' she questioned. 'Charles?'

They rose obediently. There was general movement. Rogers

and a parlourmaid appeared, to take away the tea.

'We'll go to the library and play Old Maid,' said Cicely.

'Anything but word games,' said Tommy.

But as Rogers opened the door there was a diversion. He opened it with his usual silent and deferential air and stood behind it holding the handle so that it should not swing back upon Mary the parlourmaid as she carried out the silver tray; he was therefore unaware of the impression he gave of participating in a rather grand entrance. The effect for those who did see it was comic.

'Oh, do look,' said Cicely quietly.

Everyone looked and heard the gentle flap of webbed feet. It seemed that Rogers was holding open the door for a duck.

'Oh dear,' said Ida, who recognised the bird.

Rogers, seeing Mary hesitate with her loaded tray, came out from behind the door to see what was happening. Mary stood aside, blushing with embarrassment. The duck, hardly hesitating, continued its progress between them. It was a wild duck, a young female mallard in the peak of condition.

'Ah,' said Sir Randolph. 'Rogers, I think we have need of Master Osbert.'

'How too divine,' said Aline.

'Duck, duck, come here, come on, duck.' Cicely held out her hand.

'It's no use trying to catch it,' said her brother Marcus. 'It'll only fly about and knock things over. We'll have to wait for Osbert.'

'What a naughty boy,' said Ida. 'I'm so sorry, Belle-mère.' (This was how she addressed her mother-in-law).

'Nonsense, my dear,' said Minnie. 'But I think Marcus is right. We'd better all stay quite still until Osbert comes. There are so many things to knock over in this room.'

The group, most of whom had been on their feet in the course of redeploying themselves for the next part of the evening's entertainment, now sat down again.

The bird paused, as if aware for the first time how many people there were in the room, and looked from one to the other with its head on one side.

'It's thinking,' said Cicely.

'I hope it won't come to any sudden decisions,' said Sir

Randolph.

It opened its mouth in a sort of yawn – no sound emerged – it shut it again, shook its feathers slightly, then slowly extended one leg sideways as if in a dance movement. It then stretched one wing along the length of the leg, opening to view a patch of deep bright blue feathers barred with white which had been conceal-ed beneath the speckled brown of its wing.

'How beautiful,' said Olivia.

Leg and wing were then returned to their more usual posi-tions, the feathers shaken again, and the slow contemplation of the company resumed.

'Where on earth is Osbert?' said Ida.

The duck now with a surprisingly loud spluttering sound emitted a large damp dropping. Cicely giggled. The duck walked slowly forward and lowering its head began to dabble, or graze, at a Persian carpet.

Fortunately at that moment a boy rushed into the room, scooped the duck into his arms – it quacked once in protest but did not struggle – and seemed about to rush out again. This pale, dark-haired boy was the ten-year-old Osbert, Ida's third child and second son. As he approached the door Nanny appeared in the doorway followed by Rogers, Mary and the between-maid with a mop, dustpan and brush. Relief had arrived.

'Osbert, wait,' said Ida. 'You might at least apologise to Granny.'

'I'm sorry, Granny,' said Osbert, looking hunted.

But everyone now was laughing, wanting to take an interest in the duck: only Minnie was quietly encouraging Rogers to get the rest of the tea out of the way and put out the card table.

'A duck is rather an unusual pet,' said Lord Lilburn, looking at the child from his great height, down his long nose and over his thick brown moustache. 'How did it come about?'

'I found her on the river last spring. She'd lost her mother.'

'A mere chick then?'

'She was only about four days old, I think.'

'And won't she fly away?'

'She does. She goes down to the river with the other ducks but she comes back at night and sometimes in the day time. That's why I never know when she's coming back, you see, and then she comes to look for me.'

'You'd better hang on to her tomorrow then, hadn't you?' said Charles Farquhar in his hearty way. 'If she's with the wild duck tomorrow she's for it, isn't that so, Sir Randolph?'

Sir Randolph looked at his grandson rather seriously.

'Keep her in tomorrow, Os. Don't forget.'

The boy, a frailer-looking creature than his more solid brother Marcus, held the duck tighter and nodded.

'You hear that, duck?' continued Charles Farquhar facetiously. 'If you're out there tomorrow afternoon you've had it. If I see you flying over me I can tell you you haven't a hope. Bang, bang and it will be all over.' He laughed loudly.

'If you kill her,' said Osbert, whiter than ever, 'I will kill you.'

'Osbert!' said Ida and Nanny simultaneously.

'Oho, you will, will you?' said Charles Farquhar, apparently much amused. 'And how do you propose to do that, may I ask?'

'I will kill you,' Osbert narrowed his eyes and drew back the corners of his mouth, speaking through his teeth, 'by Prayer.'

There was loud laughter. Osbert flushed. Nanny shepherded him from the room. The between-maid cleared away the duck's excreta, Mary cleared away the tea. Rogers quietly closed the door behind them all and opened out the green baize card table. General conversation was resumed.

'How I wish we had not laughed,' Olivia Lilburn said quietly to Lionel Stephens.

'You didn't.'

'I didn't think it was funny.'

'You think he means to carry out his threat?'

'Not that. Though if I were God I'd be inclined to grant his prayer.'

'Oh!' he remonstrated.

'No, but you can see he has such strong emotions, and he will have to be educated and taught the ways of the world and made to be on the side of the guns and against the ducks. It seems such a pity.'

'We all have to learn to school our emotions to some extent.'

'Of course, but who invents the rules of manly behaviour? Who says it's the height of heroism to kill? For every hero does there have to be a living sacrifice? I can see you are terribly shocked by my saying that. I am sorry.'

'I am not shocked so much as shaken. I am shaken because

although I did know – I have always known – that you had such fire, I didn't think you would ever show it, or at least not to me.'

'I feel I can show it to you because you are a true friend and won't laugh.'

'No, I won't laugh.'

'We are being very serious. I think that might be breaking one of the rules. I think it is bad form to be serious.'

'I'm quite sure it is. But no one will guess. The more serious we look the more people will think we are telling each other terrible lies about Aline.'

'We could do that later. I'm quite good at telling terrible lies about Aline. It's only that having a son of my own has made me think of other things, and of my own appalling responsibilities. And I am often aware at shooting parties how differently I feel from a man and how, more than that, I really would like to rebel against the world men have made, if I knew how to. I see the beauty of a good shoot of course and the charm of country sports and traditions, but I can't help feeling the added solemnity the whole thing gets from that sacrificial note, the note of death, of blood. Why do we have to have that, to complete our pleasure?'

'Nature includes the note of death and of blood. It is all around us.'

'We don't have to love it, and seek it out and long for war so we can have more of it.'

'Do we do that?'

'Have you never wanted a war?'

'I suppose there is something in every man that answers to the call of battle.'

'There you are then.'

'There I am. But I shall not, if I can possibly help it, shoot young Osbert's duck.'

'That I do believe.' She smiled at him.

His answering smile faltered slightly, but before she had time to wonder why this might be her husband had approached to say, 'Are you taking a hand of bridge, my dear?'

'No, I hate games. It's my lack of competitive spirit again – we've just been talking about it. I shall fetch my needlework and sit by the fire with Ida.'

'Let me get it for you.'

'Thank you, Bob, that would be nice of you.'

She stood up. Lionel Stephens did the same.

'I have some boring briefs to go through. I think I'd better take the opportunity. Otherwise it means doing them before breakfast and that's not my favourite time of the day.'

*

Evening had given way to night as Tom Harker waited for his rabbit, motionless beside the gate, one finger resting on the top strand of the net which he had stretched along the fence which bordered the wood. He could hear the bitch busy in the undergrowth. She had put up one rabbit but it had run out on the other side of him, beyond the net; one short high whistle had stopped her as she began to give chase, and brought her back to the brambles and bracken on the outskirts of the wood. She was working the ground thoroughly – among so many fallen leaves she sounded like an animal three times her size – but so far without further success. Tom was beginning to feel cold. He would have liked to light his pipe, but believed that rabbits were put off by the smell of tobacco smoke. He had many theories about the habits of the creatures he hunted; some of the theories he could prove and some he could not, but nothing could shake his faith in them. Rabbits preferred a dark night, he thought, and a wind from the north or east. Tonight was not dark enough – a view which Flo, waiting with her lantern on his doorstep, would not have shared.

Tom shifted his weight from one foot to the other – the only movement he made, and that was soundless – and was thinking he should have brought the ferret when there was one short yelp from the bitch and a louder crashing in the undergrowth. He felt the top of the net jerk. Keeping his hand on it he quickly followed it along the fence until he felt a downward drag. He dropped on his knees. The rabbit was struggling vigorously, each kick entangling it more closely in the loose net. It was just beginning to scream. Seizing it firmly at the back of the neck, Tom knifed it once, hard, through the net. It was immediately still. He unravelled it and put it into one of the big inside pockets of his long jacket. He went back to the gate and neatly rolled up the net, removing the pegs with which he had fastened it to the ground as he came to them. Net and pegs went into the other pocket. The bitch was already at his feet, fawning in her sheepdog way. He wasted no time on congratulations but turned and walked with long strides back up the hill towards the road.

*

When Lionel Stephens went into his bedroom he found a young man there, lighting his fire. This was John Siddons, a footman of the house. Lionel did not often travel with his own valet – he had brought a loader, who looked after his dog – but knew that at Nettleby where he often stayed one of the younger male staff would be deputed to look after him. John had fulfilled this function several times before; he found it more interesting than his usual duties.

'I'm sorry, sir. If I'd known you wanted to be in here I could have lit the fire earlier.'

'That's all right. I've got some papers to go through and it's nice and quiet up here.'

'I'm afraid you won't be very warm, sir.'

'I'll be all right. That fire will get going soon. This house is nothing like as cold as my own, I can tell you.'

'That's better,' said John as the coal began to glow with a livelier heat. 'I'll come back later then to put out your clothes.'

He gathered up Lionel's discarded shooting clothes, scooped up a pair of shoes to clean, and went out – whistling under his breath, which made Lionel smile.

Still smiling, he walked over to the writing table, sat down and opened a notebook which lay there.

> 'I wonder why,' he read,
> 'Though I turn everywhere to find
> Some relief
>
> There still should lie
> Your lightest word on my mind
> Like a grief.'

He groaned, tore out the page and threw it into the waste-paper basket.

He turned to a file of papers and began to read through them quickly, making occasional notes in the notebook. The case was a rather complicated one of commercial fraud. Unravelling it would be a good exercise.

He did unravel it, but had time as well to let his thoughts

wander. When John came back an hour later to put out Lionel's evening clothes he found the room empty, though the fire was burning well. The wastepaper basket was overflowing with crumpled pages torn from the notebook. John took Lionel's dinner jacket from the cupboard and laid it out on the bed. He found the appropriate shirt in the chest of drawers and choosing cufflinks and studs from the leather stud box on the dressing table – he hesitated between the rolled gold and the amethyst and chose the latter – he inserted them into the shirt ready to be fixed in place, laid out the tie, socks and shoes, with a last minute rub on his sleeve for the latter, and picked up the untidy wastepaper basket before leaving. Mr Stephens had evidently had trouble with his work. John glanced at the top sheet of paper. '. . . you, don't you see, you I should be fighting for, wanting to die for. . .' Unexpected. He might just have a proper look at that in a minute in the safety of the boiler room.

*

Sir Randolph had retreated to his study. He was very fond of his study. His nineteenth-century ancestors had been rich land owners at a time when profits from agriculture were high. In 1868 – only a few years before the beginning of the agricultural decline from which the estate was still suffering – the Baronet of the time, Sir Randolph's great-uncle, had had one or two improvements made to the house, until then a simple, early-Georgian manor. The improvements had included a new and more portentous entrance – a pillared portico leading into a high and frequently icy hall – and a wing to one side of it containing a billiard room, the study and a gun room, with servants' quarters and bachelors' bedrooms above. Sir Randolph complained a good deal about the wing. He said it made the house too big, and he ought to pull it down. Minnie objected to this idea on the grounds that it would make entertaining no fun at all – there would be hardly any room for visitors, let alone visitors' servants – and Sir Randolph allowed it to be thought that his failure to put into practice his ruthlessly efficient plan was because he did not want to upset Minnie. The true reason was that he would have hated to lose his study.

It was a smallish room, high-ceilinged and panelled half way up the walls with dark oak. The patterned wallpaper was dark too, but not much of it was to be seen because of the number of pictures hanging on it and the massive oak superstructure above the fireplace which incorporated two mantel-shelves with small supporting pillars at their sides. The shelves were crowded with a variety of objects and ornaments, and above them the carved and fluted wood allowed for an inset oval picture lit on each side by hinged candelabra. This picture, like most of those on the walls, was – only just discernibly for the pictures too were dark – a landscape with figures. This one, unlike the others which though age and tobacco-smoking owners had obscured them were by such painters as Zucharelli and George Morland, was the work of an amateur. Sir Randolph's great-aunt, an artist of considerable skill, had copied it in oils in the spring of 1864, when she and her husband had spent three months in Venice. It showed a man on a horse looking down into a sort of quarry where a woman was sitting, draped in a cloak. The horse held one leg up in front of it as if about to paw the ground, wanting to be off, and the man seemed to hesitate, and behind them to the right was a group of buildings on a hill, very solid, a large farm perhaps, and on the other side a vast and various distance stretched towards a pale sky, becoming a deep shadowy blue as it approached the horizon. It was a picture which once looked at – for the dark varnish Great Aunt Hannah had applied had darkened even more with the years and not everyone did look – seemed to draw the spectator by some kind of infinite and mysterious significance. Sir Randolph had never troubled to find out what it was supposed to represent or who had painted the original. He liked it as he liked certain pieces of music and would have hated to have had it moved, cleaned or elucidated.

His desk was in the middle of the room. Against it, on the side opposite to where he sat, was a sofa, covered with dark red plush, fringed round its feet, and adorned with several cushions embroidered by his mother in vaguely ecclesiastical designs. Beside the fire, with a painted screen behind it, was a more comfortable leather armchair. The fireplace itself was a small one suitable for burning coal; it was surrounded by painted tiles depicting trees and birds. In front of it was a tiger-skin, and in one corner of the room, beside a bookcase containing many bound volumes of the Badminton Library as well as Sir Ralph Payne Gallwey's *Letters to Young Shooters* (the history and philosophy were on the other side of the fireplace), there stood a stuffed bear, six foot high and grimacing horribly, shot by Sir Randolph's father in the Rocky Mountains in 1874 – he had been ADC to the Governor of Canada at the time.

The desk was a massive oak one, with a small polished brass rail round three sides of it. Though always neat it was usually crowded. For one thing, most of Sir Randolph's boxes were kept on it. He had a great number of these of various sizes and made out of various woods; his known predeliction for them had for years made the choice of Christmas presents easier for his relations. Some were Indian, inlaid with ivory, some French, made of fruitwood, and one of the largest, which was made of mahogany, was inlaid on the top in a pattern of darker and lighter squares and diamonds in a variety of different woods, so many that the maker had included a diagram inside the box which specified which was which – pear or apple, rosewood, date or hog plum, dogwood, black cherry, tamarind or lime. In this one he kept all the letters Minnie had ever written to him. Their interest was not so much romantic – they had corresponded little in the early days, being usually together – as scandalous. She had written to him from London, from great houses, from spas, from palaces, on many occasions when for one reason or another (one excuse or another, perhaps, for he had never shared her social appetite), he had not been with her. She was a witty and irresponsible correspondent – though she usually broke into French when she was going to be really outrageous – and her letters could have caused a good deal of embarrassment had he ever shown them to anyone. 'Missing you as ever my dear old friend' they sometimes ended, or 'Tomorrow, D.V., I set off for my dear home and husband'. Few would have guessed how sincerely she had meant it. Minnie had appeared very flighty as a young married woman.

In a smaller box, made of a pale mahogany striped with rosewood, he kept the letters he had received from the late King Edward VII, most of which were short, friendly and to the point, dealing with arrangements for sporting activities or technicalities which had been raised in discussions about such activities. He imagined that Minnie probably had a larger collection, revealing a more intimate side of the Royal nature; he had never asked her.

Beside the boxes he kept his current Game Book, which was bound in black morocco leather like its many predecessors. For years now he had had the habit of every now and then, on finishing the entry for the day, turning the book back to front and letting his pen wander with his thoughts. The first time he had done it had been in the winter of 1893 when Minnie was spending a lot of time away. One day a letter had arrived from Easton Lodge, where she was staying with Daisy Brooke, the Prince of Wales being of the party.

'So my husband is forty, or will be on the day he gets this letter. I have bought you something I think will amuse you but I shan't send it because I want to see your face when you open it' – (It had been an absurdly expensive cigar case) – 'Of course you have always been quite wise enough to be forty, and that has often made me wonder why you put up with me who am silly enough to be sixteen. How I wish I were with you.' He knew she meant it. He also knew that it would have seemed to many people that there was nothing to prevent her being with him if indeed she wished it. Nothing kept her from him but a party. Minnie's priorities, however, were different from his own and he had never felt that marriage had given him any particular right to question them. So he had turned the Game Book round – he had been filling it in when a servant had brought him her letter – and had written, 'My wife and I are very fond of each other but she cares for Society more than I do.' It was true. Their mutual disappointment only made them more tender of each other's feelings. That winter though, he had had plenty of time for the Game Book. He had had to accustom himself to being what the world considered a complaisant husband, and the Game Book had helped him a little in that respect.

The complaisance was in some ways – or in one particular way at all events – more apparent than real, but this was a detail which he considered too intimate ever to be mentioned to anyone, certainly not merely in order to save his own face. The fact was that Minnie disliked sex. The familiarity of the marital bed made his own attentions acceptable to her from time to time, and it was also possible that at some time or other a Royal desire might have been interpreted as a Royal command. He had never asked her about that, but he knew and had always known that apart from that possible exception the world's gossip was inaccurate – she was a faithful wife. The knowledge had not saved him from all distress – indeed in some ways it had added to it, by constituting what might have been a weapon on her side – but the intermittent loneliness and disappointment of earlier years had gradually given way to a more settled and contemplative melancholy which as his daughter-in-law Ida sometimes pointed out, he on the whole enjoyed.

'Aline Hartlip is a trouble-maker,' he now wrote. 'She has what Minnie would call a mauvaise langue. Gilbert is a capital fellow and a real sportsman. Lionel Stephens is a fine young man whom I admire because he works hard and is making what I understand is beginning to be a brilliant career at the Bar. He tells me he doesn't care for politics so he is doing what he does in order to lead a useful and interesting life whereas he could have sat on his perfectly pleasant little estate in Lincolnshire and gone on being an amateur sportsman and nothing else. His mother had a bit of money so he wouldn't have been badly off. Instead he saw what was happening, saw that that sort of life isn't the life for a man any more – the sort of life I lead. Everything's against us now. The politicians are determined to turn this country into an urban society instead of a rural one and in the course of the change they think they've got to take away the power of the landed proprietor. So they fling Acts of Parliament at our heads, set up town councils, parish councils, abolish residential qualifications for JPs, encourage us to sell our possessions instead of keeping them entailed for the next generation, do nothing to help agriculture out of its terrible problems – and now the Liberals are crippling us with taxes. For generations we ran the country; it did not suffer from our rule. If the landlord class goes, everything goes. It will be the ruin of rural England. Ida tells me I am prejudiced. Show me the man with blood in his veins who is not.'

Sir Randolph was feeling much better already.

'An age,' he wrote, 'even perhaps a civilization, is coming to an end – it is happening all over Europe. In the meantime it is bad for the young men. If you take away the proper functions of an aristocracy, what can it do but play games too seriously? It happened at the end of feudalism and it is happening now.'

'I think I shall write a short pamphlet,' he said aloud. 'For private circulation. Decently printed and so on.'

*

Tom Harker was in the darkness on his way home along the road when his collie, who was a few paces in front of him, stopped suddenly, then came back to walk very close to his heels. Alerted, Tom felt his pockets to make sure that nothing incriminating in the way of pieces of netting or rabbit's feet might be seen and then quickened his pace. Round the next corner, also moving at a steady pace, came a tall figure whose face he could not see in the dusk, surmounted by a wide-brimmed hat and wrapped in a thick Norfolk jacket and a long scarf.

'Good evening, friend.'

Tom was now close enough to see that the speaker also wore a grey beard and stout walking boots.

'Good evening to you, sir.'

'I wonder if you would be good enough to direct me to the nearest inn. I seem to have missed my way.'

'That'll be the Nettleby Arms, sir, in the village. You're walking away from it. If you'll walk with me a little way I can point you in the right direction.'

'That would be very kind.'

The stranger turned and set off the way he had come, hardly waiting to suit his pace to Tom's. He was a tall man with a pleasant, deep, schoolmasterly voice.

'I see you have a bad leg. Tell me if I go too fast. I have been tramping all day and have got in the way of a good speed. Were you in South Africa perhaps, in the Army?'

Tom's halting pace was due to his attempt to conceal the bulge of the rabbit in his pocket by keeping one leg straight. 'No, sir, no, it was a mantrap did it. Cruel things, they can be.'

'Good God! Don't they know they're illegal?'

'It was some time ago,' said Tom hastily. 'Not this present gamekeeper, it was the one before, a vicious man.'

'I should say so!'

'I bear no grudge. He was doing his duty as he saw it, that's what I say.'

'His duty to trap a fellow human in a diabolical contraption that might cripple him for life! And all to ensure that there should be enough poor beasts for someone else to murder. Is there much shooting then on the estate?'

27

'Indeed there is. This is Sir Randolph Nettleby's place. Some of the best shooting in the country. The King himself has shot here, though not so often as his late Majesty.'

'Good God. How ghastly.'

'Taking the food from the poor man's pot indeed as God has provided,' said Tom, changing his tone to suit what seemed to be his audience's view.

'Murder.'

'You might say so in a sense.' Tom was mystified now and spoke tentatively.

'Must we kill our brothers and sisters in order to eat?' said the other.

'I should hope not indeed,' said Tom stoutly but in total bewilderment.

'Until we can recognise the universal kinship of all living creatures we shall remain in outer darkness. In outer darkness.'

'Ah.'

'The birds are our sisters, the beasts our brothers.'

'In a manner of speaking, you could say.'

'All we need for our daily sustenance are the fruits of field and orchard.'

'They do say the Lord will provide.'

'It is quite unnecessary to eat flesh. I have walked a good twenty miles today and I could go on for another ten. No flesh has passed my lips for five years.'

'Is that so then?'

'Will they be out tomorrow about their purposes of massacre?'

'I couldn't say, sir. It's nothing to me, the pastimes of the rich class. I couldn't say if they'll be shooting tomorrow. This is where I'll be going, sir, to my poor residence. If you go straight on to the crossroads there you're in the village then. The Nettleby Arms is a hundred yards or so to your left.'

'I can't thank you enough.' The stranger shook him warmly by the hand. 'Let me give you this leaflet. It enlarges a little on what we have been saying. I can see you are a fellow spirit, a sympathizer. Good luck to you!'

Flo, the candle in her lantern burnt nearly to its end and her legs cramped from the huddled position in which she was trying to keep herself warm on Tom's doorstep, heard his uneven step, and his indignant muttering, approaching.

'Fellow bloody spirit indeed, bloody lunatic, what's he bloody think he's bloody talking about I'd like to know, murder indeed – bloody barmy if you ask me.'

Terrified, she stood up quickly and backed up against the door, holding the lantern in front of her face.

'What?' Tom was almost as startled as she was. 'What's this then?'

'I've a message from Mr Glass, will you beat for him tomorrow, 8.30 Batty Clump?'

'Hold on a minute. Here, come inside. There's a madman I've just left out on the road wants to know where they're shooting tomorrow – we don't want him to hear us. Come on in, don't be afraid, it's only old Tom.'

He led the way into the house and left her hesitating in the dark while he went through into the bedroom and put his coat, rabbit and all, on the bed before coming back into the kitchen to light the lamp on the table.

'That's better.' He turned to look at her. 'Now then, what's all this? Mr Glass wants me to beat, does he? Who's fallen out then?'

She told him about her father's back and repeated the message from Mr Glass, keeping her eyes fixed on Tom's face and trying not to look at his right hand, which had blood on it.

'What d'you think of that then?' he said nodding towards the leaflet which he had put down on the table.

'I don't know.'

'You can read, can't you? More than I can.'

'The Rights of Animals,' she read obediently. 'A Vindi ... vindi ... something of the doctor-something of Universal Kinship.'

'Rights of Animals indeed. Animals haven't got rights, have they?'

'I shouldn't think so. I don't know.'

'Except to hunt and be hunted. Spot here thinks she's a right to her dinner. Here then, look what I've got.'

He fumbled about on the chimney-piece and produced a stick of liquorice.

'That's for being a good girl and waiting so long.'

'Thank you, Mr Harker.' She took it and ran. She ran all the way home. On the way she threw the stick of liquorice into the ditch. The hand which had given it to her had had blood on it, and had he not come in muttering about murder?

*

Cornelius Cardew continued on his way much encouraged by his encounter. It seemed to him that among these country people there was a directness of understanding, an instant and often wordless appreciation, which was extraordinarily heartening. He imagined that good man by his fireside, his worthy wife ladling out some sort of health-giving hot-pot (fairly health-giving anyway, for it was too much to hope the family might be so enlightened as already to have forsworn meat) while the children gathered round to listen to the words he would be reading to them from the pamphlet in his hand, words which would strike them first as strange and then as startling and then as scintillating with a fine refulgent light which made everything new and plain and held out to them quite irresistibly the clear necessity that they, the labouring poor, exploited by the rich, should connect themselves by sympathetic alliance with the animals, exploited by all men.

His stride lengthened as the road sloped downhill towards the lights of the village. He looked forward to the night's resting place. He was used to walking long distances and found it no more tiring at sixty than when he had been a younger man, but the journey he was engaged on was a long one, all the way from the Cotswold Hills to the slopes of Hindhead in Surrey. He had walked it the other way the previous week, in order to visit a friend, a former colleague in fact – twenty years ago they had been public-schoolmasters together – who, having seen the light a little later than Cornelius himself, had only just established himself in a Tolstoyan community in the Cotswolds. Cornelius had found the visit stimulating. He very much liked the idea of people banding themselves together in order to work for a better world, indeed, naïve tho' it now seemed to him, he had in his youth seen the school to which he had dedicated his early manhood rather in that light, but none of the other societies in which he had been involved – the Fellowship of the New Life, the Fabian Society – had seemed to him quite the answer. People tended to go off in such odd directions, towards religion for example, or towards dry statistical analysis of problems he felt should not be approached entirely materialistically (he himself considered that he was a rationalist without being a materalist). It was no doubt far better to form one's own association, and now that he had found this group of like-minded spirits among whom his friend Rundle had come to settle, there seemed no reason not to do so. He had been thinking of names as he walked through Oxfordshire. The Rationalists' Guild sounded insufficiently exciting, the Brotherhood of the Free Spirit possibly erred too far in the other direction. Besides, he had a feeling that there had been some such association in Medieval times, and that it had been in some way discreditable. He could not be sure of it – his subject had been Classics, not History – but he thought it was something to do with witchcraft, or possibly sex orgies.

His mind wandered by an uncontrollable progression towards the sitting room of his cottage on the Surrey hills where the fire would be burning brightly and the lamps would be lit beside the upright Broadwood piano at which his wife, Ada, her statuesque beauty belying her fifty-two years, would be settling herself for an evening's duet-playing with their neighbour, the philosopher H. W. Brigginshaw. Of course he was very fond of old H. W., but Rational Man was only too often subject to the same unworthy emotions as Irrational Man and he wished H. W. would not roll his eyes in that silly way when he came to the tenderer passages of Schubert. Or at least that Ada would not look as though she liked it when he did.

He would write to Shaw, that was what he would do (turning his mind resolutely from thoughts of that cosy sequestered scene), after supper at the inn he would write a long letter to his friend the famous playwright George Bernard Shaw, outlining the details of his new scheme and telling him at the same time – for he would be interested to know – how extraordinarily well his woollen Jaeger rational underwear had served him on his walk. His mind already turning over the pleasant phrases of his description, he swung on down the road towards the lights of the inn.

*

Cicely, dressed for dinner, was sitting in front of the mirror so that Ellen her maid, who was also Flo Page's elder sister, might pin up her hair.

'It slips out so, doesn't it? Especially when it's just been washed.'

'I'm getting better at it, Miss. I'm using these very long pins right at the back. They were all right last night, weren't they?'

'There were wisps after dinner, I know. I was tucking them in all the time I was talking to Count Rakassyi.'

'I know it was all right at dinner. I particularly asked John when he came out after the fish and he said it was looking lovely. I hope you don't mind him saying so, Miss. I mean it was only to cheer me up, me being a bit anxious.'

'You mean you hang about outside the dining room to ask the footmen if my hair's come down? Oh Ellen, I'm sure that's not what proper lady's-maids do.'

'I don't always do it. Just sometimes, when I'm extra worried. It was Hortense, you see, she showed me how to use these long pins and I wasn't sure if I could do it as well as she does.'

Cicely crouched down on her stool so as to be low enough to catch Ellen's reflection in the mirror.

'Who ever is Hortense?'

'Oh dear, I've lost that bit now. I'll have to start again.'

'I'm sorry. It's because you're so tall. I can't see your face to talk to. Couldn't you sit down or something?'

When they had re-arranged themselves to their own satisfaction Ellen, who was indeed nearly six foot tall and quite extraordinarily angular and energetic, explained that Hortense was Lady Hartlip's French maid.

'The things she can tell you, just about ironing. I could never be as good as that.'

'Is she a frightful flirt? French maids in plays always are.'

'She has a funny manner, that I will say. I thought we were all very friendly yesterday afternoon when we had our time off and she was showing me how to use these pins, but the way she was talking to John this morning you wouldn't think she was my friend at all. I hardly knew where to look. He just stood there grinning. I could have killed him. And the way she talks about Lady Hartlip, I wouldn't do that. I mean, of course, we all gossip and we all know some people are nicer to work for than others but someone like that, I mean, she could work for anyone I should think, the positions she's had. She wouldn't have any need to work for someone she didn't like. I couldn't tell you some of the things she said, Miss, I couldn't really.'

'No, and I should think you'd better not. At least, I suppose you'd better not. Anyway, what you'll have to do is marry John quickly and then you can keep him in order.'

'Oh Miss, we couldn't. Not yet. Not without any prospects.'

'John won't be a footman for ever.'

'But if he applies for another position it would mean leaving here and neither of us would like that. I couldn't imagine being away from the village. Besides, our Dad says I'm too young.'

'You can twist your Dad round your little finger, you know you can, Ellen.'

'I usually can get him to see sense, yes. John did think of applying for a job as valet to Mr Stephens. He thinks Mr Stephens is a very nice gentleman.'

'I do too. Very nice. And yet in a funny way he's so nice, and so good at everything, and so kind and clever and elegant and – I wonder if he's quite real sometimes.'

'I think Count Rakassyi is more your sort of gentleman, Miss. He's more lively, if you know what I mean.'

'You're saying that to find out what I think of him, I know you, Ellen, you are a very cunning girl. Of course he's more my sort of gentleman, that's to say he's irresponsible, flirtatious, gossipy and – well yes – rather romantic in a way. But he's nearly thirty you know.'

'Is he? I'd never have guessed it. He's quite well preserved, if you know what I mean, isn't he. Oh do you know, Miss, Hortense says Lady Hartlip has more than fifty combs for her hair? Tortoiseshell and diamonds, and all sorts of jewels. Don't you think I might just run along and get her to lend us one? Lady Hartlip would never notice, I'm sure.'

'No, Ellen certainly not, you do have the most outrageous ideas. I suppose Rogers will never leave, will he? I mean, so that John could be the butler?'

'Mr Rogers won't leave till he retires, I'm sure of that. Besides, I don't know that John could take over even if he did. I don't know if he'd have the authority with the other staff, them having known him as just a footman. It wouldn't be easy.'

'I'll have to marry Count Rakassyi then and you and John will have to come to Hungary as valet and lady's maid and we'll gallop on fur-lined sledges across the great snow-covered Hungarian plain from one glittering palace to another.'

'I've never really fancied snow, I don't know why. Is it always snowy there?'

'You're very particular. When his father dies he'll be a prince.'

'I still won't fancy the snow though, will I?'

'It may not be snow. I don't really know much about it. It may be days of endless sunshine and no sound but the wind gently stirring the stalks of the ripe golden corn.'

'Do they have nice villages, with a church and everything – or are they Roman Catholics, do you suppose?'

'I don't know, I'll find out. Or better still, if he proposes to me I'll tell him there are a few points you'd like to clear up with him before I answer. Not that he's shown much sign seriously of being about to propose. I have to admit that.'

'I'm sure it's only up to you, Miss. Although I still think we ought to have had one of those diamanté combs.'

'You really think that would do the trick? Oh Ellen, do I want to be loved for my hair ornaments?'

Ida, coming into her daughter's room to see if she was ready to go down to the drawing room with her, heard their laughter and had expostulated, 'Children, children,' thinking that her whole family must be helping Cicely to dress, before she realised that Cicely was alone with her maid.

Ellen immediately assumed an intensely serious expression, inserted the last of the hairpins, admired her handiwork, said 'There we are, Miss. Good Evening, Miss,' and left the room, spoiling the effect by momentarily reinserting her angular form round the corner of the door to say 'Good luck Miss,' in a loud whisper.

'You shouldn't encourage her, Cicely,' said Ida, genuinely shocked.

'I don't need to,' said Cicely cheerfully. 'She does very well without.'

*

Lord Lilburn had lost his second-best set of shirt studs. His wife Olivia had gone up to her room early, before the dressing bell had rung, and having changed quickly – her widely admired 'natural look' was often achieved by the simple expedient of not taking much trouble over her clothes – had settled herself on a chintz-covered chaise-longue in front of her bedroom fire with a small leather-covered volume in her hand. Lionel Stephens had been reading it earlier that day after the shooting lunch. He had a number of these little pocket editions and she had asked him what this one was and had been pleasantly surprised to find that for once it was not Greek. 'I love Ruskin,' she had said. 'Even when I think he's talking nonsense, I love the sound of it.' Lionel had immediately taken a gold pencil out of another pocket and written 'O.L. from L.S. Oct 30th 1913'. The book was *Frondes Agrestes*, passages from Ruskin's *Modern Painters* – 'chosen', it said, 'at her pleasure by the author's friend the younger lady of the Thwaite, Coniston.'

Olivia wondered who the lady of the Thwaite might have been and thought idly how pleasant it would be to have a distinguished philosopher and sage as a close neighbour and friend and to be allowed by him to make selections from his works for publication in slim leather volumes. She had always thought she would like to be a friend to very clever people. Lionel Stephens was clever – he could talk about anything. He had another quality she liked very much, which was that he could think about anything, that was to say there was nothing he was not prepared to consider, either seriously or not so seriously, and this open-mindedness, or openness to the possibilities of things, seemed to Olivia a very attractive quality, and one which her immediate social circle – which was really her husband's social circle, since before her youthful marriage she had lived quietly among innumerable country cousins – did not freely provide. She thought Lionel would be a good example for her son Charlie to follow, and hoped that as the boy grew up she would be able to arrange for them to see a good deal of each other.

These pleasant thoughts were interrupted by her husband coming rather suddenly into her room and saying, 'That ass Mathews has left half my things behind.'

'What a nuisance. But you look very nice.'

'I've got the wrong studs on.'

'No one could possibly guess.'

'They're too smart. Frightfully bad form. Look as if I'm going to some damn ball.'

'Oh Bob, I'm quite sure no one would think that. They're so small. I think they look very nice.'

'You don't understand. You never do understand how much these things matter. Gilbert Hartlip is always impeccably turned out.'

'Impeccably boring too, I always think.'

'How can you be so frivolous, Olivia? Gilbert carries a great deal of weight.'

'Of weight? What can you mean? No one could possibly call Gilbert fat.'

'You are being obtuse on purpose. I suppose you think it's funny. Gilbert carries weight in Society.'

'Oh, Society.'

'Don't dismiss it in that way, Olivia. Society is very important. I hate going into it inadequately equipped.'

'It's not a battle surely?'

'In some ways it is not unlike a battle.'

'In which he with the too-smart shirt studs bites the dust?'

'Well. . . .' he began unwillingly to smile. 'Sustains a setback maybe.'

Olivia laughed, putting her head with its thick crown of auburn hair back against the blue chaise-longue. 'You are quite ridiculous.'

'It's all very well. You can dismiss these things if you like, but they are the structure of our lives and if we lose respect for them we lose respect for ourselves.'

'My self-respect is not in the slightest bit connected with your shirt studs. But what you mean is I can afford to be frivolous because I am sustained and maintained by you and the position you confer on me by making me your wife, and I see that that is true and I always do know perfectly well that it is true, although at the same time it makes me feel quite extraordinarily leaden inside. So I try not to think about it and to think about Charlie instead, so here I am reading about education. It says here that he must be brought up in close communion with nature, Bob. We could manage that, now couldn't we? And what about this?' She opened the book at the place where she had left the marker and read out, '"I believe an immense gain in the bodily health and happiness of the upper classes would follow on their steadily endeavouring, however clumsily, to make the physical exertion they now necessarily exert in amusements definitely service-able. It would be far better, for instance, that a gentleman should mow his own fields, than ride over other people's." What about that, Bob?'

'You are trying to provoke me and I shall not rise. Who is this ape? John Ruskin – well, there you are then. Art and life are two very different things, as I believe he found out when he tried mar-riage, did he not? Where did you get this rubbish?'

He looked at the inscription on the flyleaf. Olivia blushed.

'Lionel Stephens was looking at it today when we were out shooting, and he gave it to me when I said I liked Ruskin.'

'Good man, Stephens, very good man indeed.'

Olivia had noticed before that as long as the proprieties were observed her husband seldom evinced any signs of jealousy. She was sure that this was admirable and rebuked herself for feeling faintly disconcerted.

All the same she spoke a little wistfully.

'You care very much for good form, don't you, Bob?'

'Certainly,' he said briskly.

*

They were all gathered in the drawing room. Harry Stamp and his wife Mildred had come over from Corston, ten miles away, and Philip Ormston who also lived near and was in the Grena-diers with Tommy Farmer was there too, handsome and sport-ing but more intelligent than Tommy. Ida, who knew nothing of Cicely's notions about winter palaces and fur-lined sledges, con-sidered him an eligible young man.

The Stamps had lived at Corston as long as the Nettlebys had lived at Nettleby. The inherited genes and the environment having been through the years much the same, it was possible that the Nettlebys had always been irritated by and rather despised the Stamps and the Stamps had always been puzzled by and rather admired the Nettlebys.

'Well Randolph!' said Harry Stamp, in a hearty, rallying sort of tone.

Sir Randolph wondered why Harry Stamp always greeted him as if he were a dog. He did not feel like a dog, least of all the friendly sort of trusting retriever Harry Stamp seemed to be addressing.

'My dear Mildred.' Sir Randolph turned instead to greet Mrs Stamp, taller and stouter than her stocky, weatherbeaten little husband, daughter of a Leicestershire landowner, Boadicea in the Corston village pageant since time immemorial, *bête noire* of Minnie. She was wearing a dress of heavy purple brocade with a curiously asymmetrical neckline.

'How charming you look my dear,' said Minnie, putting an arm in hers and leading her over to be introduced to the other guests.

'It is rather nice, isn't it? It's this wonderful little woman in the village.'

'Fascinating,' breathed Minnie, rolling her eyes at Sir Reuben Hergesheimer as she introduced him. Minnie's scarcely concealed insincerity in all of her encounters with Mildred Stamp deterred the latter not in the least; she considered Minnie Nettleby one of her oldest friends, and a wonderful woman if a little on the wordly side.

So studded, jewelled, feathered, draped, they went in procession to dinner, and there was not one of them that did not feel some slight, however brief, lifting of the heart as they did so, for even in a ceremonious age to prepare for and then to undertake the opening movements of one more ceremonial the perfection of whose design you did not question, was pleasant. After the opening movements there did for some lurk the spectre of boredom, leading to dread, leading in the end perhaps to that questioning of purposes which had been at the beginning absent; but that was only for some, for Sir Randolph, who had been brought up to a simpler life, for Lionel Stephens, who could not altogether control that capacity to think about anything which Olivia Lilburn so admired in him and who was anyway unsettled by the overwhelming nature of his feeling for Olivia, and for Olivia herself, in whom the whole thing was tentative, the questions half-formed and the answers, though guessed at, unspoken, because she was young, ill-educated and wished to be a good wife. The spectre, though, was altogether absent from Cicely's view of things.

'Now in Hungary,' she said to Tibor Rakassyi, who was sitting next to her, 'there is always snow, I suppose?'

'Always snow? My dear Miss Cicely, it is not Siberia.'

Minnie and Aline Hartlip had Harry Stamp sitting between them, but they were old hands at keeping boredom at bay. They had invented an infatuation. Maisie Arlington, they said, adored him. Maisie, the most up-to-date and generally admired of young London hostesses, had stayed a night or two with her husband at Nettleby in September on their way back from Scotland and had been taken by Minnie to see the gardens at Corston.

'She told me about it,' Aline cried, clasping her hands excitedly as if she were recognising the description. 'She told me a divine man had shown her round and been too fascinating for words.'

'There you are,' said Minnie. 'That's exactly how it happened. I've never seen her so bouleversé. Maisie of all people. It was a coup de foudre.'

'Oh I say – really? Do you mean it?' Harry Stamp turned from one to the other in high excitement. 'I must say I did think she was most charmingly – well, responsive, if you know what I mean –'

'Responsive? She was mad for you, mad for you, Harry,' said Minnie quite throatily. 'And she has all London at her feet. What a conquest for you.'

'Well, I don't know about that, I'm not sure you two ladies aren't pulling my leg.'

'How could you think that?' Aline looked hurt. 'I'm not at all that sort of person, am I, Minnie? Don't I simply hate ragging and all that sort of thing?'

'Of course, my dear, Aline would never tease. No, no, it's love at first sight. The truest love of all, I always think. Of course, you will have to follow it up. She will be in despair if you don't.'

'Follow it up? You really think so? You think I ought to follow it up? What, send flowers or something?'

'My dear man, not yet,' drawled Aline. 'Flowers come after, not before. You must call.'

'Call?'

'Of course. She's always at home in the mornings. About

the tallest trees were clearly visible.

Spot the dog sat outside the privy, facing the wide misty valley. Lately her master had been thatching ricks in a farmyard some five miles from the village and her day had been bounded by the walk to and fro, so that when the intermittent humming from the little building was succeeded by sounds denoting satisfaction (like many people who live alone, Tom Harker had a tendency to give himself a certain amount of vocal accompaniment), she got to her feet and began slowly to wave her tail, and when he emerged she was ready to dance round his feet in anticipation of their now setting off.

He was in a good humour and did not rebuke her, but when he had removed the rabbit stew from the stove, where it was already beginning to smell appetizing, and stoked up the fire, strapped on his leggings and eased on his heavy boots and his thigh-length coat, he chained her by her kennel and left her. Disappointed, she watched him until he was out of sight, his long stride taking him steadily up the hill, still humming, towards the Park.

*

Breakfast in the gamekeeper's cottage was a more elaborate affair, involving a clean tablecloth and a big teapot with a pattern of flowers on it, matching plates, piles of toast and two boiled eggs each. Dan made the breakfast while his father was outside feeding the chickens and ducks and collecting their eggs.

Mrs Glass had died five years ago and the older children, two boys and a girl, had left home. One boy was a forester on a big estate in Yorkshire, one who had a mechanical bent had gone to work in the Morris factory in Oxford and was living in lodgings there. The girl was in service near Bicester. Mrs Glass's married sister who lived in the village and whose children were old enough almost to look after themselves, came three times a week to clean the house, do the washing and leave something cooked for them. This she did in return for eggs and vegetables and a good share of the game with which Glass as one of the perquisites of his job was plentifully provided. Otherwise the two of them looked after themselves and Dan was as neat and methodical

54

twelve is the best time. And if she says she's not at home you must persevere.'

'Call again the next day sort of thing, what?'

'And the next and the next and the next,' said Aline, knowing that her friend Maisie simply detested being called on before 4 o'clock in the afternoon.

Minnie laid one soft, jewelled hand on his.

'I am so happy for you, Harry. Some people go all through life without it happening to them. The real thing, I mean.'

'Yes, but look here you know, I'm a happily married man and all that.'

'So is she, so is she. But we are all of us helpless before the storms of passion. The real thing, Harry, the real thing cannot be denied.'

'It can't,' he cried, quite persuaded. 'It can't be denied. But I don't know when I'll next be in town, dash it.'

'You must make a special journey,' said Aline. 'Without any doubt at all. 38, Princes Gardens. That's her address. What was it she said to me about small red moustaches? I wish I could remember – bruising one's lips on a firey-blossomed cactus, was that it?'

Fearing that all this might be getting out of hand, and leaving Harry Stamp expostulating delightedly to a straight-faced Aline, Minnie turned to Gilbert Hartlip on her other side.

'Have you noticed how easy it is to have the most outrageous conversations at dinner? Everybody is so busy being polite to their immediate neighbours no one has time to listen further afield. Have you observed my little granddaughter at all? She's becoming quite a flirt.'

'I don't suppose that pleases her mother.'

'No, but I never think a grandmother's advice has to be as responsible as a mother's, do you? I tell her she should be as naughty as she likes – within the bounds of propriety of course – and as cruel and heartless to young men as she cares to be. It will be such fun for her to remember afterwards, don't you know.'

Her benign glance wandered from Cicely's animated face to Olivia's fuller and more serious countenance, which at that moment was turned towards Lionel Stephens with a questioning expression which yet held, on the grounds of nothing more than perfect proportion and moulding, complexion, colour, and the light and shadow thrown onto it by the shaded candles on the table in front of her, a kind of authority, and with it and because of it a kind of reserve.

Lionel had been so delighted at finding himself seated next to her that he had been momentarily disconcerted, and had covered his confusion by talking first to Aline Hartlip who was sitting next to him on the other side. He had been placed next to Olivia at almost every meal since his arrival, and his disorientation was caused by the thought that this might have been because Olivia had asked Minnie for such an arrangement. Minnie had in fact needed no prompting; she loved beauty, and considered the furtherance of romance between the possessors of it the least of the services she could perform for it, but Lionel was ready to seize on anything which might seem to show some awareness on Olivia's part of what had happened, of the event in which they shared. He could not believe that she could continue to meet his eyes and not recognise the truth which was written in them.

Minor pleasantries having been exchanged with Aline, he turned to Olivia, watching for an opportunity to join her conversation with Philip Ormston who was on her other side (this was when Aline began to tease Harry Stamp), and hearing mention of the Russian ballet managed, by the mildest mention of Stravinsky, discreetly to insert himself into the discussion, in which before long, Cicely having claimed Philip's support in a disagreement with Tibor Rakassyi over the opposing advantages of hunting in Ireland and in Leicestershire, they were left alone.

'It's a very calming and good little book, the one you gave me,' she told him. 'And it's because of the rhythm of the sentences more than because of what they say, just as I thought it would be. Like music. I was going to be disagreeable and because I had been reading it I was not. Not very, anyway.'

'Art makes us better, of course. It's the sort of flat truth one's supposed to be too sophisticated to acknowledge. Why were you going to be disagreeable?'

'I was going to be airy and whimsical and superior, and fail completely to understand the fact that if things which don't mean anything to one do mean something to someone else, it is not necessarily the someone else who is at fault. More than that I couldn't possibly tell you because of the unutterable banalité of it.'

'I feel certain you're being too hard on yourself, but without more of the facts of the case I can't prove it to you.'

'What about your fraud case – was it a fraud case? Is every little wicked twist of it securely stored away in your brain now?'

'I suppose so. I shan't be sure until next week when I try to call it all out again for the benefit of the astonished and admiring Court. I didn't spend much time on it. I found myself writing a very long and pointless letter to a friend.'

'Pointless?'

'Because I knew I should never send it.'

'Then perhaps it was a pity to make it so long.'

'I had so much I wanted to say to her.'

Olivia found herself unexpectedly moved at the thought of Lionel caring for someone – she had somehow never considered him in that connection.

'Does she love you?'

The concern with which she asked the question, softening the directness of it, made it all the harder to answer.

'I don't think so.'

'If you had so many things you wanted to tell her I'm sure she would have wanted to hear them.'

'Do you think so?'

'Why don't you tell them to her instead of writing? Though of course it is nice to get letters.'

'I shall one day. One day I shall have to. Will you be walking with the guns tomorrow?'

'I suppose I shall. In the afternoon anyway.'

'Will you stand with me?'

'I should like to. I feel rather proud when I stand with you.'

'I feel very proud when you stand by me.'

That look Minnie caught. She caught it as it started from Olivia's eyes and as it was reflected back there again from Lionel's, and it seemed to spread with Minnie's own glance as she looked round the table at the candlelight and the faces and the silver and the crystal (they had champagne with the fish) and said to Gilbert Hartlip, 'In spite of everything, one manages to enjoy oneself, don't you think?'

*

Osbert was dreaming of a great black lake surrounded by trees. Between the trees snow had fallen onto the banks by the water and in the snow he could see the footprints of prowling foxes; he knew he must be careful.

He had always had strong dreams. He had been sent away to a preparatory school at the age of eight – the school where his brother Marcus had spent five apparently contented years before him – and from the first had formed the habit of sleeping underneath his bed. He was not unhappy, he said, he had no complaints, but every night he would start off tucked up in bed like all the other boys in his dormitory and every night he would be found later by Matron on her last rounds crouched on the dusty boards underneath the bed. Nothing short of physical force would induce him to come out. Every afternoon he was beaten by the Headmaster for disobeying school rules (a rule about sleeping in rather than under beds having been hastily made to meet the occasion), and every night the same thing happened again. He was quite unable to explain himself. He felt better under there, was the most he would say. Finally the Headmaster wrote to his father and said that he was a disruptive influence in the school and that he had never come across a boy so hardened in his resistance to discipline. Osbert with his white face and long bony legs was settled at Nettleby to be tutored by the Vicar.

'Sometimes Mr Fortescue is Mr Fortescue,' he said to his grandmother once. 'And sometimes when he is standing up and leaning over the desk to look at a Latin exercise on a sunny day he isn't Mr Fortescue at all but something quite different, a sort of big black spidery thing.'

'Now, Osbert darling, I do hope you are not going to become affected,' Minnie had said. 'Mr Fortescue is far too fat to be a spider.'

Another time he had been walking in the woods with Sir Randolph, and they had stopped to sit down on a fallen beech tree and Osbert had said, 'Sometimes I dream of great huge turning circles, thick and blankety and slowly turning, and so, so big, and some have spikes on them and some are smooth and they go on and on for ever.'

'Is that a nice dream?'

'It's awful. The most awful thing you can imagine.'

'Did you ever dream about them when you were at school?'

'Every night.'

'But you never told anyone?'

'In the day time I forgot them.'

Mr Fortescue found him polite but hopelessly forgetful. Ida wondered whether she should take him to see an expert: she had heard there was a man in Heidelberg who was very clever. Sir Randolph said, 'Leave him alone. There's no malice in him. Give him time and he'll come along all right.' He spoke as he might have spoken of one of his black, curly-coated retrievers, and like the retrievers Osbert in due course came along. Mr Fortescue found an unexpected interest in common with him; they both liked weak puns. At least, Mr Fortescue's puns were weak. Osbert, by his irresponsible attitude towards the sense of the thing, occasionally achieved real wit—or as his grandmother put it 'a jeu d'esprit.' It turned out that he had a memory after all and did not seem to mind memorizing lists of Latin vocabulary; the more remote from his own daily concerns the lessons he had to learn the more he liked them. Latin and Maths became his preferred subjects; Mr Fortescue soon saw no reason why he should not in due course follow his brother to Eton.

He stayed at Nettleby with Violet and Nanny while Cicely and Marcus went with their parents to Paris, where their father was en poste. The borderline between dream and what he understood was to be taken as Real Life became clearer to him. His dreams became less overpowering.

Thus the dark lake and the foxes' footprints in the snow between the trees were not frightening although they were important. They required of him an effort which he knew he was capable of making. Somewhere on the black water or in the reeds which bordered it his duck was sleeping, her greyish-green beak tucked so far under her speckled feathers that the tip of it showed behind the wing: the footprints in the snow showed that she was in danger, but he did not doubt that he would find her in time to save her. In his dream he began to walk slowly round the lake, searching as he went. His bare feet (for he was in his pyjamas) made no mark on the snow. I am lighter than the foxes he thought, therefore I have power over them, and even when he heard the sound of running feet he was not afraid. They were running too fast to be stalking one little duck, they must be after something else – but as he turned to look at them he saw they were not foxes but a pack of wolves, snarling and shouting 'Stop, oh stop, you beast,' and as he stood aside to let them pass one of them noisily opened his bedroom door and holding it half open inserted a soda water syphon round it and spurted a hissing jet of soda water into the room.

'Tommy, you half-wit, that's Osbert's room, of course there's no one in there. Go away.'

'Gosh, sorry.'

'What's that?' Osbert was sitting up in bed.

'Go away, Tommy.' Cicely rustled over to kneel beside the bed, putting her arms round her brother. 'It's all right, we're only playing hide-and-seek. Poor Osbert, did it give you a frightful shock?'

'I knew it was you playing hide-and-seek,' he said, which was true because in his dream he had known. 'Did Granny let you?'

'Hush. She's playing bridge. Go to sleep.'

Tibor Rakassyi, scornful of these childish English games, looked in and saw in the light from the landing the kneeling figure clasping the child and heard the reassuring whisper followed by muffled laughter and thought, really she is very endearing, perhaps I should let myself become a little interested.

*

When he had finished his work, John the footman went down to the boiler room to see if Mr Stephens' boots had dried. At least that would have been his excuse if anyone had happened to ask him what he was doing down there; in fact he knew from experience that Mr Stephens's boots would be drying quite satisfactorily (they had not even been very wet) and that it was not necessary for him to clean them and put them out by the gun room until early next morning. He liked the boiler room. It was warm and private. He liked the roar of the big furnace; even the acrid smell of coke fumes did not strike him as unpleasant. When Ellen wrote him a note it was usually in the boiler room that he read it. This time it was not a note from Ellen that he wanted to read, but the letter which he had found discarded in Lionel Stephens' waste-paper basket and which he had put into his pocket for later perusal. It was torn in half and crumpled but quite easy to piece together.

'My dear,' it began. 'I couldn't look at you when you smiled – did you notice?'

Confirmed in his guess that it was a love letter and without the slightest feeling that he ought not to be reading it – on the contrary congratulating himself on having removed it from the waste-paper basket rather than let it lie about with the other rubbish where anyone might see it (the kitchen maid for instance was a very silly girl) – he read on. 'There is a certain smile you have which I cannot meet – not because it dazzles me, though it is dazzling – but because it is so innocent. It's as if you didn't know how much I love you, how much – for it must be so – you love me, or are going to love me. It's not for nothing – how could it be? – that all those ordinary hesitancies which veil people from one another were never there between us. From the first we looked at each other from heart to heart – oh how we looked – "My face in thine eye, thine in mine appears And true plain hearts do in the faces rest." We may be talking about anything – trivialities, gossip, reading – or it may be one of those other times when suddenly we say so easily things that really matter to us – but always we look. I have never known anyone whose eyes I could meet in the way I meet yours. Isn't there another Donne poem where he has a line "And while our souls negotiate there"? Well, when we look at each other our souls are negotiating. And it's only when you look at me as if you didn't know, when you give me that sweet warm friendly smile you give so many people, and which is so beautiful it hurts and so kind I want to cry, that I have to look away. It's not for me that smile. I know too much.

'I was rather shaken anyway by what you had just been saying – about war and so on – because of course you are right and I adore your rightness and yet – and yet – there's a kind of inevitability about the other thing. If there were to be a war I should want to fight in it. I don't suppose it will come. People say something must happen about Ireland; other people say the militaristic regime in Germany is going to insist on a trial of strength sooner or later. On the other hand we've had two or three crises in the last few years which have blown over and come to nothing. Who knows? I can't say I positively want a war; and yet one gets a feeling sometimes – life is so extraordinarily pleasant for those of us who are fortunate enough to have been born in the right place – ought it to be so pleasant? – and for so few of us? And isn't there sometimes a kind of satiety about it all – and at the same time greed? We seem to have become money-mad – there's never been so much gambling, speculating, fortune-hunting – yet were we not all educated to be heroes (Roman ones at that)? Supposing it did come, some great trial, might it not cleanse us of our materialism, our cynicism, our lax lazy hypocrisies, make us gird our sinews and find simplicity again? And then should we not be fitter afterwards to make a better world? For that we must be what we are here for, to leave the world a better place than we found it.

'And if it came, you see, my dear, it would be you I should be fighting for. You would not thank me for it, you might even – tho' God forbid – *blaze* at me, as you briefly did when we talked of battles, but you could not stop me. A better world – everything better – *is* you, for me. You are Truth because you are Beauty – or Beauty because you are Truth – and you cannot stop me dying for you – although I would much rather live for you, if you would let me . . .'

John read this letter several times. Then he slowly folded it and put it in his pocket. He went over to stand with folded arms, leaning back against the big deal table on which the gentlemen's boots were standing, and gazed for some time at the furnace from behind whose doors the glow of the burning coke escaped. The letter gave him a good deal to think about. In the first place there was the mundane consideration that if Mr Stephens were in love then the likelihood was (for there was no indication in the letter as to the identity of the lady) that he would soon be getting married, and in that case he would no doubt need to enlarge his establishment, and would be looking out for a hard-working young couple as valet and ladies maid. It was not that, however, which was making John so thoughtful. It was rather the feeling he had of recognising certain emotions which until that moment he would not have known how to express. The letter seemed to him to be true; obviously that was how Mr Stephens would feel when he was in love and now that John had read it he understood that that was how – in a slightly different sort of way of course – he felt about Ellen. They did look into each other's eyes, and she did stand for everything good in his life. Not being educated people they did not go much on poetry – that he thought they could probably do without – but as for fighting for her and for a better world, with a touch of personal glory no doubt thrown in – well, if there was a war and Mr Stephens went to it, he would go with him.

These inspiring thoughts made him feel more cheerful. He had been briefly and rather vaguely downcast at the thought that he and Ellen were perhaps not getting it quite right. Naturally Mr Stephens and his lady would tend to feel the whole thing on a more high-flown level – this was all to do with education and knowing more words for things. He had no objection to that, but he did wonder whether perhaps he and Ellen missed something by being such friends. They had known each other such a very long time and though there were times when it was all rather solemn – on summer evenings perhaps when they walked hand-in-hand by the river looking at the dragon flies and the swallows and the occasional darting kingfisher – even then they did tend to try to push one another in, or simply to give each other hearty slaps on the bottom. He did not think Mr Stephens and his lady would slap each other on the bottom. He and Ellen did it often; even when they were working and passed in the passage. But she did tell the truth, Ellen, and it was one of the reasons he liked her. She was truthful and brave and as unlike the silly kitchen maid as she could be. He had never told her that she was Truth because she was Beauty or Beauty because she was Truth because it had never occurred to him to do so, but now that he knew it could be done he saw no reason not to remedy the omission.

*

Aline Hartlip sat at her dressing-table wearing a dark blue satin peignoir and polishing her nails with an ivory-backed nail buffer. She was not happy.

A tap on the door nevertheless made her heart beat distinctly faster in the expectation of its being Charles. Before she moved she looked at herself in the mirror and saw that her pale cheeks were slightly flushed and her eyes bright.

'Bitch,' she whispered to herself. The self-hate in the whisper was mingled with self-love. Lips parted, she rested her tongue for a moment on her lower lip and let her gaze feed on her own reflected lust; then she moved slowly over to the door, conscious of the touch of the satin on her naked body as she went, and slowly opened it.

'Gilbert!'

'I'm sorry, my dear, I didn't mean to bother you. I wondered if you had any of those sachets, the ones that French doctor gave you – my head's agony again.'

She walked – quite a different sort of walk – to her dressing-table, and found the little packet.

'Aren't they some terribly dangerous drug? You ought to be careful.'

'It's only laudanum or something isn't it, opium, chloroform, I don't know. They didn't do you any harm. I must have something.'

'Poor thing, I'm sorry. I didn't know the men had come up. Weren't you going to smoke a cigar?'

'I didn't feel like it with this head.'

'Wasn't the blotting-paper any good?'

He sighed. The blotting-paper had been suggested to him by his German brother-in-law on whose estates in Silesia he had been shooting earlier in the season; it was supposed that chewing blotting-paper until it became a sort of paste and then inserting it between the front teeth and the upper lip prevented the vibration of the skull which caused shooting headaches. Gilbert had not found the method effective.

'Perhaps German blotting-paper is different,' Aline suggested. 'Did you try it while we were there?'

'No. He didn't tell me about it until the last day.'

'That must be it then. I'll write to Maud and get her to send me some German blotting-paper.'

'That's nice of you. It might do the trick.'

He lingered, flexing his fingers.

'I could stay a bit if you liked.'

'My dear, it's not one of our weeks. Besides you need rest if you're to do yourself justice tomorrow. It's no use letting people think Lionel Stephens is a better shot than you. You know how people love to talk. You don't want that sort of thing going around, do you?'

'What do you mean? Is that what people are saying?'

'I don't know that they're saying it exactly. Don't look so shocked. You know you've been thinking about it.'

'Nonsense. What did they say? Tell me what anyone has said.'

'No one has said anything. Please don't yap at me Gilbert.'

'I am not yapping. Someone must have said something, otherwise you wouldn't have thought of it.'

'Yes I would. I thought of it. Why not?'

'You never think about my shooting.'

'Of course I do. At least I do if I see someone else trying to be as good as you. I may not be interested in everything you do but I am always loyal, you know that.'

Gilbert's face, which at the moment was pale, habitually wore an expression of distant hauteur, brought about by his natural arrogance and aggravated by the malfunctioning of his sinuses, but at the thought of his wife's loyalty a pleased smile crossed his features, giving them briefly a liveliness they too often lacked.

'I'll show them. I'll get a good night and I'll show them. You'll see.'

'Of course you will. You can beat Lionel Stephens any day, conceited young fool.'

'I don't think he is a conceited young fool. I will beat him though.'

'He is conceited. And a prig.'

'You are only saying that because you are getting bored with Charles and would have liked a flirtation with Lionel. Whereas perhaps he has other preoccupations.'

'That is the sort of bitter remark we agreed we would never make to each other.'

'It was not meant to be bitter. I don't feel bitter. I did once, but I'm getting used to it now.'

'Please don't try to sound pathetic. We made an agreement and I have kept to it. You started it, with that disgusting old hag in Maida Vale.'

'It is quite usual for men to have distractions which don't affect their devotion to their wives.'

'My distractions don't affect my devotion to you. I have never said anything disloyal or in any way let you down in public.

Please go now, I'm getting a headache too. It must be infectious.'

He looked at her, remembering almost affectionately how angry she used to make him feel, remembering also with a sense of relief that he no longer found her particularly attractive.

'Yes, I'll go. Thank you for the sleeping draught.'

He closed the door quietly behind him. He was sleeping in a room a little further down the passage, Minnie's forethought having given the Hartlips the Red Room, that was to say the one furthest separated from the dressing room that was usually used with it. Charles Farquhar's room was on the other side of the Red Room, not next to it but two away. Minnie could be relied upon to get that sort of thing right.

*

The remaining men were seen to their rooms by Sir Randolph. He did this every night, wandering from room to room – 'Got everything you want?' – giving a poke to the fire, glancing round the room. Minnie would usually have done the same with the women; she would have thought it odd for any of them to go to bed except at the moment ordained by her. Some of the men, on the other hand, might stay up later than their host to play cards or smoke; for one of them to go to bed earlier betokened ill-health. Sir Randolph knew that Gilbert Hartlip's headache must be a bad one. He had known him sit up, white-faced and expressionless but maintaining some sort of conversation, rather than make his excuses and leave his fellow guests to comment upon his weakness. As if it mattered, Sir Randolph thought. He knew a number of men who shot as much as Gilbert and suffered from headaches as a result. He saw no shame in it, and considered Gilbert an odd, cold, proud fish of a fellow. Nevertheless he was a superlative sportsman and Sir Randolph was honoured to have him as his guest – out shooting, that was to say. In the evenings he was not very lively company, unless of course one talked about shooting. He had many fascinating things to say on that subject, but it was uncivilised to talk about sport when the ladies were there.

In his own room Sir Randolph opened the window wide and leant out. It was a clear night and seemed colder – there might even be the first slight frost of the season. He breathed deeply. From the trees on one side of the lawn over which he was looking, the vixen whom he knew to frequent that particular copse suddenly emerged and crossed the lawn, stiff tail straight out behind, at a steady trot, preoccupied with her own concerns, indifferent to his.

He half closed the window, undressed and folded his clothes neatly on his chair; then he climbed into his high, many-pillowed bed and reached for his bedside copy of White's *Selborne*.

'Good little fox,' he said aloud, without bothering to think what it was about the fox which so merited his approbation.

*

It was hardly light when Tom Harker got up and went into his kitchen to rake out the embers of his stove and coax it back into flame. He filled a kettle and a big saucepan with water and put them on the stove, before he went outside to let out his dog and push some food through the wire door from behind which his foul-smelling, yellowish ferret's pink eyes stared at him without blinking. He pee-ed onto the path beside the cabbage patch – the privy was half way down the garden and not worth the walk except for more serious concerns – and set up a brief plume of steam. There had been a slight ground frost and the air was still cold, although the rapidly brightening sky was clear and it looked as though it would be another fine day.

He went inside again and set about skinning the rabbit; the stove would take some time to heat up and he could not make himself a cup of tea until it did. His sharp knife moved with precision. Soon he could remove the skin like a jacket and lay it flat to be salted. The bare, bloody rabbit was quickly disembowelled, cut into joints and put into a pot with some onions and carrots. He put it on the stove in place of the saucepan of water, which he now moved onto the table and into which he put, having first removed them from his feet, the socks he had been wearing all night. After a moment's thought he added the handkerchief he had been wearing round his neck. He went into the bedroom and put on a clean pair of thick woollen socks, then reached under the bed, grunting slightly, to find another dirty pair and two more handkerchiefs. These he added to the contents of the pan, then fetching a piece of hard yellow soap from the kitchen cupboard began to rub them vigorously, humming through his teeth in a kind of tuneless buzz.

When the kettle boiled he made himself a pot of strong black tea and cut himself several thick slices of fat bacon, which he ate with brown bread. He hung his washing on the line in the garden; it was full daylight by now and the low morning mist was beginning to clear. Still humming, or buzzing, he walked down the path between the beds of vegetables, of which some were weeded and some were not, and went into the lavatory.

His mother had brought him up to go to the lavatory every morning after breakfast. His father had died when he was five years old and he had little recollection of him. His mother had gone out to work every day in the fields and had generally been too tired to give him much attention, but there were certain things about which she had always been strict, and this was one of them. Since he had had a tendency to be constipated as a child, it had meant that he often had to get up earlier than he would otherwise have done to allow time for this duty to be properly performed before he set off to walk to school. In spite of this the privy was in no sense a place of punishment for him; rather the contrary. It was a substantial brick building, and because the ground behind the cottage sloped downhill, and because the privy had two steps leading up to the door, it had in effect two stories, one containing the large wooden seat and one at least six feet beneath it from which once a year, a door at the side of it being opened, the ordure could be collected. The size of the seat and the length of the drop beneath it had meant that as a child he had had to be careful not to fall down the hole; the slight element of fear this introduced only made the place more wonderful in his eyes. Other boys did not have privies so large they were afraid of falling down them.

Opposite the seat, at a convenient height from the point of view of the sitter, was a small square window, from which could be seen a row of bean poles and beyond the bean poles, and much further away, the woods on the opposite bank of the river towards which the green field beyond the cottage garden continued its gradual slope. This morning the woods were still partly obscured by the mist rising from the river, so that only the tops of

about the housework as he was about his botanical drawings and his notes on natural history.

These last had become a point of contention between Glass and Sir Randolph. (Dan, though not indifferent in the matter, was undecided as to which side to take.) It had all been started by Cicely, who a year ago when Dan had still been at school had seen one of his Nature Notebooks there. Minnie was always happy to let someone else take over her duties in the village. Whenever they were at Nettleby, Ida and her daughter did most of the visiting which Minnie in fact, though no one would have guessed it from her manner, found a bore. Cicely went to the school one day, was shown the children's work, and came back much impressed by Dan Glass's skill. Sir Randolph asked to see some of the notebooks and when Dan left school and was taken on as an assistant under-keeper to work with his father (at a yearly wage of £20), Sir Randolph, whose interest in the boy had been aroused, soon came to the conclusion that although he would undoubtedly in due course become a very good game-keeper, there was something not only about the skilful methodical drawings and notes which he still kept in a succession of notebooks, but about his cautious attitude towards his observations which seemed to Sir Randolph genuinely scientific in spirit. He thought it would be a pity if this aptitude were to be left without further training, and offered to finance Dan's education. He suggested a grammar school in Oxford – could he not board with his brother the mechanic? – and held out the hope of University. Glass, embarrassed and finding it difficult to explain why he felt so strongly opposed to the idea, had so far politely but firmly rejected it. Dan did not know what to think. He was perfectly content with his life as it was, but to work on the subject which seemed to him more interesting than anything in the world with other people who felt the same would obviously be wonderful. On the other hand, the prospect of more school seemed less wonderful, and he did not want to leave his father. He was as yet a stranger to worldly ambition, except in the sort of dream-like way which requires no action. The question stayed in the air. Glass had said no, but his conscience nagged him. Sir Randolph insisted the offer was still open. Dan tried to forget about it, expecting that Providence must surely speak, one way or the other.

After breakfast Glass became restless as Dan piled the dishes by the sink.

'Leave them be. Let's go.'

He was beginning to fuss, as he usually did before a big day.

'It's not seven yet,' Dan said, calmly beginning to wash the plates.

'We need to be there before the rest of them. I want to go past Tom Harker's place, make sure he's coming.'

'He'll be coming. Flo would have come back if he hadn't been there or couldn't come. Besides, he likes coming.'

'Darn him. He likes having a good look at the ground, that's why.'

'He likes the sport too. And the dinner.'

But he consented to leave the rest of the dishes and go to put on his boots. He knew Sir Randolph was as much of a perfectionist as his father, and it was as well to be on the safe side.

*

Ellen hurried up the back stairs with four shining, brass hot-water cans, two in each hand, and four clean, white, linen face towels, two over each arm.

John, who was walking along the passage ahead of her, carrying several pairs of clean shoes, stopped to watch her slightly perilous progress.

'You'll drop them.'

'I won't unless you make me. Watch out! What are you doing?'

'I'm putting a letter in your pocket.'

Ellen bent her long legs and crouching at his feet, rested the hot-water jugs on the floor. She looked up at him questioningly.

'A letter?'

'I want you to read it when you're alone. It's quite long.'

'Is it very serious?'

'Yes.'

'Oh no, what is it, John? You can't do that, when I'm in such a hurry too. What does it say?'

He was pleased by her anxiety. 'You'll see.'

The menacing figure of Hortense sprang immediately into her mind's eye.

'You don't care for me any more. That's it, isn't it?'

'Of course I do, silly. That's what it's about.'

'Oh, well that's a relief anyway. Holding me up and giving me such a fright.'

'Why d'you carry so many? You're bound to spill one of them.'

'I never have yet. And it means I get round in half the time, doesn't it?'

She gave him an exaggeratedly patient smile and hurried on her way.

She put the hot-water jugs by the sink in the housemaid's cupboard, covered each one with a sort of tea-cosy and laid a face towel on the top of that, so that they were ready to be collected by the various other servants who would be coming along in a few minutes. She herself would be coming back for one of them to take into Cicely's room and put in the big china bowl on the wash-stand when she had been downstairs to fetch the early-morning tea tray. As she hurried back along the passage with this purpose, she was surprised to see Osbert coming towards her in his pyjamas and with one very muddy leg.

'Master Osbert, whatever are you doing? Does Nanny know?'

'No. I'm just going back to get dressed. The thing is I went to feed the duck and I was just moving the cage so as to let her get at some better grass because I meant to keep her in all day and it tipped over and I fell in the pond. But it will be all right.'

'You were moving that big heavy cage all by yourself? What about the duck?'

'She flew off. She thought I meant her to. But she'll come back soon. She hasn't had breakfast. She always has lots of wood-lice and meal and stuff before she goes so I know she'll come back soon. I've left it open and I'll keep on looking out for her.'

'You're dripping on the carpet, look. Never mind I'll wipe it when I come up. Listen, I know where all the wild duck are. They're down by the bridge, I saw them the day before yesterday when I had my evening off. If she's not back after lunch I'll come with you and find her. Does she come if you call her?'

'Yes, when she can see me.'

'That's all right. You'd better run then. Don't let Nanny catch you.'

Ellen knew as well as anyone that the last day of a big shooting party ended with a duck shoot by the river at dusk. She also knew that the rules of sport and the rules of entertaining were both inexorable. Even Sir Randolph could not be expected to refuse to offer his guests the opportunity of shooting at wild duck just because a child's tame duck might have chanced to be among them. She hoped fervently that Osbert was right about the attractions of the wood-lice.

*

Cornelius Cardew lay on his back in his hard bed at the Nettleby Arms and stared at the ceiling, which was discoloured by damp. Before he went to bed he had given the innkeeper's wife a packet of peppermint tea with instructions to make a pot of it and bring it up to him at eight o'clock the following morning. It was now eight-fifteen and there was no sign of the tea.

He felt he needed it. The previous evening's discussion in the public bar had not gone well, and he had been forced to the conclusion that the villagers' political and philosophical attitudes were more influenced by their suspicion of outsiders than by their desire for reform. He had seldom come across a group of men who agreed with each other so consistently. 'You're right there, John,' 'What Jed says is right, sir,' and so on, all through the evening. 'Where you're wrong, sir, to my way of thinking.' He'd had to drop the question of animal rights almost immediately – that had aroused positive hostility – but they had hardly seemed more responsive on the matter of their own rights. 'They'd never give the vote to such as we,' seemed to be their view, but they also averred in the first place that political meetings were perfectly enjoyable and you could make a lot of noise at them without the vote, and secondly that if they got the vote then a lot of other much less sound people would get it too, 'towns-people, slum-dwellers and that, gypsies,'; this was not at all the sort of class-solidarity a good Socialist expected. Land Reform interested them a little more, and he had the feeling that he might have roused them there had they not already written him off as a crank.

The trouble was, he thought as he stared at the ceiling, that these were not the sort of people from whom the agitation for Socialism was going to come; it was not to be expected. It was the urban poor who were going to benefit most from Socialism. But the thought that was depressing him as he waited with decreasing optimism for his peppermint tea, was the thought that his own vision of the just society was that the urban poor should be living lives not so very different from these villagers' lives, except that they would be paid a fairer wage for their labour and would own their vegetable gardens instead of being dependent on the whim of a landlord; and if he were to be honest with himself, he would have to admit that in the first place he was not at all sure as to the economics of the thing and secondly and more worryingly he was not at all sure whether it would really accord with the notions of the urban poor themselves.

He was brought back again to education. Because of course if people were educated to see the excellences of such an Arcadia all would be well. If one was to do without the hierarchy of command, one had to work towards a common understanding. Education had been his first love. He had been a good teacher, a personality. Each class had been a performance; he had consciously played up his eccentricities, and when he heard boys imitating him he was pleased. There was a certain 'We don't *know*' on a rapidly rising inflexion which he often used in trying to open their eyes to the wonders and mysteries of the world. 'What is the secret of the Universe? We don't *know*. How does the human brain function? We don't *know*!' When he heard boys in the passages saying to each other 'What's for supper? We don't *know*. What did he set us for Prep? We don't *know*', he felt that this showed he was getting through to them, and that their imaginations were quickening even though they were as yet only manifesting their new awareness through an appreciation of the farcical.

One of the ideas thrown out by his friend Rundle and the Tolstoyans had been the possibility of starting an experimental school. Cornelius had been against the idea for the reason that had made him give up teaching before, that one was only reaching a tiny élite of those who could afford the fees; but now the more ambitious thought struck him that if they were able to secure enough financial backing, they might be able to offer half their places free. Of course this would mean an incredible amount of hard work and persuasion; but hard work and persuasion were two things at which he considered himself to excel.

Already the phrases he would use in his first fund-raising manifesto were running through his head.

As if to confirm him in his new optimism and preceded by a tremendous crash on the door, his peppermint tea arrived. The girl who brought it, who had pale spotty features, holes in her thick black stockings and a terrible cold, put the tray down on the bedside table, drew the curtains (which released a small cloud of dust from their folds), and withdrew, banging the door, which immediately re-opened.

'Door!' he shouted.

It banged again, and this time stayed closed.

He wrinkled his nose at the pungent reminder of her visit she had left upon the air, and sighed heavily. Humanity could be very disappointing. But as he sipped the invigorating tea his glance fell on the stout stick with which he had walked all yesterday, and he remembered that he had planned to hoist one of his Universal Kinship posters on it and interrupt the shoot. He had imagined himself followed by a small crowd of sympathisers, but this it now looked as if he might have to do without. Perhaps the point was more dramatically made by a single individual. And now as the peppermint tea took its refreshing course through his sytem and the open curtains disclosed a glint of sunshine, his imagination leapt ahead to the possibilities of the day. What if there were to be a philanthropic millionaire among the slaughtering landowner's guests? 'I congratulate you, Mr Cardew, on the independence and moral worth of your protest. Allow me to offer you a small cheque towards the expenses of any of your endeavours, more particularly should they chance to lie in the educational field.' Or Royalty. He had been told that the King often shot there. A pity English Royalty was always so philistine. What about the King's foreign relations, an archduke, the Kaiser himself maybe? The Germans were often very good on education, though sometimes a little on the authoritarian side. 'Allow me, Herr Cardew, to set up a small international trust, with unlimited funds for co-educational progressive schools, the vanguard, the prototype so to speak, of the new world order.'

'Your Imperial Majesty is too kind.'

Laughing wildly Cornelius jumped out of bed, made an elaborate obeisance in front of the cracked mirror, then going to the door shouted energetically for the girl to bring him some hot shaving water.

*

Sir Randolph, up early as he always was on shooting mornings and thinking he might deal with one or two letters before breakfast, walked along the passage towards his study. He was surprised to hear voices from the billiard room; even more surprised on opening the door to find Gilbert Hartlip, accompanied by two men of unfamiliar aspect, in the act of aiming a gun at the head of Julius Ceasar which surmounted a large wall cupboard containing billiard cues.

'Ah Gilbert, yes, yes, sorry, I didn't realise it was you.' Sir Randolph, embarrassed, attempted to retreat.

Gilbert, also embarrassed, smiled his never very convincing smile.

'My dear fellow, do forgive me. I wasn't about to take a pot shot at a Roman Emperor. One of my loaders hasn't been with me very long and with these new guns I thought we'd just have a minute or two's drill, don't you know.'

'Shouldn't have thought you needed it, seemed to go like clockwork yesterday.' Sir Randolph backed out of the room, hand on the door knob. 'Wouldn't have mattered anyway. Caesar I mean. Only one of those casts, you know, one gets them at the British Museum. No value, no value at all. Not that you'd have been loaded anyway.' He shut the door. 'At least I hope you wouldn't,' he muttered, continuing on his way towards the study. He supposed there was nothing like being a perfectionist. He was a funny fellow, Hartlip, all the same.

The study caught the early morning sunshine – it was the only time the sun did reach into that room – and this morning it was full of pale light as the sun broke through the mist outside. Already dusted and tidied, the room invited him to spend some hours there, sorting out his thoughts as he occasionally did in the mornings. This room, which changed so little from year to year, now made him feel nostalgic for the shoots of long ago, of his boyhood, when no one came but country neighbours and the occasional visiting cousin, when the birds were fewer and not always even driven and the bags were smaller and the old Queen was still on the throne, and nobody had ever heard of Lloyd George.

Sitting down at his desk he gazed through the sunlight in which the dust slowly circulated at the picture above the chimney piece, where the dimly discernable horse and rider chafed to leave on their nameless quest, and the blue distance – containing, it was to be presumed, the dragon, the dark tower, or the ideal city – stretched away towards the unknown horizon. Freed from time, he felt influenced towards a familiar state of watchful calm, from which he was aroused by the slow crescendo then rapid diminuendo of the breakfast gong being sounded by Rogers, an acknowledged master on the instrument.

*

Batty Clump was more or less in the middle of the park. The long drive to the house passed it, at this stage bordered by a fence of post and rails to prevent the cows and horses from wandering onto the drive. Nearer the house and over a cattle grid, the drive was unfenced, the flock of dark brown Welsh mountain sheep which kept the grass smooth and well-cropped being considered less of a hazard. Batty Clump was a coppice of mixed Scots firs and deciduous trees, which had been planted during the re-landscaping of the Park by Sir Randolph's grandfather a hundred years before; it afforded good cover for pheasants, and it was usual on the morning of a three-day shoot to send the beaters through it to drive the birds towards the belt of woodland on the outskirts of the Park. Two other clumps were driven in the same way. When the guns arrived the thick belt of wood on that side of the Park was driven towards them, and so by a precise plan of campaign each piece of ground which offered cover was driven towards a succession of stands, until in the afternoon there only remained the great wood which sloped down to the river. Wide green rides had been driven through this wood at intervals, affording stands over which the birds were known to fly high and fast, and culminating in the last stand of all at the end of the wood, where there were sometimes so many birds that even when the guns were placed three deep they were all kept fully occupied.

At precisely half-past eight the beaters, or rather that proportion of them who had been called for at this early hour – for another forty men were to meet them an hour later to start beating the bigger woods – began to walk slowly through the clump, tapping the tree trunks with sticks as they went and emitting a mixture of low-pitched churring, whistling and whooping sounds according to their various preferences. They wore long smocks made of thick whitish drill which came below their knees and gave them an antique look. The purpose was not picturesque but rather to give each man a distinguishing protective covering and to prevent unauthorised persons joining them – poachers spying out the land, vagrants hoping to claim a wage at the end of the day, even curious spectators.

Glass felt happier now that his army was on the move. His two dogs at his heels, he glanced along the line at the man next to him to make sure that no one was going too fast and moved resolutely forward through a tangle of bramble bushes.

Tom Harker further down the line was whistling a high clear whistle every now and then and occasionally giving his nearest neighbour a scornful look. It was quite clear the latter had been drinking. His unshaven face was blotchy, and it had been only too obvious to anyone standing near him while Mr Glass was issuing his instructions that his breath was still heavily laden with beer. Judging by his unsteady progress through the wood and the occasional echoing belch he was hardly sober yet.

'The Lord have mercy on his soul,' said Tom Harker quite loudly, raising his eyes heavenwards. As he did so he saw a red squirrel watching him from a high branch. It turned with a flick of its tail and clawed its way up the tree trunk, ran along a thin undulating branch, jumped to another far below and disappeared.

'He'll get you if he can,' said Tom Harker. 'Nail you to a fence he will. Just like our blessed Lord. For stealing an egg or two to keep body and soul together.'

He had not meant to imply that Christ was a stealer of pheasants' eggs; what he meant to convey (if only to himself) was the important point that just because they had dressed him up in a frock and were going to give him a few shillings and a decent bowl of stew and a baked potato (he hoped), it was no use anybody thinking he was going to forget which side he was on.

*

There were nine guns out that day. Sir Randolph considered eight to be enough and was proposing to be self-effacing. At a big shoot he often concentrated more on the organisation and the placing of the guns than on his own share of the sport; he often said, though not in front of Glass, that he considered himself a first-class head-keeper. He set off in the brake with Lionel Stephens beside him. Bob Lilburn and Charles Farquhar, sitting opposite each other, were reminiscing about hunting, Sir Reuben Hergesheimer and Gilbert Hartlip, side by side, opposite their host, dissected one of the previous evening's bridge problems. Behind the brake the three others followed in a smaller dog-cart, drawn by Minnie's favourite fat black cob. Marcus and Tommy were listening to Tibor Rakassyi's account of shooting parties on the estate of a certain bachelor uncle of his on the borders of Hungary and Bohemia; they shot partridges and hares all day, there would be a wonderful lunch spread upon tables in the shade of the acacia trees and a peasant band to play to them while they ate it, and then in the evenings, after dinner, every bachelor when he went up to bed would find a peasant girl from the village, ordered in for the night by the superintendent, tucked up there waiting for him. Tommy was embarrassed by this story. He was not sure why, because he went to brothels with his brother officers, so it could not be that he was prudish; it was probably because he thought Marcus was too young to hear that sort of talk or perhaps just because it was too soon after breakfast – anyway it seemed a bit foreign to him. Marcus also thought he was too young to hear that sort of talk and wished Tibor had not begun it. At the same time he hoped he might one day be asked to stay with this uncle, but not too soon, perhaps in about five years' time. He had a schoolfriend who had been to a brothel in London twice, but he himself thought twenty quite early enough to be introduced to vice. Rather cleverly he thought, he managed to steer the conversation in another direction by saying how jolly it had been in Vienna when his father was en poste there, when he himself was only ten. Perhaps he might even have met this lively uncle, but it was unlikely that he would have remembered.

'I was only Osbert's age. Not that I was as vague as he is.'

They were approaching the starting point of the day's sport,

64

in front of the Home Farm buildings. A small crowd of beaters was already there, with Glass and the under-keepers standing a little apart from them. The men talked in groups as they waited. Tom Harker stood immobile, both hands on his tall stick, looking straight in front of him. The idle exchanges going on around him were of no interest to him. He had known most of these men all his life and though he was prepared to be loquacious should anyone raise what seemed to him to be a serious subject – the Drink Question, or the reform of the Poor Law, or the habits of game – the domestic trivialities with which they concerned themselves bored him; he was not prepared to join in their facetiousness or the bantering friendliness with which they exchanged small pieces of information about their families. He sniffed the wind and waited.

Sir Randolph went over to greet Glass and the other keepers while the shooters, their loaders forming another sub-group in this apparently heterogenous but in fact multifariously differentiated collection of men, walked about slowly in the chilly sunshine.

Bess and Sam waved their tails while their master conversed with Sir Randolph. Bess, had she not been checked, would certainly have planted her front paws on the waistcoat of one or other of them; but Lorna, Sir Randolph's own dog, merely trembled, her eyes fixed on his face. She had been brought down by Charlie Pass, Sir Randolph's loader, from the kennels in the stable yard by the house, and as he talked Sir Randolph held out a hand for her leash and she moved quickly to sit at his heels as Charlie passed it over. Sir Randolph slipped off the leash: it was unnecessary. He trained his own gun dogs and was famous for it; articles on his methods had appeared from time to time in sporting journals and his advice was often sought by breeders and head-keepers. He had had a succession of black, curly-coated retriever bitches, proclaiming them more intelligent than pointers, more dignified than spaniels. One of his maxims was that you should never speak to a dog unnecessarily. Nothing annoyed him more than to see one of his grandchildren making a fuss of Lorna, stroking her, kissing her ears.

'Don't fawn on her,' he would say. 'It insults her.'

And Lorna, who had been receiving the attentions with every sign of enjoyment, would look ashamed, not having the wits to remember how often, when she might have been expected to be shut away in her kennel, she had lain in front of the fire in the study listening to her master's voice – or on these occasions only half listening, for she knew that the tone of voice he used in his animadversions on the state of the country, or his reverberating readings in the works of Tennyson or Swinburne, was not really meant for her. Out in the field, however, he kept his resolution, with the result that she was in a state of continuous concentrated attention, ready at a nod or a raised hand, a whistle or a short word of command, to perform miracles of interpretation. He swore that a retriever was the only gun dog you could train to think for itself. 'When it comes to a decision in the field,' he said, 'if she's left to herself and knows your ultimate aim, nine times out of ten she'll get it right.'

Gilbert Hartlip walked over to greet the keepers. Sir Randolph suggested that they should walk to the first stand. The beaters were already moving off in the direction of the wood.

'Looks as though we should have a good day, what?' said Gilbert Hartlip to Glass.

*

Aline Hartlip was writing letters in her room. She was wearing a morning dress of blue serge with a lace fichu round her neck – it was not yet time to change into the tweeds she would wear when she joined the men for lunch.

'Mon petit ami,' she wrote. 'You make me very unhappy by being unhappy – it is not at all what I expected of you. You were to be gay and carefree, always laughing, and a little bit unkind – don't you remember? We used to wonder if you were ever going to be capable of True Feeling. Mon petit soldat bleu, what happened to the hardness of your heart? As to the injustices of which you complain, I don't in the least understand you. I had not said I would be at Rumpelmeyers at four o'clock, I had said I *might* be there. You did not call, I received no message, I did not go. Where is the betrayal? I stayed at home. George C. called and bored me to tears with his effusions. Voila tout. If you wish to be forgiven call on me next week when I am back in London – but no horrid moods – I cannot bear them. Your misjudged friend. . . .'

She sighed as she folded the letter and put it into an envelope.

Younger admirers were very sweet of course, but so tiring – they were so serious, so easily offended – really sometimes she thought she only kept up with some of them because it seemed to be expected of her. It was part of what she represented to her small but devoted circle that when distinguished statesmen called, or foreign ambassadors, or young politicians with their way in the world to make, there should be a young man with her looking serious and offended. It was part of the background against which her pale beauty stood out at its most exotic and treacherous; it was what her world required of her.

'Dear Mr Van Fleet,' she wrote – she had small firm writing and covered the page quickly – 'I am very disappointed in the performance of the shares which you recommended to me. I understand from a source very close to the company concerned (I cannot say more) that shares in Hergesheimer Gold Mines are likely to rise sharply within the next few weeks. Please sell the shares you put me in and buy Hergesheimer Gold instead. I intend to take the profit on some at least of these and to finance the dealings thereby – meanwhile please ask your Accounts Department to desist from sending me begging letters.'

She screwed up her face as she folded the letter. It annoyed her to be reminded of the necessity for money: Gilbert as a financial provider was as correct as in every other way, Charles was occasionally generous, others too, but an existence so exquisite as Aline's needed unlimited finance, nor was she at all clever at remembering what she had spent or where. She was too often reduced to having to concern herself with affairs she thought would have more properly been dealt with by a man, largely because to have secured this happier state of affairs would have involved explanations she preferred not to make: apart from anything else, neither Gilbert nor Charles had any idea of the extent of her gambling losses.

'You know what life is like here,' she now wrote, adding to a letter she had started the day before to her cousin and best friend Everilda Shakerly. 'Of course too heavenly – but no men in the mornings – I think darling Randolph considers conversation between the sexes immoral before lunch, like reading novels. Even Minnie has never been able to persuade him to ask a few non-sporting men to keep us amused during the day. Never mind, yesterday the two boys, Tommy Farmer and the schoolboy grandson, were given a day off because Randolph thought he should ask a couple of boring neighbours to shoot in their places. We went bicycling by the river – so pretty. I didn't tell le petit Farmer all I knew about you and son Papa – he has not half the father's dash but something could be made of him – he has a sort of calf-love for Cicely the eldest granddaughter but it won't come to anything – he's to be in London next year – rather surprisingly loves Wagner – would he do for your Agnes, do you suppose? He is the eldest son and there is coal beneath the Park. . . .'

*

Olivia was reading about ancient Rome. The governess who had given her lessons as a child and who was a remarkably ignorant woman had nevertheless told her that the correct thing to do was always to follow 'a course of reading', which meant having on hand one serious book and one less serious. The French governess who had succeeded her for a year when Olivia was sixteen had added the necessity for something in that language as well; so that Olivia's present taks were *The Grandeur that was Rome* by F. W. Stobart (she had read *The Glory that was Greece* the year she was pregnant with Charlie) and Turgenev's *Smoke* in the Garnett's translation. She was enjoying both of these very much, but she detested Victor Hugo's *Les Miserables* and sometimes cheated by reading a poem out of a small book called *Les Cent Meilleurs Poèmes* instead. On the whole, though, she was strict with heself, did not skimp or skip and left Turgenev until last; she was even struggling to produce an English version of Lamartine's *Le Lac*, but she was not at all satisfied with it. Turgenev she adored. She felt there was no English novelist, even George Meredith, who created women she could so much admire or who showed such true perception about feelings. She wished her husband did not despise such reading; it seemed to her very important that people should understand about feelings and recognise them in themselves. By studying feeling, she thought, you would get better at it. It seemed to her as important to feel truthfully as to think truthfully. The novels most of her friends read and enjoyed seemed to her sentimental and it worried her that she was unable to explain the difference between that sort of novel and Turgenev to her husband. He read political biography he said, and the newspapers.

'Then what about *With Rod and Gun through Mesopotamia*?' she had said indignantly.

But it seemed there was no such book, though she was sure she had seen something very like it. It seemed that to go with rod and gun through Mesopotamia would be for some reason very silly, the sort of thing no English gentleman would dream of doing – perhaps it had been big game shooting and perhaps it had been India.

Olivia's reading was interrupted by Cicely who put her head round the door to say 'I must tell you something. May I? It's so intriguing.' She was wearing riding clothes and her hair was as usual in wisps about her face. 'It's a lovely day for riding. I wish we hadn't had to come back but it's almost time to change for lunch. I had such a funny conversation with Ellen, that's what I wanted to tell you about.'

Olivia put down her book. She liked Cicely and was amused by the friendship which had sprung up between them and in which she was cast as the understanding older woman, a role with which she was unfamiliar but which she was prepared to like. She had often noticed how men encouraged boys, once they were of public-school age, in sporting activities particularly but also in matters of manly behaviour, as if the older man, whether or not related by blood, considered it his obligation gently to initiate the younger into the customs of the tribe. She thought this charming and wished that women did it as well. Too often married women seemed to find young girls merely a bore, or worse than that a potential object of jealousy. Olivia did not find Cicely boring. She liked her liveliness and suspected her of having more courage than she herself had ever had. Cicely might well choose to be unconventional; something to which Olivia had never aspired, in her actions at least. Her thoughts, generally speaking, she kept to herself.

'She's had an extraordinary letter,' said Cicely, sitting on the window seat.

Olivia looked at her attentively.

'Tell me who Ellen is. And then about the letter.'

*

Minnie, having finished her morning consultation with the cook, was out in the garden talking to Ogden the gardener about the replenishing of the herbaceous border. This vast bed, backed by a high yew hedge, extended down one side of the lawn which spread before the classical garden front of the house. Four men and a boy were working on it while Minnie conferred with the head gardener. They were giving it its autumn grooming, cutting down dead stems, removing canes and stakes to be stored for the winter, forking over the soil between the plants, planting out seedling wallflowers and forget-me-nots, Canterbury bells and Sweet Williams.

'The asters,' said Minnie. 'Look how they've spread. Shouldn't they be divided now? Some could go into the kitchen garden for picking.'

'Best not lift them now, not until the spring. They won't thank us for it.'

Minnie never argued with Ogden. He was not always right, but the brief triumph of proving him wrong was seldom worth the ensuing coolness. The last time she had insisted on having her way there had been, though it was the height of the season, an extraordinary falling off in the number of ripe peaches available for the house from the greenhouse. She had thought it better not to refer to it but had taken the point. After all he was a good gardener and good gardeners were known to be on the despotic side.

She turned instead to greet Violet and Nanny who were setting off across the garden for their morning walk.

'Are you going fishing?'

Violet was carrying a net and a jam jar.

'I'm going to catch a stickleback and look for Elfrida Beetle so Osbert can go and get her when he's finished lessons.'

'Who is Elfrida Beetle?'

'She's very naughty, she hasn't had breakfast.'

'It's the name they give the duck,' Nanny explained.

'It's a silly name, that's why we don't call it her.'

'I think it's rather a nice name. How did she get it?'

'She used to be called Alfred and then when she turned into a female she was going to be called Alfreda but Nanny said it wasn't Alfreda but Elfrida and then she'd just swallowed a beetle and elle is French for she.'

'I see,' said Minnie, prepared to let it go at that.

'She freed the beetle,' explained Violet. 'By swallowing it. She freed it from the miseries of life. Elle freed a beetle. Elfrida Beetle.'

'Ah,' said Minnie.

'It's a silly name but it is her name.'

'And she has run away?'

'She thought Osbert meant her to go to the river but he didn't. But she will come back because she hasn't had breakfast.'

'I hope she does.'

'She'll be back,' said Nanny. 'I never saw such a greedy animal.'

'Bird,' said Violet.

'No need to be pert,' said Nanny.

Violet held her arms out sideways and ran in zig-zags across the lawn saying in a silly voice, 'Pert bird, bird pert, perty birdy.'

Nanny shook her head and followed doggedly.

'I suppose the youngest always does tend to get a bit spoilt,' said Minnie, turning back to Ogden.

'They do that.' He smiled. For this apparent taking of him into her confidence he was prepared to overlook the bold remarks about the asters.

*

They killed sixty-two pheasants on the first drive. The mist had all cleared by the time the guns were allotted their positions. They waited, fifty yards or so away from each other, in silence, their loaders, with or without dogs, behind them. Bob Lilburn sat on his shooting stick, relaxed in his tweeds, a big fit man, a figure of kindly authoritarianism, eminently capable of fulfilling all the obligations of the day's sport. He was a good shot – 'How did you do?' Olivia would ask him, 'Got my share,' he'd say casually – was never in doubt as to any of the small points of procedure or etiquette, when to leave a bird for someone else to shoot, how much to press into Glass's hand at the end of the day – details which still worried young Marcus and even sometimes Tommy Farmer whose father the General had no shooting of his own. It was a familiar world to Bob Lilburn and he moved at ease in it – some people might have said he was at his best there. Sir Reuben Hergesheimer, next to him, smoked a cigar while he waited, his face expressionless apart from a faint weariness. Two of the Nettleby men waited with him as loaders. He was an indifferent shot, though not a positively bad one. Shooting was something one did for purely social reasons, and social reasons to him were adequate reasons.

Lionel Stephens was about half way along the line, Gilbert Hartlip at the end. Looking along the line, Percy Maidment, Lionel's chief loader, could see Albert Jarvis waiting behind Lord Hartlip.

Percy Maidment was a Lincolnshire man, of agricultural labouring stock. The land he knew best was flat and seemingly interminable, broken only by low hedges and solitary elms and long barrow-like heaps of stored sugar-beet; he hated the land. This implacable loathing was probably the strongest and certainly the most constant emotion of his life. He had volunteered for the army at the time of the South African war but had been rejected as unfit – he was undersized and under-nourished. He had worked on Lionel's Lincolnshire estate ever since that rejection, and found partial escape from his bondage to the land in two directions – as a driver of Lionel's mother's Wolseley car and as a loader for Lionel when he went shooting. Lionel's mother was responsible for most of the estate management in Lionel's absence in London. She was known locally as a terror, just as the agent Mr Hopkins was known as a hard man: curiously perhaps, in neither case was the reputation generally felt to be a bad one. As a loader Percy Maidment had quickly become adept. Not only was he neat and quick in his movements but he was fiercely competitive. Lionel was unaware of the strength of this feeling. He smiled on the rare occasions when the usually taciturn Percy revealed anything of it, and put it down to a rather charming loyalty, but it was something more than that. Secretly Percy was maddened by Lionel's lack of competitive spirit; the notions of gentlemanly sport were inimical to him. The object of shooting parties, he considered, should be to shoot more game than anyone else. He wanted his man to beat Lord Hartlip. He had bet Albert Jarvis ten shillings that he would.

As they waited in silence for the birds to break, a silence soon broken by the sound of the beaters crackling, tapping and whistling their way towards them through the wood, only Charles Farquhar and Tibor Rakassyi were without feelings of tension – or almost without them. Charles was a man who for the time being was getting everything he wanted out of life – that was to say a sufficiency of hunting, shooting, food, drink and women. His affair with Aline had given the finishing touch to his never exactly faltering confidence. The difficult temperament which had driven former lovers to despair bothered him not at all. He put it down to women's moodiness and ignored it. She was beautiful, fashionable and physically in love with him; through her he was getting asked about more than ever before. To be positively liked by an old oddity like Sir Randolph as well as all that was more than he hoped for. He preferred Minnie anyway; she was, as she would have put it herself, more sortable.

Tibor Rakassyi's self-satisfaction was less personal. He was pleased with himself for being not so much what he was as where he was. The English nation seemed to him the most prosperous and secure in the world, and the English upper class the most enviable. To move at ease in that society, and to be accepted by it, seemed to him one of the chief joys of the cosmopolitanism to which his membership of the European aristocracy gave him access. He would have been surprised to learn that Sir Randolph, unlike Minnie who aspired to it, considered cosmopolitanism a vice. It was all right to know your way around Paris, Sir Randolph thought, and to visit Italian picture galleries or the relics of the classical world, but generally speaking a man should stick to one country and be proud of it. If one wanted to travel there was always the Empire.

In ignorance of his host's view on nationality, Tibor waited in his new Norfolk jacket (perhaps a little more tightly belted than an Englishman would have worn it) with his gun (made for him by Mr Henry Holland in Bond Street) casually pointing skywards over his shoulder, his heart and his stomach both in good order. An English autumn morning, prospects of sport, pleasant companions, hints of a flirtation to be pursued later on, what more, Tibor Rakassyi would have said in his excellent English, could a fellow want?

The first shot came from Lord Hartlip, immediately followed by the thump of a pheasant hitting the ground from a considerable height. For a few seconds there was only the sound of the approaching beaters, an alarm call from a running pheasant in the undergrowth, a scattering of blackbirds from the bramble bushes, then the loud whirr of wings and the birds began to fly out, at first in ones and twos and then in rapidly succeeding groups high and fast. Eyes forward, legs slightly apart – one in front of the other – left hand well forward along the barrel, each shooter discharged his two barrels, held out his gun to be exchanged and fired again with intense concentration for the space of about six minutes. The beaters, noisier now as they roused the last birds unwillingly to flight, reached the fence at the edge of the wood and faced the guns. With a final swing Lionel Stephens brought down a high bird a few yards behind him; it could be heard hitting the ground in the renewed silence. The drive was over.

'Fifteen,' muttered Percy Maidment to his companion, a Nettleby boy. 'Agreed?'

'Agreed.'

*

Sir Randolph was always relieved when the first drive was over. He could tell from that, he felt, how the day was going to go. On this morning's showing, the day was going to go perfectly.

He walked towards the next stand with Gilbert Hartlip, anxious to show him that any coolness he might have noticed in his manner when he had discovered him practising changing guns in the billiard-room that morning was to be attributed solely to the earliness of the hour. Of course, Gilbert was a capital sportsman; how could it have crossed his mind even for a second that he could possibly be anything else? He was looking better this morning too.

'Rotten luck those headaches you get. I'm so glad to see you looking fit again this morning.'

'I borrowed some medicine of Aline's last night. Seemed to do the trick. Got me a decent night's sleep anyway. I'm sorry I had to go up early like that.'

'We didn't stay up late. Even the card players turned in soon after you did. And the Stamps have never been night birds.'

'I hear he's thinking of letting.'

'Letting? Harry Stamp? What, letting Corston, d'you mean?'

'So he was saying last night.'

'Really? Good Lord. That's very bad news. Harry Stamp letting. I'd never have thought it of him.'

'Can't keep up with the costs, he was saying.'

'Of course he can't keep up with the costs, none of us can keep up with the costs. I'm mortgaged up to the hilt, I can tell you. Half my property is mortgaged. Who's he found to let it to then? Some damned newspaper proprietor I suppose. Somebody who'll do nothing but entertain his friends from Town and not give a thought to his obligations. The countryside needs all the help it can get in times like this. I'd never have thought old Harry Stamp would run out on it. What's he going to do then? Live in Dieppe, I suppose, like the Martins. Good God. In a boarding-house, I suppose.'

'I don't know that it's as bad as that. I think he was only talking of a few months, not more.'

'I should hope not. Don't suppose he can even speak French, Harry Stamp. He was always thick-headed. The boy's the same, isn't he, Marcus?'

He waited for his grandson, who was walking a few yards behind him.

'Isn't he? Harry Stamp's grandson? Isn't he pretty fat-headed?'

'I hardly see him. He's older than me. He's usually drunk whenever I do see him. Or fighting.'

'No discipline at Eton these days,' said Sir Randolph, his good humour, which had been shaken by the news of Harry Stamp's intended defection, apparently quite restored by the thought of the ineluctable genetic imperfections of the Stamp line.

*

At eleven o'clock, John the footman carried a silver tray into the morning room. On it was a bottle of Vichy water, together with one glass and a plate of the special ginger biscuits from Biarritz of which Minnie was so fond. Having finished her domestic interviews, Minnie, as she usually was by that time of the morning, was sitting at her desk. Her letters today, however, held nothing of particular interest to her, and she was glad enough to be interrupted by Aline.

'I knew I should find you here. Am I interrupting you? Are you halfway through a divinely elegant billet-doux?'

'My dear, I am much too old for that sort of thing. I do nothing but stare at bills.'

'Don't talk to me of bills. Look, this is what I came to show you. Isn't it divine?'

She held out a piece of delicate cream-coloured lace.

'Too pretty. Nottingham?'

'Bruges. An old admirer, the sweetest thing. A Norwegian, can you imagine? I went with my sister and a governess years ago, when I was a girl and Dolly was still in the school-room. We stayed in a pension and were supposed to be improving our French and he was staying there too before going into the Army and he quite fell for us. We used to go for bicycle rides by the canal. I think it was Dolly he really fell for. She had such lovely golden hair, right down her back – of course she didn't use to put it up then, and he used to gaze and gaze at it – and then of course she died, poor darling, of that beastly diptheria, and he still writes to me every now and then even after all these years. The other day he sent me this because he was going through Belgium for some reason – I don't know why, he's an army officer now – but it's pretty, isn't it?'

Minnie took the piece of lace and spread it out on her knee to see the intricate pattern.

'What a touching story.'

'But what shall I do with it, do you think? It's too good to put on a petticoat or an under-bodice and there isn't enough for a pair of sleeves.'

'You're so clever at that sort of thing. Those shoes with lace appliqué you were wearing last night were too fascinating. If it were me I expect I'd just trim the bodice of a dress with it. Haven't you got anything being made you could use it on?'

'Well yes, but I was thinking of not getting in touch with my dressmaker for a bit. I may have to be a bit elusive to one or two people of that kind for a month or so.'

'Bills?'

'My confounded bookmaker mainly. I've never known a man so stingy with credit. He knows he'll get it in the end.'

'I could probably let you have a little something for a few

weeks if it would help.'

'My dear, you are too sweet, I couldn't possibly. I can't bear looting my friends. If only I hadn't had such a rotten Cesarowitch. I can't tell Gilbert because I promised to give it up. I could let you have it back very soon, that's the only thing, because he pays me part of my dress allowance on the first of December.'

'Of course I can let you have something till then. It's so horrid having to worry about money.' Minnie reached for her cheque book, wiped her pen on her green leather pen-wiper, dipped it into the ink and held it poised.

'One? Two?'

'You're too sweet. If you could make it two.'

Minnie filled in the cheque for two hundred pounds, saying as she did so, 'What about a hand of whist? We shall get quite enough fresh air this afternoon and we've plenty of time before we need to change.'

'Divine. As long as you don't make it double or quits.'

'No, no, no,' said Minnie, ringing the bell for someone to put out the card table. 'Gambling at cards before lunch? What immorality. Certainly nothing over sixpence a point.'

*

All morning the sound of shooting came intermittently from the Park, moving gradually closer to the thick belt of woods which descended to the river. A breeze had come up, and carried the salvoes of shot across the orderly landscape of the Park to the garden, where the men still working on the herbaceous border heard them, and through the window of Olivia's room, which she had opened to let in the smell of autumn with the sunlit air: she did not listen, concentrating instead on the tale Cicely had to tell her. The sound of shots carried no message of alarm; it was nearly two hundred years since a party of redcoats had skirmished in those woods with a hopelessly ill-organised group of supporters of the Old Pretender; more than two hundred and fifty since an ancestor of Sir Randolph's, surprised by an ambush in a hedgerow just beyond the confines of the Park, gave his life for his King and became thereby the inspiration for one of the most perfect pieces of prose in Clarendon's *History of the Civil*

War. The sacrifice now was not of men but of birds, handsome creatures, bred up in every luxury a bird could wish for by Glass and his men, fed, protected from predators, set loose for a few months of life in what it was to be presumed might be a pheasant's Eden, only to be cast forth by a whole host of rustic angels, bearing not so much flaming swords as sticks and whistles, forced to take to the air reluctantly – heavy birds, a flight of more than a few feet exhausts them – forced up and out to meet a burst of noise and a quick death in that bright air.

'Good high birds,' the shooters said.

'Plenty of them.'

'That was a real rocketer you got on that last drive, Gilbert,' said Bob Lilburn.

'A lucky shot that one.'

'You're too modest. I heard you once had seven dead birds in the air at once. I've always wanted to ask you if it was true. At Sandringham, was it?'

'Yes, well, conditions there are so good one tends to find one's best form. Especially when there's such a virtuoso as the present monarch to spur one on. I know one had better not say a word against the late lamented King in this household, but the present chap's a much better shot.'

'I've only shot with him once, at Lowther. We had the Kaiser that day too. Very Royal.'

'He doesn't do too badly does he, considering he only uses a 20-bore because of the arm?'

'I always have a feeling you can't rely on a fellow with a withered arm. Irrational, I suppose.'

'He can be very charming. Arrogant, of course. Great friend of mine's got a withered arm. Mauled by a tiger in India. Nothing wrong with him.'

'That's different. Not born with it. Does he shoot?'

'Who, George? Not any more. He's a first-rate helmsman though.'

Two tall men in tweeds striding across the plough talking of the great days at Cowes, the new twelve metres, Sir Thomas Lipton's Shamrock, the America's Cup.

'Too loud,' muttered Sir Randolph to his grandson. 'Don't know why people have to chatter so when they're out shooting.'

'Not as bad as Cicely.'

'If your sister talks when she comes out this afternoon I shall send her home. Last time she seemed to think it necessary to squeak every time the fellow she was standing next to let off his gun.'

'I couldn't seem to hit a thing at the last stand. Did you see me at all?'

'You vacillate. Doesn't do to be indecisive. When they're coming over fast, choose one and aim. I think I caught you looking at your loader too, didn't I?'

'I might have.'

'Never look at your gun or your loader. Keep your eyes forward. Your swing's improved a lot though. You got a good cross-flyer a couple of drives back.'

They waited in the plough facing a coppice of mixed soft-woods which sloped slightly downhill towards them. Because of the mild autumn many of the leaves were still green: only the horse-chestnuts and ashes were russet. The silence had just begun to give way to the sound of the approaching beaters when a roe deer suddenly appeared at one end of the wood, crashing noisily out of the undergrowth where it had been hiding. It ran towards the line of guns, saw them and turned back towards the woods. When it heard the beaters it hesitated, head high, eyes and nostrils dilated, then with occasional long leaps ran the whole length of the line and away across the Park to the bound-ary of beech trees. Tibor Rakassyi had raised his gun, but being towards the centre of the line had time to notice that no one else had done so, so did not shoot. A smile seemed to be passed along the line in the wake of the animal. Tibor accordingly received it from Lionel Stephens and passed it on to Tommy Farmer, rather as if it were an item, a slipper perhaps, in one of those mysterious games which Cicely would insist on playing after dinner.

The roe deer had been started by Dan Glass. He had been walking down the edge of the wood and had seen it run from him between the trees. He knew there were roe deer about because he had seen tracks and droppings but they were extraordinarily elusive and it was some months since he had seen one. It was a young male half-way through its autumn moult. He paused for a moment to take note of the exact position – it would be a good place to come back to with some plaster of Paris and make a mould from a fresh footprint – then hurried to bring himself level with Tom Harker, who was next to him in the line of beaters. Tom, who was whistling and tapping rather mechanically now, looking forward to the break for lunch, had taken care to change his position in the line; he did not want to walk next to someone who had succumbed to the evils of alcohol. The man of whom he thought in these disapproving terms, a woodman by the name of Walter Weir, was up towards the other end of the line, where Glass had noticed his condition and hoped he might soon sweat it out. The steady progress over sometimes rough ground was hot work, and even those men who were free of the particular disadvantage under which Walter Weir was labouring found the pauses between drives a relief. Then they could feel the fresh breeze, and the slight chill as the sweat dried on their faces.

Glass was preoccupied by his responsibilities. Well though he knew his job, he knew also that this day – the last day of the biggest shooting party of the year – was the culmination of his year's work. Of course, there would be other shoots. The second big shoot at Nettleby was towards the end of November but traditionally the important one – the one to which the best sportsmen were invited – was during the last week of October. The fact of some of the leaves being still on the trees was a welcome challenge: less expert shots preferred to come later in the year. Apart from the two big parties, extending each over three days, there would be day shoots, and after Christmas there would be two or three days for shooting cocks only, but none of this was anything like as important as the October shoot. The October shoot was the one for the crowned heads and the famous sportsmen, Lord Hartlip, Mr Stephens, Lord Lilburn: when Royalty was here, the last two drives down by the river were often watched by a crowd of spectators lining the opposite bank to see the performance, constituting incidentally one of his worst worries. They could not be relied upon to keep quiet, had been known to call out comments or encouragement. He would never forget the day, the last time the late King had shot at Nettleby, when a loud and none too sober voice from the crowd had shouted, just as the first birds flew out, 'Come on, Teddy, give 'em what for!' He had never been able to find out who it was.

There had been nothing like that so far today; only the fact that a small body of beaters, all from the hamlet of Upfield, had lagged behind on one drive and caused a slightly ragged presentation of the birds to the guns. He had told them they could all go home if they could do no better than that, separated them from each other and had no further trouble. The morning pursued its course with apparently faultless organisation, but Glass knew he could not relax his vigilance for one moment.

As the first shots were fired on the last stand but one before lunch, Percy Maidment and Albert Jarvis gave each other one quick little glance before their full attention was required by their respective champions. Sir Randolph, quite reassured – now that Gilbert looked so calm and the morning was taking its course so pleasantly – that the spirit in the air was sporting rather than vulgarly competitive, had placed Gilbert and Lionel side by side at the end of the line, since the lie of the land was such that there was usually a great concentration of birds in that corner and they could expect some excitement. He himself stood well back, midway between the two of them, to pick off any birds that sheer pressure of numbers might oblige them to leave.

As he had expected, the birds came over fast and high. Even so the two experts in front of him were so quick and accurate that not many passed them. Intent though he was on his own shooting, he had time to notice the exhibition of skill in front of him.

'Well, Charlie,' he said to his loader when the drive was over. 'You don't often see shooting like that.'

'I never seen anything like it, Sir Randolph,' said Charlie Pass with true admiration.

Sir Randolph watched Lorna about the task of picking up the birds and noticed that Albert Jarvis and Percy Maidment were busy doing the same with a haste which seemed almost frantic. Hardly straightening their backs between picking up one bird and the next, they hurried to and fro across the small area of ground which was most thickly strewn with corpses as if they themselves were under fire and in danger of imminent destruction. Sir Randolph looked at them in some surprise and was even more astonished to see Lorna, on her way back to him with a bird, being waylaid by the two of them, each attempting to grab the pheasant. Lorna let them have it and went back to look for another, whereupon the two began to quarrel loudly as to whose bird it was.

Sir Randolph, hesitating to reprimand them when it seemed

to him the responsibility of their own masters to do so, was relieved when Gilbert Hartlip, who had begun to walk away towards the group of other sportsmen, evidently heard the raised voices and turned back.

'What's all this Jarvis?'

'I'm sorry, my lord, this was your bird, my lord, what I was just picking up.'

'My impression was that it was Mr Stephens's bird, my lord,' said Percy Maidment doggedly.

'Where was it lying?'

'Just here, my lord.'

'That was one of mine. Pick it up would you, Jarvis.'

He nodded dismissively to Percy Maidment, who went quite pale with suppressed rage, but turned at once obediently and went to pick up another bird.

Sir Randolph, disappointed (he would have preferred to see Gilbert rebuke both men equally), caught up with his guest. 'That man of yours seems rather jealous on your behalf.'

'He's a good enough man, Jarvis. Been with me for years. He's not usually wrong about that sort of thing.' Gilbert spoke with careless assurance. Sir Randolph did not like to object further. It seemed appropriate to his mood that the first cloud of the day had crept up to cover the sun.

*

Cornelius Cardew had heard the last burst of shooting, and was making his way briskly between the hedgerows in the direction in which he had calculated the morning's campaign must be going. The last drive before lunch, it seemed to him, must be on the outskirts of the small wood which was the last group of trees in the main part of the park, before the big wood and the descent to the river. He had already ascertained from enquiry in the village that lunch was likely to take place in the boat-house.

As he strode along he noticed with pleasure the small flurries of finches among the hawthorn berries in the hedge, and the flash of a yellowhammer darting ahead of him; he had time to notice a tiny wren making her way along the inside of the hedge towards a pleasant tangle of bramble, hawthorn and dogrose in which several blue tits were already finding nourishment; a pair of magpies were churring at each other (or at him) in the field just over the hedge, and the rooks in the tall elms by the gates of the park were settling back into the branches from which the shooting had earlier disturbed them. Once he had been master in charge of the Ornithological Society, but that was a long time ago, before he had discovered Socialism, before he had married.

'Is Miss Tremlett interested in birds, sir?' the boys had asked him with simulated innocence.

That was Ada, the Headmaster's daughter, serene and swan-like by the river's edge.

'Quite, I think,' he'd answered, assuming indifference.

'Only quite, sir? She seemed very interested the other evening, sir, when you were looking for moorhens' nests.'

'She has a particular fondness for water birds, Watkins. Have you finished your identification sheet for the woodlark?'

Watkins had been a little beast, he remembered, with a filthy mind and a maddening capacity to jabber in Latin verse; he was certainly a don by now. Cornelius had seldom cared for the clever boys. Given books, they taught themselves; he preferred the boys who needed him. He sometimes wondered whether Ada needed him. Ada had been taught only to play the piano, sew and read Emerson's *Essays*; and yet he often had an uncomfortable feeling that she was much cleverer than he was. He had encouraged her to read widely since their marriage, but that had only seemed to mean that she had more to talk about to H. W. Brigginshaw when he came over to play duets. She did not like to talk to Cornelius about ideas. She said they made him too excited and then he would start all that nonsense. Cornelius had thought that married life would include all that nonsense quite frequently but it seemed that Ada preferred to keep it to a minimum. As a devoted husband he respected her wishes and continued with admirable disinterestedness to campaign for freer sex for everyone else, only occasionally leaving a particularly eloquent pamphlet on her writing table in the hope that she might read it. Her preferred cause, however, was Votes for Women.

Reaching the end of the Park wall he continued some way beside the fence of post and rails which succeeded it and which ran along the outskirts of the big wood. Reaching a wicket gate which opened onto a well-worn path into the wood he turned in, and as he closed the gate behind him was horrified to notice that the fence beside it had had two higher rails added above it for a space of five or six feet and that this structure, conveniently placed as it was by a path from which one might turn either towards the house or towards Glass's cottage, constituted one of the gamekeeper's gibbets. It was crowded with corpses in varying degrees of decomposition. The topmost rail held a row of small mammals, some of them hardly more than a leaf-like shape of dried skin or a bedraggled tail, moles mostly or squirrels, and next to them, some obviously more recently killed and still smelling powerfully of rotting flesh, were weasels and stoats, five or six of each. Below these were the black feathers and evil beaks of crows, magpies with their tail feathers gone and a couple of brightly coloured jays which could not have been there for more than a day or two. Below again came the multifariously speckled feathers of kestrels and sparrow hawks, miniscule and soft on their breasts, long and curved for swiftness of flight on their wings, their fine-boned heads mostly skeletal, eye sockets void; and beneath them hung the owls, three tawny owls and a barn owl, wings hanging open, swaying from time to time as the breeze touched them.

'Cads,' said Cornelius Cardew, facing the rows of dead. 'Unspeakable cads.'

He turned away. Grasping more firmly his long blackthorn stick and the square of cardboard he held under one arm, he followed the path through the wood to where another less well-used track led away from it uphill. This he calculated must be the way to the boundary between the River Wood and the Park. He hurried, afraid that his estimate of the time it would take beaters and sportsmen to re-position themselves for the last drive of the morning might have been wrong, but when he came to the edge of the wood and paused he could see the beaters waiting at one side of a thick coppice of mixed ash, wych-elm and beech with a belt of dark spruce planted on the outskirts. Keeping to the shelter of the trees he fixed the piece of cardboard – on which was written in large red letters THOU SHALT NOT KILL – to the top of his stick and waited for the beaters to disappear into the wood. At a signal from Glass they began to move. As soon as they were well in among the trees, and screened from him by the thick spruce, Cornelius walked quickly across the intervening open space and into the wood at the corner furthest from the beaters. He had not yet seen any of the waiting guns, but peering now from behind a tree towards the Park on the other side of the coppice he could see Gilbert Hartlip not many yards away from him, with Albert Jarvis and a young boy attentive behind him. Further away stood Bob Lilburn and his loaders, with Tommy Farmer yet further on and Sir Randolph standing behind and between Gilbert Hartlip and Bob Lilburn. The sound of the beaters making their way through the wood could already be heard. The waiting figures were silent and alert. It was hard for a moment to remember that the keen concentration of their hunting instinct was not directed at their fellow man. Cornelius grasped his stick and waited.

The beaters were coming nearer, pushing their way through the undergrowth, breaking twigs and branches, whistling, tapping, irrevocably advancing. Trapped (though wilfully) between this approaching army and the tense figures waiting in the open space beyond the wood, Cornelius felt the whole wood alive around him. Two jays flew over his head, screeching, followed by a single green woodpecker; blackbirds were hurrying through the brambles, a stoat ran almost over his foot without noticing him, then turned back into a thick tangle of bramble, ignoring the two or three rabbits which were running close behind it. Dozens of pheasants were running through the undergrowth, reluctant to fly; some of them moved quietly and without haste, perhaps survivors from earlier onslaughts who had learned cunning. Finally with a whirr of wings a handsome cock bird flew out of the high branches, over the outlying ash trees and on into the sunlight. Lord Hartlip's shot stopped it instantly. Such had been its impetus that the lifeless bundle of ruffled feathers seemed momentarily suspended in the air before it fell with a thump to the ground. Lorna trembled but did not move. Two or three shots came from the other end of the line but close though the beaters now were the pheasants still held back, running from side to side or flying low through the branches. Two broke out close to Cornelius; both fell to Gilbert Hartlip. Another flew over high and fast and fell, he could not see to whom. Suddenly a hare appeared from behind him and dashed out onto the grass at a tremendous speed. Shot in the hindquarters it rolled over and began to scream. Another shot sent it somersaulting over and over before it died. And then suddenly the air was full of pheasants. In twos and threes and then in larger groups they flew out, away from the beaters and high over the guns. The shooting was continuous now; Cornelius could smell cordite; scattered pellets fell all round him, pattering onto the branches and the fallen leaves.

'Enough of this,' he said loudly.

At the same time an astonished voice from within the wood called out 'What the...?'

But he had gone. Grasping his banner firmly and raising it above his head he stepped out from the trees and marched towards Gilbert Harlip. A few yards away from him, he turned sharply right and began to march straight down the line in front of the guns.

Gilbert did not falter, his eyes fixed on the air above Cornelius's head.

'What the hell is that man doing?'

Bob Lilburn stopped shooting.

'Look out, you fool!'

Gilbert's glance moved to his left for a second only then returned to the air in front of him. He held out his gun, hot-barrelled, received its re-loaded pair, raised and fired it in one movement, swung and fired the second barrel, held it out again. The interruption had not caused him to lose a single shot.

'Out of the way, man,' shouted Bob Lilburn.

Cornelius walked slowly forward, his gaze fixed straight ahead.

'Fetch that man up here, would you,' said Sir Randolph quietly to Charlie Pass.

At the same time Glass, who from the end of the line of beaters had seen Cornelius set off from the shelter of the trees and had immediately shouted to Walter Weir to move over so as to take his own place, broke out of the wood at a run. Walter, sober now and anxious to redeem himself, moved over quickly, calling out to the man next to him to fill the gap. Glass ran heavily towards Cornelius, reaching him at the same moment as Charlie Pass; each seized one of the intruder's arms.

'Let me go!'

Waving his banner wildly in the air Cornelius resisted their attempts to march him towards Sir Randolph.

'Let me go I say!'

The sound of his own voice, high and nervous, struck him immediately as inadequate. They were pushing him about, making firm but reassuring noises as if he were a bullock that had strayed into the wrong field.

He made an effort to speak louder and lower.

'Leave me alone!'

'Can't do that, for your own safety, sir,' said Glass, no less firmly but slightly more respectfully; he had noticed the educated accent. 'If you'll just come along and have a word with Sir Randolph now, that would be the best thing.'

Lord Lilburn and Tommy Farmer, in front of whom the altercation was taking place, had both hesitated for some minutes in their shooting, partly because their concentration had been broken by the interruption and partly because they wanted to make sure that they were not likely to hit anybody by mistake, but now reassured by the sight of Glass and realising that shots aimed at birds so high above the heads of the men in front of them were no serious danger to the latter, they turned their attention back to the pheasants. None of the other guns had faltered. The noise and the continuous light rain of falling shot all round them, as well as the danger of being hit on the head by a dead or dying bird, weakened Cornelius's resolve. He allowed the two men to propel him in the direction of Sir Randolph, who though deprived of his chief loader was still picking off most of such pheasants as escaped the fire of Gilbert Hartlip and Bob Lilburn. As they passed Gilbert Hartlip, his loader Albert Jarvis, though fully occupied and indeed trembling with the keeness of his concentration, still had time to mutter out of the corner of his mouth with a sibilant viciousness which surprised Cornelius, 'Silly sodding bugger.'

Sir Randolph lowered his gun and looked at Cornelius.

'You don't approve of our sport, I fear.'

'It is not my idea of sport. It is my idea of murder.'

'Ah yes. That's all right, Glass. We'll go on down to the boathouse when this drive is over. You've caught us just at the end of our murderous morning, sir, and we're about to join the rest of our party for our ill-earned lunch. Tell me, are you from these parts? I don't think we've met before, have we?'

Cornelius, his arms freed, stuck his stick firmly into the ground, paused for a moment to straighten the cardboard placard so that Sir Randolph should be face to face with the third commandment, and produced from his pocket a pamphlet, the same he had given Tom Harker on the previous evening.

'My own work.'

'"The Rights of Animals, a Vindication of the Doctrine of Universal Kinship." I see. These pheasants of course, if one wanted to be legalistic about it, wouldn't be here at all if we hadn't put them here, got the eggs, hatched them out, reared the chicks – you might say we give them life and then after a bit we take it away again – abrogating to ourselves somewhat God-like powers I must admit. But let's not bother with all that. This is a very well-produced pamphlet, Mr Cardew. Tell me, where do you get such a thing printed? Is it very expensive? I hope you don't mind my asking?'

'Not at all. There's a very good printer in Dorking, near where I live, an excellent man of anarchist views. He gives me very good rates.'

'Special terms, ah. I shouldn't get such good ones, I suppose.'

'Are you a pamphleteer, sir?'

'I was thinking of making some sort of foray in that direction. I'm very concerned about the neglect of rural life in this country. People don't understand its importance you know, don't understand, if I may say so, its traditions – in which I would include its sports. I'm perpetually expressing myself on paper on these subjects. I thought I might put together some little thing for publication, a pamphlet yes, a polemic really, a polemic I think is probably the right word.'

'Rural life, I see. Would you include economics, the plight of the agricultural labourer and so on?'

'Certainly. Unless we support our agriculture the people who work on the land will soon be as poor as the Irish. Half of them live in hovels as it is, eating nothing but boiled pudding.'

Cornelius nodded. 'The decay of rural life, a polemic. I'm sure I could interest my printer friend. The decay – the ruin even would you say? – would you say the ruin?'

'The ruin, if you like.'

'The Ruin of Rural England. A Polemic. A diatribe. Could you make it a diatribe?'

'Certainly I could make it a diatribe.'

'The Ruin of Rural England, a Diatribe!'

'Precisely.'

The drive over, those nearest Sir Randolph strolled towards him, curious to observe the intruder; the men picking up the birds or urging the dogs to do so eyed him suspiciously. All were surprised, none pleased, to see Sir Randolph and Cornelius Cardew facing each other with satisfied smiles over the militant title at which they had arrived. Their pose struck no one as appropriate.

'That man deserves to be shot,' said Bob Lilburn loudly as he approached.

'He damned nearly was,' said Tommy Farmer, supportively indignant.

'Perhaps we might continue our discussion some other time?' murmured Sir Randolph. 'These murderers are a hot-blooded lot you know. If I may keep this? I shall certainly read it. And perhaps it has your address?'

Cornelius looked round, and noted that Lord Lilburn in his tweeds looked remarkably large and fit. He felt hurriedly in his pockets.

'My card.'

'Thanks. Hindhead, how charming. We'll certainly be in touch. You'll broach the matter with your printer friend?'

'He shall send you an estimate, without fail. Good day to you, sir.'

Cornelius cheerfully hoisted his placard and set off towards the wood. On the way he passed between various groups of shooters, dog-handlers and beaters, and turned from side to side to greet them with a confident wave and a more or less playful shake of his stick. He was greeted by stares which expressed varying degrees of unfriendliness. Only Sir Randolph, watching his irregular progress which was interrupted by pauses to re-adjust the placard – it had a tendency to slip askew on the stick when he raised it in the air – and to lift his wide-brimmed hat to the more formidable in appearance of the shooters – he had a particularly wild smile for the tall and stony-eyed Lord Hartlip – only Sir Randolph smiled benignly.

Bob Lilburn approached his host.

'You'll have him up in front of the Bench, I imagine.'

'He had to get back to Hindhead,' said Sir Randolph vaguely. 'Pretty place, Hindhead. Do you know it at all?'

*

Down by the river there was a cool breeze. Nanny wished she had made Violet put on her woollen gaiters.

'Come along now, we'll be late for lunch.'

Violet was hanging over the bridge, scuffing the toes of her shoes on the stone wall. Under the bridge the river slid smoothly and fast towards a shallower passage of miniature rapids, through which it splashed its way with a variable rippling haste from which Violet found it hard to remove her gaze once caught. Beyond the rapids came deeper water, flowing apparently more slowly towards the shaded bends and quiet pools where chub and trout moved lazily among the long strands of straight green weed.

'She isn't here, what shall we do?'

'She's probably at home by now.'

'We promised Osbert we'd find her.'

'We can't find her if she's not here. She'll be at home, eating up her food, that's where she'll be. Come along.'

'We promised.'

'He can come down himself after lunch. He can miss his rest. There now.'

'He doesn't rest anyway.'

Violet reluctantly allowed Nanny to take her hand and lead her back towards the road.

'Don't dawdle so, Violet. He does rest. He reads his book.'

'I have to rest with my eyes shut.'

'So did Osbert at your age.'

'He used to creep out and do naughty things. He went out into the Park and got knocked over by a sheep.'

'That's one of his stories. You shouldn't believe him.'

'It stamped its foot at him, and then it knocked him over with its nose. I'm tired, I can't walk any further.'

'I know someone who got out of bed the wrong side this morning.'

'I didn't get out any different side from what I usually do. Oh look, that's Granny's car.'

They had been walking along a footpath beside the river and

now reached a wooden stile which led on to the road. A car was approaching them, moving rather slowly. Violet hopped up onto the stile and waved. Patten the chauffeur was driving the big Daimler down to lunch. He had already transported first of all the housekeeper and two maids to prepare the boat-house and light the fire and then Rogers and two footmen with the lunch, some of it in hayboxes to keep it hot; the housekeeper and the maids had been returned to the house, their duties completed. Now he had Cicely beside him in the front, while behind the glass screen Aline and Minnie and Ida, wearing their tweeds, talked about her marriage prospects, and Olivia, who had put on a brown velvet jacket above her long dark tweed skirt, with a brown fur hat and muff, looked out of the window and wondered whether she would find herself sitting next to Lionel Stephens at lunch.

Aline had asked whether the Hungarian could be considered a serious contender for Cicely's hand.

'We're not thinking of it,' Ida had answered.

'Couldn't we look on him as just a little bit sur le tapis?' Minnie suggested. 'Just a foot, just a toe? He is so handsome.'

'Her father's against her marrying a Continental,' said Ida. 'He says things are too unsettled at the moment to risk her marrying anyone except an Englishman.'

'If there was a war we'd all be on the same side,' said Minnie comfortably. 'After all, all the Royal Families are related. They can't possibly have wars with each other. And the Rakassyis are so wonderfully rich.'

'An English match would be much more secure.'

'I suppose so. And all those foreign relations would be rather a bore. Foreign aunts and cousins are usually deadly, much worse than English ones. Besides, we can enjoy a year or two of speculating, can't we?'

'What does she think about it, I wonder?' said Olivia.

Minnie smiled at her.

'She will enjoy speculating too. She is not like you, with those high ideals which make you the princesse lointaine for so many admirers. Very few of us are like you, dear Olivia, that's why we cherish you so. Most of us are dreadfully mundane.'

'Oh.' Olivia protested; she was genuinely surprised.

Cicely tapped on the glass partition, laughing and pointing to the side of the road. Violet was standing on the stile waving, with Nanny beside her. Patten slowed down but did not stop. Violet saw Cicely laughing, her mother and grandmother waving, Olivia smiling, Aline's raised hand from the shadow of the back seat.

'If we start walking up the road Patten will give us a lift on his way back,' said Nanny.

In the car Olivia was saying, 'I do hope they found the duck.'

*

The boat-house was largely Minnie's creation. Ten years ago she had looked at the simple structure which at that time provided shelter for a couple of punts and an old rowing boat and had said, 'What we need here is a rustic summerhouse.'

Accordingly, on the top of the long low brick building which jutted out over the water so as to house the boats in an area half river and half bank, there had been constructed a big, gabled, half-timbered room with lattice windows looking out over the river. The land approach was through a wicket gate beside the path and across a lawn edged with neat flower beds to an entrance under a wooden balcony held up by pillars in the form of tree trunks; woodbine now mingled with the clematis which had been planted to clothe these rugged columns. Inside was a lobby, a serving-room and a room for keeping such necessities as fishing tackle and card-tables – Minnie had been known to call for these immediately lunch was over – but mainly there was the big, light room, its unpolished wooden floor covered with Indian rugs and its many windows looking out onto woods and river. There were trees, tall beeches mainly, on the opposite bank as well as on the side where the boat-house was built; so that river, sky, leaves and branches were all that could be seen.

In the summer Minnie liked to bring picnic parties here. When she was younger she sometimes took friends for a walk through the woods and led them to the boat-house as if by chance, throwing open the door triumphantly (just as they were feeling tired and wishing she would lead them home for lunch) to disclose a delicious meal laid out on a white table cloth and Rogers and the two footmen standing behind the chairs with just the right mixture of deference and shared pleasure in the guests' surprise. The children came there too, to bathe or picnic or fish; in a long spell of fine weather the boys might be allowed to spend the night.

For a shooting lunch in late October the fire had to be lit and the place aired the day before; even so there was a slight smell of damp. Minnie loved the boat-house nonetheless. She hurried in ahead of the others, congratulating Rogers on the preparations, re-arranging cushions and chrysanthemums, exclaiming, 'It is pretty though, isn't it? Olivia, Aline, you must admit it's pretty. Don't you love it?'

Yes, they said, they loved it.

A log fire was burning in the open fireplace (smoking a little, it had to be admitted, but not so as seriously to affect the eyes), a grandfather clock was ticking in one corner of the room, and round the walls were dark oak dressers with blue china on their shelves. Immediately in front of the fire were two handsome bronze dogs on which to rest the fire irons, and grouped around the fireplace were several basket chairs with cushions covered in the same flowered cretonne as the curtains. In the middle of the room was a long narrow refectory table laid for lunch and surrounded by Windsor wheelback chairs.

'Just like the three bears!' cried Aline.

'Rather more than three,' said Cicely. 'And far too many Goldilocks'.'

She went over to kneel on the window seat looking out at the river.

'This cushion's damp. I bet it's been used in the punt.'

'The young are so critical,' said Minnie without rancour. 'I think we could open one bottle of champagne, Rogers, before they come. Lady Hartlip looks cold. Come by the fire, my dear, and have a little glass of champagne to warm you up.'

'They're coming,' said Cicely from the window. 'I can see Glass with Sambo and the game cart. I shall go and kiss his darling old nose.'

'Cicely, Cicely,' her grandmother remonstrated.

'She means Sambo's nose,' explained Ida without smiling.

'Even so. . . .'

*

93

Lionel felt quite strange, walking along the path through the trees, turning in through the open gate towards the entangled rustic columns and the wooden balcony and the painted gable, an enchantress's dwelling certainly, so deep in the woods and close to the quiet-flowing river. As soon as he had seen the building he had felt this strangeness, faintness almost. All morning he had been concentrating on the familiar and satisfying routine of shooting, a routine in which the alternate demands of technique and good manners meant that one had little time left over for dreaming; the sight of the boat-house brought the dream immediately to the forefront of his mind. She would be there already.

Lionel had known Bob Lilburn slightly for many years, but had not met Olivia until Maisie Arlington had happened to ask them all to the same dinner party only a few months ago before a ball at the Russian Embassy. He had thought her beautiful and good, clever and kind, but it seemed to him that there were many married women of his acquaintance to whom those four adjectives could aptly be applied. The mystery was as to how the foolish creatures in their first or second season next to whom he often found himself sitting at dinner could turn apparently overnight into such exquisitely civilized beauties. Of course, they were quite endearing, the girls, with their touching determination to keep talking at all costs and their tendency when one saw them at home in the country to relapse into their former ways as the tomboys of the schoolroom, only pulling themselves up short from time to time when they remembered they were young ladies now with their hair up and a duty to keep younger brothers and sisters, governesses, ponies and dogs at an appropriate distance, but he found them insufficiently serious and was afraid that as a result they thought him a prig. But a wife, he thought, who was to be one's life's companion, had to be someone to look up to. He felt in himself a capacity for adoration which loosed on one of these insubstantial creatures might be expected to frighten her to death. How could he lay upon one of these children the responsibility of personifying the Ideal? So he went home to Lincolnshire and his mother, whose acid tongue did not prevent him from seeing her as having always held out for him the supremacy of beauty and honour, this being it seemed to him a considerable part of what women were for. At a slightly different level he took actresses out to dinner. He gained thereby a reputation (to which he was indifferent) as a man about town, but most of them were respectable girls and when they were not he usually felt rather a beast afterwards. That the beastliness and the capacity for worship might one day unite and both be bent upon one chosen object had begun to seem less and less likely. His third meeting with Olivia had achieved it.

'It must be so, mustn't it?' she had said.

She had been expressing some view, as usual putting a better construction upon things than anyone else, and then she had turned to him and said 'It must be so, mustn't it?' and he had seen in her eyes for the first time that question which he now recognised as underlying so much of her being. It was her longing for goodness combined with the slight desperation with which sometimes, failing to find it and in spite of her wish to be clear-sighted in facing realities, she turned for reassurance to others, which he found so touching. For though she could be definite in her views, scathing in her criticisms, it was when she faltered, when her brightness was occluded by doubt, that he most adored her.

Lionel knew Bob Lilburn as a practical man, a sportsman, a good landowner. No one could have called him imaginative. Olivia would have expected more understanding than he had to give. She would have expected it because he looked like a hero; but he, Lionel, could answer her questions better than Bob could, because he could say 'Yes, it must be so, and if it is not so I will make it so', and because in appealing thus to one side of his nature she also appealed to the other, because her short upper lip trembled slightly as she raised her eyes to his and the impulse to crush the doubts with an abundance of kisses seemed over-whelming. He soon recognised himself as being in the grip of a tremendous passion. Small indications had made him believe she knew of it; his one object (beyond the attainment of which he did not even speculate) had become to make her admit what she knew.

*

When Cicely kissed Sambo's nose it set up a frightful tickling around his whiskers. He blew down his nose but failed to ease the situation. He stretched out his neck to its fullest extent and drew his lips back from his yellowing teeth to make an expression like a disdainful camel's, then as if embarrassed by the laughter this caused he lowered his head and rubbed his face against the front of Cicely's tweed jacket, almost knocking her over.

'Your manners, your manners,' she expostulated.

Tibor Rakassyi had approached, smiling.

'He is not used to being kissed by pretty young ladies.'

'It's a funny reaction, to make a face like a camel.'

'If you would care to experiment I can make some very pretty faces.'

'And you always do, when kissed on the nose?'

'Almost always.'

'You must look funny. How was the shooting?'

'Perfection.'

'Not for the pheasants, I suppose. Are you hungry? There is a delicious lunch.'

The shooters were making their way slowly into the boat-house, in twos and threes, talking. Lionel Stephens hung back, finding himself at the last minute unaccountably afraid of setting eyes upon Olivia, as if he could not be sure what might happen when he did.

Servants were carrying out a heavy cauldron from which hot rabbit stew was to be dispensed to the beaters, who were already forming themselves into a straggling line along the path by the river some little distance from the boat-house. Albert Jarvis and Percy Maidment finding themselves adjacent moved by un-spoken agreement further apart; they were hardly on speaking terms, so acute was their rivalry.

Albert Jarvis came from Derbyshire. The Hartlip estates were close to coal-mining country on the Yorkshire border, and the Jarvises were a mining family. Albert had failed to find a job down the mine on leaving school and had become an agricultu-ral labourer and then an under-keeper instead. He had a keen admiration for his employer, whose remote manner when dealing with subordinates only added to his authority in Albert's eyes. A good shot himself, Albert's respect for Lord Hartlip's skill was unbounded; he looked on him more or less as his personal champion. A bachelor, living in lodgings and seldom visiting his family, working long hours for low wages, his sense of identification with his employer – with whom his function as loader put him at certain times of the year and unlike the other under-keepers into the relation of personal servant – was in many ways his essence; it was as if Lord Hartlip did his living for him. Albert had quickly recognized in the tense little form of Percy Maidment a similar determination that his man should be pre-eminent. It set them apart from the others. They were like two greyhound trainers among a crowd of onlookers who had not even bothered to place bets.

Tom Harker held both hands cupped round his baked potato and waited for his stew; he had no complaint. The food smelt good and behind and beyond the food the fallen leaves, the dark earth and the river smelt good; so did his own old coat and the hands he held up to his nose, warming them round the potato. They smelt of earth, sweat, the pheasants he had carried over to the game cart and which had left a smear or two of blood behind, and the onions he had cut up that morning to put into his own stolen rabbit stew. The morning's exercise left his body feeling easy; he had no thought beyond that and the satisfying of his hunger – except perhaps a hardly conscious regret that his collie was not with him. Being a fool, she'd not exercise herself; he'd have to walk her round the field when he got back, tired after the day's work. Besides, she liked the woods.

'See the deer?' he asked Dan Glass.

Dan nodded.

'I saw them in Bowlers Plantation last, a month or two back. A couple of young they had.'

'They've bred there before. It's the bracken up the top they like. They hide the young in there. You can walk right on top of them before they'll move.'

Dan smiled, not saying, 'And what might you have been doing in Bowlers plantation, Tom Harker?' though he thought it.

*

'There was this letter,' Cicely said. 'It said such wonderful things – you wouldn't have believed it.'

'What sort of things?' asked Lionel Stephens.

'That she was Truth because she was Beauty and Beauty

because she was Truth and that there was going to be a war and he was going to gird his loins and fight for her sake.'

Lionel Stephens looked serious. 'Where did she find this letter?'

'He gave it to her. John, the nice footman who was here a minute ago. He wrote it and gave it to her.'

'Do be careful, he'll hear.' Olivia was standing by the fire facing Cicely and Lionel.

'He's taking lunch out to the beaters. But really though, don't you think it's romantic? She couldn't believe it. He'd never done anything like that before. It was quite unlike him, she said.'

'Perhaps someone else wrote it for him,' suggested Lionel.

'But who? Sometimes the village people do ask the Vicar to write a letter for them when they can't do it themselves, but an you imagine Mr Fortescue producing anything so poetic?'

'It sounds a little overdone to me,' said Lionel. 'What would you think if you were written such a letter? Would you be pleased?'

'Pleased? I should be too fascinated.'

'And you?' Lionel asked Olivia.

'I should be dreadfully embarrassed.'

'Why?'

'I should feel ashamed. I should know I wasn't in the least worthy of it.'

'Wouldn't you be secretly just a little pleased?'

She shook her head, smiling, a little flushed. She would have liked it he thought, I ought to have sent it.

'Ellen was pleased,' said Cicely.

She saw her grandmother looking at her across the room. Minnie had an uncanny capacity to listen to other people's conversations while appearing to give undivided attention to her own. Knowing this, Cicely understood immediately from an almost imperceptible shake of Minnie's head that she was to change the subject. Even Cicely did not ignore that kind of directive from her grandmother.

'But you haven't told us what this morning's bag was,' she said at once to Lionel. 'Were there plenty of birds about?'

There were certain subjects one did not talk about because they were not amusing. Minnie had had to speak to Cicely before about bringing Ellen and her affairs into the conversation. Whoever could be supposed to want to talk about servants?

Sir Randolph was saying, 'Can't we sit down?'

'Oh he'd like to have nothing but a sandwich,' Minnie said. 'When I first came here they had nothing but hard little sandwiches and a glass of beer. Standing up, in the rain. It took me years of nagging to get him to change.'

'I daresay a certain Royal guest was quite a support in that way,' said Lord Lilburn (rather sycophantically, Minnie's daughter-in-law Ida thought).

'He liked a proper lunch.' But her smile, though fond, was brief; it did not encourage further conversation on the subject. Bob Lilburn had not been part of that set – he was too young for one thing – and Minnie only cared for reminiscences with others of the late King's intimates – or rather, such others as had been her friends, for there were one or two whose names even now Minnie did not like to hear mentioned, one or two whom she considered to have been disloyal, even treacherous, and though the dreadful details of their offences were never these days enumerated, certain now ageing – indeed in one notorious case deceased – ladies were by no means forgiven. Minnie, a good friend, was not one to forget an enemy.

'Very well then, we shall sit down, but you are not to hurry us. If I catch anyone gobbling their food I shall be very upset and I shall blame it all on you.'

'No question of gobbling. Plenty of time. Quarter-past two, I told Glass.'

'He is a terrible disciplinarian, my husband. He ought to have been in the Prussian Army. Aline my dear, sit beside him and distract him for goodness' sake.'

Aline had been looking out of the window. She had meant to be cold to Charles Farquhar – he seemed to her to be in a tiresomely jovial, boyish mood – and at the same time to remind him, by presenting him with a view of her profile, which was famous, of who – even (in the sense that she was a phenomenon) what – it was that he was treating so lightly and with such scant respect. It was Grecian, her profile; the line of forehead and straight fine nose was like a statue's; only her chin, according to Sir Randolph, was too long.

'Gilbert was telling me,' he said to her, 'that Harry Stamp last night was talking of letting Corston. Were you there when that conversation was going on?'

'No, but he did say something to me to the same effect. I can't remember why he said he wanted to do it.'

'Economy, I suppose. That's why most people do it. Doesn't seem the right thing to do to me. Seems a bit rat-like.'

'He looks more like a ratter than a rat,' said Aline. 'One of those little ratting dogs you know. A terrier or something. Jack Russells, aren't they? He seems more like a Jack Russell terrier than a rat.'

Lionel, following Minnie's indication that he should sit next to Olivia who was on Sir Randolph's right, joined in the conversation as he sat down.

'If he can recoup a bit that way, isn't it a sensible thing to do?'

'These people who take houses,' said Sir Randolph. 'They don't care twopence for the places. They don't take an interest. They just enjoy themselves. Why not? That's what they've taken the place for – it doesn't mean anything to them. It's not their house, their land, their village, their tenants, estate workers, servants. What do they care? But these are hard times for all these people. The agricultural depression's getting worse all the time. Nothing will induce the politicians to bring in protective tariffs, the only thing that might save us; we've just got to sit it out, retrench and sit it out. Letting your house and allowing your land to go to pot is not the right way to deal with it.'

'Is it really so bad?' asked Olivia. 'The countryside looks so beautiful and the people so happy.'

'They're having a hard time. We hear a lot these days about factory workers and conditions in slums. No one bothers about rural poverty – we deal with it locally of course as best we can but when there's no money in land there's no money for charity. No one cares about country people. All the attention goes to the towns.'

'I should have thought that every English person's deepest idea of England was of the country. Doesn't England mean a village green, and smoke rising from cottage chimneys, and the rooks cawing in the elms, and the squire and the vicar and the schoolmaster and the jolly villagers and their rosy-cheeked children?'

'It has not existed for many years now.'

100

'It must exist. How could we all believe in it so if it didn't exist?'

'Exactly. We believe in it. That is why the idea is such a powerful one. It is a myth.'

'If it is a myth, you are part of it.' Olivia was pleased with this idea. 'You are part of the myth, you see. That's why you say you don't believe in it, because you are inside it. It doesn't look the same to you, how could it?'

'You flatter me.' But he smiled, looking at her animated face. 'I'm not part of a myth. But I think there is a myth and I think it will be difficult to change it. It will lurk there at the back of our minds, disturbing our dreams of becoming a Twentieth-Century nation.'

'Is there no way of turning the myth into reality?'

'It would mean working againt the whole current of history. We are going to have a very different world, a world in which you and I, my dear, in our different ways, will each of us be dodos.'

'I think you will make a very distinguished dodo. I don't know that I shall do it as well. I shall have regrets, and remember that I once could fly.'

Aline, who had been talking to Tibor Rakassyi on her left, happening now to turn back towards her host and overhear Olivia's remark, looked questioning.

'Before I become a dodo,' Olivia explained.

'Didn't you adore that book?' said Aline, taking it as a reference to a recent novel. 'I like books one can swallow in a mouthful, like a chocolate, guiltily.'

'Anyone less like that Dodo would be hard to imagine,' said Lionel quietly to Olivia.

She thought he was referring to Aline.

'I'd have thought there might be similarities,' she answered.

'I meant you.'

'Oh, I am not half so dashing. But I'm shocked to hear that you read frivolous novels. I thought it was nothing but the Real Thing for you.'

'One can't have the Real Thing all the time. One can't live up to it. Besides my mother likes Mr E. F. Benson's works and I find them by my bed when I go home.'

Sir Randolph found that he could listen to Aline's conversation – some tale she had to tell about an incident in a bookshop, how she had seen someone with someone else and how that gave the game away – and at the same time let his mind wander, his imagination having been aroused by the mention of his favourite subject and by the sympathy revealed in Olivia's wide, blue-green, mysteriously dazzled (for she was short-sighted) eyes, which while her lips gave out the obligatory frivolities spoke of deeper feelings, larger understandings.

He did feel, if not yet a dodo, at least at the end of something; he did feel, looking round the room in which the watery light filtering through the beech leaves and reflecting the river gave everything a soft luminosity becoming to the unpainted faces of the women and the muted colour of their clothes and the blue and white of the china on the dark shelves behind them, that beyond the river and the trees, beyond the boundaries of his own estate, there was a whole clamorous violent disorderly process going on which was to bring about the end of an idea, an idea started by people whose combination of poetry and political acumen, curiosity and love of pastoral life, made them seem, he'd always thought, though Florentine, rather English. He believed – of course he believed – that Renaissance man had been best embodied in the eighteenth-century English gentleman, and it was this figure, standing in his library, a book in one hand, the other resting lightly on a piece of classical sculpture, gazing out over a landscape harmoniously ordered by himself and under his guidance his tenants, in the consciousness that from time to time he would be called upon to play a part in the government of his country or its defence, and that in due course his eldest son would take his place and stand at his library window and deal with his tenants and show his visitors the improvements – it was this figure which in Sir Randolph's mind accorded so ill with striking industrial workers, screaming suffragettes, Irish terrorists, scandals on the Stock Exchange, universal suffrage. If the hierarchy to which he belonged were to be swept away by absolute democracy what could his son the diplomat expect to inherit? Or his grandson Marcus, the schoolboy? His imagination ran suddenly far ahead, past bankruptcy, past expropriation, past the roused rabble and the barbarian horde, to the outposts and lonely places of the world, the faint torch of truth, the wide white light of the island of Iona.

'Now why are you smiling?' asked Aline.

102

'Because I was telling Olivia a few minutes ago my gloomy prognostications about the future, and the extraordinary thing is that sometimes when my thoughts about the future become very gloomy indeed, I find myself feeling more and more light-hearted about it. Do you find that at all?'

'I never have gloomy thoughts about the future. I can't afford to at my age, it would give me wrinkles.'

'I suppose I have always rather fancied the idea of having to take to the hills.'

'What hills? There aren't any round here.'

'We're not all that far from the Chilterns. But I suppose I mean that metaphorically. Taking to the hills when barbarian hordes overrun us, that's what I meant. I think I should enjoy it.'

'Minnie would simply hate it. I really think taking to the hills is not at all a suitable thing for Minnie to do. She and I will just have to stay behind and try to make friends with the barbarians.'

*

Sir Reuben Hergesheimer was describing to Minnie how a lunatic had appeared waving a placard and how he had taken for granted that it must be a suffragette and been astonished to find out that the agitation was on behalf of animals. 'Votes for pheasants, I suppose.'

'How absolutely disgraceful, the man should be horse-whipped,' said Minnie vigorously.

'He was just a crank,' said Bob Lilburn. 'There was really no cause for alarm.'.

Sir Reuben smiled. 'It is very hard to alarm Lady Nettleby.'

'What an ungracious thing to say. I am very easily frightened. That six in spades you called last night made me feel quite faint with terror.'

'You hadn't seen my hand. We made it, didn't we? You should have trusted me.'

'I trust you in every possible way except at the bridge table. I have learnt to trust no one at cards. What about that time when you called three hearts to my one club and we lost the rubber to that terrible Russian couple?'

'But that was fifteen years ago.'

'Of course. In Marienbad. I have a memory like an elephant—

more than an elephant, a brontosaurus – but only for cards. Now what about this horrible lunatic? Has he been shut up somewhere?'

'I think Sir Randolph rather took to him.'

'Took to him? What an extraordinary notion. How could he have done such a thing? He loves his shooting.'

'It seems they had certain other interests in common. When I came on the scene the man was promising to introduce your husband to an anarchist printer in Dorking.'

'That is so unlikely that I see at once it must be a perfectly convincing explanation for everything. How could they have got onto the subject, do you suppose?'

'It was a bad show,' said Bob Lilburn, still in tune with his hostess's former mood and unable to understand how her view that the man should have been horse-whipped could co-exist quite comfortably in her mind with the idea that it was rather delightful of her husband to have done nothing of the kind.

'The man had some literature,' said Sir Reuben. 'I only caught a glimpse of it but it was something about universal unity – no, kinship, that was it, universal kinship.'

'Good Heavens, ordinary kinship is bad enough, if one thinks of one's relations, without having to have the whole universe as one's kin. But still I can see that it might lead to just the sort of conversation Randolph likes. In fact, I'm astonished he didn't bring him to lunch. I shall ask him about that, I shall chide him, I think, don't you? He should have brought him to lunch. It might have been amusing.'

Bob Lilburn laughed, showing his even white teeth and thinking, really these grand old ladies are sometimes extraordinarily frivolous.

*

The lobster vol-au-vents consumed, the chicken mayonnaise with boiled potatoes before them, champagne or lemon squash in circulation, the conversation took its course with as much vivacity as was possible in view of the unevenness of numbers.

'But tonight,' Cicely said to Tibor Rakassyi, 'tonight there will be four beautiful ladies you have never seen before.'

'Four? What excitement. Tell me about them.'

104

'They are Mrs Walker Kerr, the Egeria of the Oxford academic world, and her two daughters. Please don't ask me who Egeria is, or was, I only know that is what Mrs Walker Kerr is of Oxford. She is very tragic and handsome and a widow and her daughters are my best friends, and so is Grizel Warburton who is the other person who is coming.'

'I thought best friends came singly. Can one have three at once?'

'Certainly. I have seven. We are all going to be each other's bridesmaids.'

'How charming. Are they all as pretty as you?'

'No, but some are prettier. Grizel Warburton is the prettiest person I know, of my age, I mean.'

'Is she the daughter of Lord Warburton?'

'Yes.'

'I have met Lord Warburton. So I am already more interested in Miss Grizel than in your other friends.'

'Oh, but the Walker Kerrs are perfectly well connected too. Mr Walker Kerr was a son of Lord Craven. He was killed in the most ghastly circumstances in Africa.'

'How terrible. What sort of circumstances?'

'He was eaten. By a huge black Zulu.'

'Oh really, Cicely,' Ida who was on the other side of the table had caught her daughter's last remark. 'You are naughty. It was nothing of the kind. He was killed in a perfectly straightforward manner in the Zulu wars.'

'Exactly,' said Cicely, undaunted. 'In a perfectly straightforward manner. For a Zulu.'

'I'm sure Zulus aren't cannibals,' said Ida, looking rather flustered. How could Cicely expect to make a good match if she persisted with this pert manner?

'Granny told me,' said Cicely. 'Ask Tommy to ask her if it's not true.'

Tommy was duly asked to pass the message to Sir Reuben who was next to him.

'Of course he was eaten by cannibals, poor man. Too dreadful,' was the answer.

Ida wondered whether Cicely and her grandmother were good for each other. Perhaps it was just as well that Cicely had invitations to house parties most of the winter.

*

Gilbert Hartlip was talking to Marcus about guns. His own Purdeys he said were the best he'd ever had – made to fit him – nothing like Purdey for smoothness and finish – yes, perhaps to fit a difficult customer, funny shoulders, one eye better than the other, Henry Holland had the experience, the patience – but he'd never go anywhere but Purdey now. Cogswell & Harrison, made when? – a very good beginner's gun, he'd got his first elephant gun there – Indian tigers – Maharajas – staying with the Viceroy – Oh Africa, yes, Kenya, good sport – a marvellous country – Scotland, had he done any stalking yet? – he'd enjoy it – rabbits? no need to be deprecating about rabbits – a rabbit, said Lord Hartlip, was a thoroughly sporting little beast.

He drank only lemonade. There was an occasional flash of pain at his right temple, sharp, but so brief that he hoped by ignoring it to prevent it from developing into a real headache. The worst thing, he had discovered, was to think about it. Marcus's artless admiration, his eagerness, like a good schoolboy, to learn, was the best possible distraction. At the same time Gilbert was not at ease. He was always tense and nervous when shooting – it was the ability when in action to keep this nervousness under an icy control which made him not just a good shot but a brilliant one – but today there was also a curious underlying feeling of dissatisfaction. It was something to do with what Aline had said to him last night, and the thought that she had probably said it on purpose to annoy made it no better; he did not think she would have invented it.

People were talking about him, were comparing him with others, doubting his supremacy. He had been one of the best shots in England for many years. He had few rivals, and those he had he liked and respected. If he had heard that people had been saying that Lord Ripon shot better than he did he would not have minded; he knew quite well that on some days Lord Ripon indeed shot better than he did, on other days he shot better than Lord Ripon. It was quite different to be compared adversely with Lionel Stephens. Lionel Stephens did not even shoot very much – he certainly did not take it as seriously as Gilbert did. More than that, he was probably half Gilbert's age; so that though he might have the advantages of youth – quick reactions, steadiness of hand and eye – the older man's infinitely greater experience could be expected easily to outweigh them. Gilbert had overheard Cicely, in one of her never-failing conversational gambits, asking Lionel which he considered his best sport, expecting no doubt that he would say shooting or hunting, and he had answered 'Billiards.' Billiards!

Not that there was anything against a man's playing a good game of billiards. In billiards you needed a good eye, a steady hand and an ability to place your weight where it was needed. Of course Lionel Stephens had all that – it was just what preeminently, being a strongly built, fit, physically well-balanced young man, he did have: it was the balance that was important, making it easy for him to control his strength. He was well built, there was no doubt about it, bound to excel at all forms of sport – of course, but to talk of him in the same breath as the famous Lord Hartlip, who was pursued by gun-makers, begged to accept their finest weapons as gifts if he would only mention their name, besought by the makers of shooting equipment to lend his imprimatur to their coats or game bags or spats (there was something on the market called the Hartlip hip-flask – ironically, since he never took alcohol until the sport was over) and invited by the owners of the finest shooting all over the world as their most honoured guest – to talk of Lionel Stephens as a possible rival – this was surely ridiculous? And yet Aline had told him that this was what people were doing, talking of them as if they were rivals, on equal terms. If he had heard of it, no doubt so had the young man; he was probably being egged on by the women. Cicely, Olivia Lilburn, the lot of them.

'Go on, you can beat old Gilbert, it will do him good.'

Impatient to be off, Gilbert looked at his watch. It was only half-past one. The sharp little hammer in his right temple struck again. Just let him get back out there and show them. Thank God he had Jarvis picking up for him. Jarvis would never let another man get the credit that was due to him. He'd seen that ratty little fellow of Stephens's trying to add a bird to his score that wasn't his. He'd tell him.

'Jarvis,' he'd say. 'We're out for a high score. Right?'

That sort of talk had to be put a stop to, straight away, before it spread.

*

By the river it was very quiet, except for the sound of the water flowing over the stones in the shallower part just past the bridge, and the occasional splash of a water vole or croak of a moorhen. Osbert walked slowly along the bank, eating an apple. Nanny had made him take an apple because he had missed his pudding, insisting on leaving before the end of lunch to look for his duck. Nanny's jurisdiction over Osbert was questionable, he having passed long ago from nursery to schoolroom and being therefore supposedly under the sway of Mr Fortescue instead, who took, Nanny considered, far too little interest in his manners, caring only that he should be sure to read in bed for at least half an hour before going to sleep at night (in Mr Fortescue's view there was nothing wrong with Osbert's manners anyway), and Osbert accordingly felt free to ignore her injunctions to wait. To please her, though, he took an apple.

Afternoon for Osbert started towards the end of lunch, as his thoughts turned to what he was going to do afterwards. Lunch was a hiatus which separated the morning from the afternoon to such an extent that any anxieties which the afternoon might hold went on seeming a long way away until the meal was nearly over; then suddenly what had seemed sufficient unto the afternoon and therefore hardly to be bothered about in the morning became an immediate preoccupation. He had been certain all morning that by afternoon the duck would have come home; but suddenly before the pudding it seemed to him that it was already afternoon and the duck was not back, so he stood up and pushed in his chair and said 'I shall have to go.' Nanny's hands were full anyway, restraining Lucy from going with him.

Walking by the river took him into the river world, changed the scale of things so that the river seemed vaster and more varied, its bends and beaches, deeps and swamps more extensive, its life more self-sufficient, the threat of unseen guns accordingly more darkly terrifying. Osbert had seen duck shoots and knew how deadly the slaughter in the dusk could be; he had seen a female mallard turn back into the fire towards her wounded mate, veering from side to side bewildered as he fluttered on the ground for the moment before both were killed. Afterwards he had asked his brother if when he was old enough to shoot it would be all right if he only shot pheasants, and Marcus in his reassuring way had said it would.

There being no sign of any ducks, Osbert sat down on the bank to listen. He threw his apple core into the river and watched it bob along in the current until to his surprise a gentle splash over by the opposite bank was followed by the appearance of a small brown bead. A water vole, nose well up, had set off at a good speed towards the apple core, leaving a widening 'V' in the water behind it. A short-sighted animal, it failed to notice Osbert motionless on the bank, and swimming strongly grabbed the apple core firmly in its mouth, swam back to the side and disappeared among the reeds. Osbert stood up and began to walk slowly along the path. There had still been no sight or sound of ducks.

*

Peaks of whipped cream shot through with pale chestnut purée.

'Ireland,' said Ida. 'Oh dear.'

'Ulster will fight. Ulster will be right,' said Charles Farquhar.

'I don't think the Conservatives should start the fight though, do you?'

'I don't see why not. Nothing to be gained by shilly-shallying. Show of force is what's needed. Whiff of grapeshot and all that. Carson's the man for me. Fantastic brain you know, that chap.'

'I think he lacks subtlety as a politician.'

'Subtlety's all very well in its place. You need a sledge-hammer too at times. Subtlety's more for private life I'd say. The boudoir what? I'm all for subtlety in the boudoir.'

Looking down the table towards him, Aline Hartlip thought, how could I?

'It's very worrying, Ireland,' said Ida, looking responsible.

How could I want him so, Aline thought, with his little eyes and his moustache so much greyer than his hair (his hair neatly smoothed, parted just left of centre, turning up a little above each temple with a suggestion of a curl), his coarse stubby hands, how could I? But I must be in love with him, otherwise why should I mind so when he eyes Cicely, pushes up against her going through a gate – I saw him yesterday when she came out with the guns in the afternoon – why should I have written him those silly letters when I thought Maisie Arlington was after him? I wish I didn't write so many letters.

'I abase myself, I lie at your feet and hope you will walk on me. Don't you see, dearest Charles, there is no one, no one on earth, who will crawl to you as I do. . . .'

She had written that to him. She, Aline, so controlled and perfect in her person, so meticulously spiteful in her conversation, had written that to Charles, who was stupid and self-satisfied and a little brutal. The arbitrariness of love never ceased to surprise her, nor the cruel dictatorship of desire to constitute a large part of its fascination for her. She was a slave to passion. For some reason this seemed to her a justification for her existence.

'The Land Acts,' said Ida, 'could work. Not here though, of course. I don't mean such a thing would be suitable here. But peasant proprietors, in Ireland, that could be right, don't you think?'

Ida was in every way conventional – she had come to the conclusion that the Irish Land Acts might be all right only when she had seen that they were being brought forward by the impeccably aristocratic George Wyndham and supported in Ireland by the quite enormously grand Lord Dunraven – but at the same time she was a serious woman and she found Charles Farquhar difficult to talk to. He was not at all like her husband, who was in the habit of discussing his diplomatic work with her and finding her ruthlessly down-to-earth judgments about people helpful. John Nettleby was not the son of his parents for nothing and had a tendency to romanticize the possessors of charm. It was perhaps his desire to guard against this tendency which had encouraged him to marry Ida. 'At least,' Minnie had said, who had hoped for something a little more dashing in the way of a daughter-in-law, 'he'll be able to trust her.'

Ida was eminently trustworthy, and it was a small contributory factor towards the absolute correctness of her husband the diplomat that from an early age he had had at the back of his mind the idea that his mother was not. Whether right or wrong, this view had made him correct, because it had made him cautious, and where emotions were concerned so cautious as to be almost cold; but Ida looked up to him, and was uneasy when she discerned in the children characteristics unlike his, and which she feared might have skipped a generation. Frivolity might be expected to have come from Minnie, but there was a kind of whimsicality which in Ida's view was no better and which she found in Sir Randolph. It was just when he least seemed to mean what he said that he was being most serious, that was what she sometimes suspected, and that was what she sometimes seemed to see in Osbert. Contrariness, Nanny called it. Whatever it was, Ida thought, it was calculated to annoy.

Charles Farquhar was not interested in Irish land reform. Hearty agreement with Ida's view seemed the easiest way out of a prolonged discussion.

'Rather,' he said, with the emphasis on the last syllable. 'I should jolly well say so. And what does Miss Cicely think, I wonder? I'll bet all she cares to know about Ireland is that you can get some dashed good hunting there.'

Cicely was opposite him across the narrow table. She acknowledged politely that she'd had a week in West Meath, but privately resented being interrupted in her conversation with Tibor Rakassyi: they had been talking about polo, and he had been telling her that he was renowned and feared throughout Hungary for his ferocious play. She had thought his boasting delightful and was flattered by his anxiety to impress her. She would have liked to enlarge in similar style upon her exploits over the Irish banks, but felt her mother's eye upon her. Ida disapproved of showing off.

'I'm so bad at playing the Irish whistle,' said Cicely, rushing as she thought to the opposite extreme (her mother recognised it as being nothing of the kind). 'I wish I could play it though, I love all that, and the fiddling....'

Tibor had always liked animated girls. She seemed at the same time, compared to the girls he knew at home, almost ethereal, all spirit – only the spirit was the spirit of fantasy and laughter. He thought of her dancing down the long passages of the gloomy palace above the Danube, gleaming at him across the crowded formalities of Viennese receptions, galloping across the plain on hunting expeditions.

'When I go to stay with my uncle, who is a Russian Grand Duke, we go wolf-hunting in the forest with a pack of Borzois.'

Her eyes enormous at the thought of the romance of it, she

only breathed an appreciative 'Oh!'

His family, Tibor thought, would be quite well disposed towards a marriage with an English girl of good family. Perhaps this evening if they played games after dinner, there might be a chance to drop a hint, see how she responded?

'You're looking pleased with yourself,' Aline murmured to him from his other side. 'You are making a face like a rose bud.'

*

Cornelius Cardew strode through Oxfordshire, and the feeling of elation which had possessed him as he left Sir Randolph and made his way through the unfriendly sportsmen, slowly faded. By the time he reached the hamlet of Cowfold a mile or two from the borders of the City of Oxford, it had evaporated altogether; he could not imagine what could have induced him to entertain such feelings. He supposed that as usual it had been a question of personalities. He had noticed in himself more than once a tendency to take a liking to an adversary; it was regrettable. Things were achieved, he knew, advances made, advantages won, by people banding together for the good of a cause and once banded remembering which band they belonged to. Just because he could not help feeling a certain sympathy with anyone who confessed to wanting to write a polemical pamphlet and have it privately printed, there was no reason to waver in his loyalties. Cornelius was opposed to blood sports, Sir Randolph Nettleby therefore was not; they were on opposite sides. Cornelius was opposed to private ownership of land, Sir Randolph most palpably was not; therefore they were irrevocably divided.

Nevertheless, nevertheless – for Cornelius was a firm believer in the power of persuasion – was there not, or might there not be, some common ground? Sir Randolph regretted the decline of rural life, the coming disappearance as he forsaw it of a fullness and vigour of existence which might be expected in the face of the materalism of the new age to become an absolute loss. It was only as to the method of retrieving the loss before it was too late that they differed. Might not Sir Randolph be induced to consider the problem from a different point of view, a point of view it had to be admitted in absolute opposition to his own interest; but then any man, Cornelius optimistically considered, any

112

man who wanted to write a polemical pamphlet must be of a philosophical turn of mind, and therefore must be capable of seeing things not only and exclusively from the point of view of his own interest. They should have talked more about the land. Cornelius, walking now between low hedges and with the towers and spires of Oxford already in sight, hesitated, felt in the pockets of his Norfolk jacket, almost turned back. He had a pamphlet on Land Reform. It would only take him an hour to retrace his steps. Or would it be better to write? He paused between the grassy verges, despising his own irresolution; then thought of a crust of bread, a pint of ale, some cheese.

An hour or so later, having refreshed himself at the White Hart Inn in Cowfold, he was striding along the road again, Oxford behind him and the woods of Nettleby some considerable distance in front. As he went he sang the Liberal Land Song, to the tune of While We Were Marching Through Georgia. One might as well try, he thought.

Workers in the fields, bending over their task of lifting roots, straightened their backs to stare at the bearded head and swinging shoulders which appeared over the hedge.

'The land! The land! 'Twas God who gave the land!
The land! The land! The ground on which we stand!
Why should we be beggars with the ballot in our hand?
God gave the land to the people!'

The October breeze carried away the reedy tenor. The men and women in the fields bent again over the soil whose deeply familiar demands, questions of ownership apart, dictated their lives.

*

Goodwood, Cowes, Scotland, the parties of the Little Season, the visits to country houses, the shooting, the hunting, the prospects for next year – and never an unfamiliar name. Olivia could hear her husband all the way from the other end of the table (his voice was quite loud), running through with Minnie the points of the Social Calendar they had jointly or severally most recently passed – so amusing or such a bore – and who'd been there (but everyone, of course) – and who was too beautiful for words, who had quite lost her looks, who was drinking too much and had made a frightful floater the other night in the House only luckily it was after dinner and no one had noticed – and she knew him to be doing no more than a kind of ritual checking of the points of the compass. He and Minnie were like two engines idling, keeping themselves turning over so that they should be ready to move the machine in a new direction when the exigencies of the occasion required it. Minnie was at the same time looking round the table to see whether everyone had finished eating and whether Sir Randolph was beginning to look impatient. Bob Lilburn was already mentally checking through his equipment for the afternoon's sport.

'The Barlows,' he nevertheless continued, 'at Rothermuir. Such views.'

'We were there with the Charlesworths. You and Olivia had just left.'

Olivia had noticed that this checking of the compass points (or listing of names) seemed to constitute quite a large part of her husband's conversation, and that often when engaged in it with another such practised hand at the game as Minnie, he could go on for what seemed to her a quite extraordinarily long time without feeling it necessary to extend his comments on the occasions or people mentioned beyond the most perfunctory kind of categorising. The object of the thing appeared to be ennumeration rather than enlightenment. Once she had said to him, 'Supposing there are some other people somewhere, people we don't know?'

He had looked at her seriously.

'What sort of people?'

'Perfectly charming people. Really delightful, intelligent, amusing, civilized. . . . And we don't know them, and nobody we know knows them. And they don't know us and they don't know anybody we know.'

Bob had thought for a moment and then he had said, 'It's impossible. But if it were not impossible, then I don't think I should want to know such people. I don't think I should find anything in common with them.'

*

Sir Reuben Hergesheimer looked across at Lord Lilburn and

then let his eyes wander down the table past young Marcus and Gilbert Hartlip to Cicely's luminous pale face and large, bright, slightly protruding eyes which at this moment were fixed teasingly on Charles Farquhar opposite her – teasingly but with a look in them which was not really amused nor even particularly friendly, for she did not altogether like Charles Farquhar. Sir Reuben thought how English all those faces were, seeing Lord Lilburn's regular well-shaped features and luxuriant moustache, Marcus's fair complexion and blue eyes less protuberant and less sparkling than his sister's, Gilbert Hartlip's thin, long-nosed, slightly ascetic air; and there came into his mind's eye a very different face he would have liked to have seen there, a sallower skin, dark eyes, eyes if heredity had anything to do with it slightly turned down at the outer corners, giving an expression of subtlety and religious calm quite at variance with the looks of these English sportsmen, the face of the young man who would have been his son if only he had ever had a son.

He had married once, in 1883, in Johannesburg. He had been thirty, his bride ten years younger. She had been Susannah Mordecai, the daughter of his then employer in the mining corporation through which he was in those years in the process of making his fortune. She was a handsome gentle creature, but it turned out that she was unable to bear children and though he was fond of her it became increasingly easy to spend time away from her and increasingly difficult when he was with her to listen to what she said; she was quite stupid. Her father from being his employer became his partner and then his ex-partner. There was no real ill-feeling over the thing – Reuben Hergesheimer had always been generous in victory (that is, as long as the victory was total) – but inevitably relations between them had grown cooler. Susannah was fond of her family, fonder no doubt than if she had had children of her own, and when Reuben's business interest took him so often to London that he decided to settle there she did not follow him. It was some years before they both accepted that the separation was final, some years again before she asked him for a divorce in order to marry a childhood friend, a widower with whom as far as he knew she had settled down happily in Johannesburg; it was years since he had heard from her.

By the time the divorce had been arranged he had become

used to a way of life which was not adaptable to dynastic ambitions; it accommodated a mistress more easily than a wife. He had been introduced by a fellow financier to the Prince of Wales; the love affair which absorbed most of his emotional energy in those years was his love affair with England. The wealth, stability and dignity of the country of his adoption (he had assumed British nationality) never ceased to give him satisfaction. Not only was its captial the financial centre of the world, but its heir to the Throne (soon its King) would have made an excellent business man himself. These were the years in which Reuben Hergesheimer managed not only to control what soon became a vast and complicated financial empire of his own, ranging from mines to shipping, docks to railways, but to hold himself available as banker, financial adviser and companion to the King Emperor of vaster terrains. He could be called upon at short notice to provide a quiet but delicious dinner and some discreet gambling at his faultlessly run house in North Audley Street, or to make up a party for the races, or a game of bridge, or even a yachting expedition. He was always the same, quiet-voiced and shrewd, uncensorious, worldly but at the same time romantic; the King Emperor had his absolute allegiance, as did the splendid society over which he ruled. To Reuben Hergesheimer English society seemed the best in the world, confident, stable and stupid; in every way open to exploitation by himself. Exploitation in Reuben's vocabulary was a good word – it meant 'to make the best of' and not at all 'to take unfair advantage of' – it led to expansion, which was another good word.

So in these years of opportunity the founding of a dynasty was deferred. By now, the best years over, he faced the fact that it was too late. He had become so discreet, in a sense so solitary, that the thought of sharing his life with anyone, however much he might use his wealth to secure himself some distance, was simply an impossibility. Besides it was not fair to the putative son to give him an old father.

He regretted his lack, not only because as he grew older it seemed that an empire without an heir apparent had less to hold the interest and concern of its founder, but also because in recent years he had begun to think of putting some of his money into land.

During the busy years with King Edward he had not seen a

116

great deal of Sir Randolph. Minnie had been his friend and bridge partner, his ally in the sometimes demanding task of keeping the Sovereign amused. Sir Randolph had been the husband in the background, the wry accommodating country squire who produced the occasional unexpected witticism or abstruse piece of information, and had the capacity to offer once or twice a year an excellently organised shooting party at which he seemed only too pleased to be, as he frequently put it himself, the head gamekeeper. It was only after the King's death that Sir Reuben had come to know and like Minnie's husband. Through him he had come to admire a sub-section of the eternally fascinating English class system with which he had not previously been so familiar. He had known grandees, such of the high aristocracy who were intimates of the King's, and he had known naturally the financial world of the City, the bankers and merchant princes, but he had not much come across the country gentry, though he was familiar with their historic role. He saw them now as a class which could command his sympathy. He saw Sir Randolph as a representative of an admirable way of life, now threatened by forces which he himself had done a certain amount to encourage. What could have been more appropriate than that some of his own gains should have been brought in as reinforcements? He could have bought a country estate – there were plenty up for sale – and his son could have inherited it, together with the millions to sustain it in sufficient style.

At this point in Sir Reuben's imaginings a vagueness sometimes crept in. He was not sure how he would wish a son of his in such circumstances to behave. Should he become totally assimilated, should he ride, shoot, fish, sit on the Rural District Council, administer English justice as a magistrate, marry the daughter of a neighbouring squire? Or should he remember his ancestors in the Polish ghetto, forswear baptism into the Christian Church, observe the feast and fast days of an alien faith? Although Sir Reuben was rationally inclined to the former view, the latter appealed to his imagination. It was perhaps fortunate that it was a dilemma he would never have to resolve. Thinking about it had led him more than once to wonder whether there might not be an easier way to satisfy his desires in this direction.

He had many god-children. The small matter of his belonging to a different faith had not prevented his practical English friends from placing theoretically at least several of their off-spring under his spiritual surveillance. The benefits they anticipated being in fact financial (and to be discovered on the reading of his will), those of his god-children who were not girls were younger sons. Some of them had little in the way of prospects, everything being destined for the elder son, and if one among them had shown signs of becoming an appropriate heir Sir Reuben would have been glad enough to have looked around for an estate, broached the matter in due course with the parents, taken an interest in the boy; but the fact was that none of them particularly appealed to him, pleasant enough though most of them were, and he did not want to make a mistake, so darkening his declining years. He waited.

Lately he had found himself increasingly drawn to the idea of an unexpected candidate, unexpected because he was not a god-son, was younger than would have been ideal and not at first sight that solid predictable English character he had supposed himself to be seeking. It was perhaps this last which in fact attracted Sir Reuben, the boy's nervousness, imagination and dark intensity of looks being after all more appealing than the typical English qualities of Marcus, the elder brother.

Apropos of nothing, and apparently interrupting Bob Lilburn's conversation with Minnie, Sir Reuben said suddenly, 'Where is Osbert today?'

'Osbert?' Minnie was surprised by the question since the children were seldom anyway seen by the guests until after tea. 'I expect by now he will be looking for his duck again unless the silly creature has turned up. It was lost this morning.'

'If it should fail to appear I should feel honoured to take on the responsibility of providing a successor.'

Minnie rested her plump white hand on his arm.

'You're the kindest person in the world. But let's hope it won't come to that.'

*

Looking over the heads of Aline Hartlip and Tibor Rakassyi at the blue china on the dark shelves and the flickering sunlight on the beech leaves beyond the latticed windows, Olivia said 'Wouldn't it be lovely to live here always?'

118

'You mean in this little house?' said Lionel.

'Yes. Don't you think so?'

'I should like it well enough if I could have my books with me. And if I were in love with my companion. And if we could keep it warm.'

'It would have to be an idyll then, for you. I don't know that I would ask so much. I think I could be happy here alone.'

'That would be a waste.'

'A waste of what?'

'Of you.'

'I might be becoming wise. Then it wouldn't be a waste.'

'We are meant to share our lives not develop in isolation. Besides I think you are wise already.'

'You can't know me very well if you think that.'

'Perhaps I don't. But then why do I feel as if I do?'

'I don't know.'

'You know me too. You know everything about me.'

'But that's impossible.'

'Yes, it is impossible. But it's true. We know each other because our souls knew each other before.'

'Did they? Where?'

'Oh, in Heaven or somewhere, I don't know.'

'You seem very sure of it.'

'Yes, I am sure. Quite, quite sure.'

'I think it's more as if ...'

But she had begun hesitantly and at the pushing back of chairs which followed from Minnie's catching Aline's eye and rising to her feet, she stopped.

As they stood up he said, 'But you will walk with me?'

*

Tom Harker stood apart from the other men, watching the boat-house door. Although the sun was still shining, under the beech trees one could feel that it was afternoon, and autumn. He was ready to go. He rested his bony chin on his clasped hands which were folded on top of his tall forked stick, immobile, his gaze fixed. He was aware of the men sitting in groups under the trees or on the river bank relaxing for a few more minutes before the call to action, smoking and talking quietly; they were as familiar

119

to him as the other natural phenomena by which he was surrounded. He would have answered for them all if necessary as
good enough fellows, given the unfortunate tendency of human
nature towards error and iniquity, but he did not think it necessary to exchange small talk with them. He had given young Dan
Glass his views on the Game Laws, to Dan's considerable
embarrassment since whatever the faults of the Laws it was his
father's duty to enforce them and Dan did not want to be disloyal
to his father, least of all in conversation with Tom Harker.
Albert Jarvis the Derbyshire man and Sir Randolph's loader
Charlie Pass had embroiled him somewhat against his will in a
political argument: they had exposed themselves, in his
opinion, as ignorant men, both claiming that it was the Tory
Party which had the interest of the agricultural worker at heart,
and remaining unswayed by his eloquent exposition of a quite
different view. He had told them that the landlord was the cause
of crime. 'He invents the laws and invents the punishments for
breaking them. Now if the land belonged to us all, it stands to
reason, there'd be no law of trespass.'

'Belongs to us all means belongs to the Government,' said
Charlie Pass. 'If you ask me I'd rather sweat for a bugger I know
than a bunch of bloody politicians.'

'That's it,' said Arthur Jarvis. 'After their own interests, politicians.'

'That may be so. That may very well be so of most of them. But
you get your man of the people and you must follow him. Lloyd
George has said . . .'

But Lloyd George was a Welshman and Albert Jarvis didn't
care for Welshmen. They'd had some Welsh miners up in his
parts, came up because they were short of work in their valleys,
taking jobs that should have gone to Derbyshire men, getting
themselves in with the employers with a lot of smooth talk.
Never trust a Welshman, that was Albert Jarvis's view. Charlie
Pass had anyway heard enough of Tom's quotations from Lloyd
George's speeches – they'd done a job together stonepicking
before the last spring ploughing. He moved away on the pretext
of asking Mr Glass how his bitch was coming along – seemed
excitable still, not much sense – and Tom, unsurprised by their
folly and prejudice which were only what he'd expected, walked
in his slow way (with his long even stride like a man used to the

hills and valleys of infinite distance, though it was not known that he'd been far outside the confines of Oxfordshire), and stationed himself on the grassy ride under the beech trees in a good position to see the first signs of activity from the boathouse, when they came. He did not have long to wait.

Sir Randolph emerged first and walked towards Mr Glass. Passing Tom, he stopped to ask him how he was keeping.

'Can't complain,' was the answer and then with a roll of his eyes heavenwards; 'His mercies are manifold.'

'Indeed they are. That was a fine piece of work you did on that roof at Hamlingham. I was over there the other day.'

'Oh yes?' Tom's smile, perhaps because it appeared too infrequently, was surprisingly diffident; it gave his stern features quite another aspect. 'It was in a terrible state.'

'They're in a poor way, some of those cottages. I'm glad to see they've started to do something about them. We've got a couple in the village here we want to do this year. Did Mr Dawkes mention them to you?'

'He did.'

Sir Randolph nodded, exchanged another word or two about the prospects for the afternoon's sport and moved on to talk to Glass to whom, after confirming the arrangements for the next drive, he said amusedly, 'I see you've got one of your favourite characters out beating today,' moving his head slightly to indicate Tom Harker.

Glass did not smile.

'Against my better judgment, Sir Randolph, against my better judgment. The last thing I want is him nosing around seeing where the best game's lying. But Page has hurt his back and there was no one else I could call on at short notice.'

'I like him,' said Sir Randolph truthfully, though he privately thought no one would ever stop the man poaching.

The other shooters were ready. Olivia, Cicely and Aline, who were to walk with them for a few drives, were with them. The beaters moved off first, the others followed. It's like an army, Olivia thought, we have bivouacked and are moving off now to the front line. War might be like this, casual, friendly and frightening. Like before a cricket match (at home in Norfolk where she had been brought up they had been great cricketers). Olivia was excited. She was not sure why, though she knew it was something to do with the sunlight through the trees, and the groups of men moving through the trees and converging on to the wide green ride by the river, and the whining of Glass's dog Bess, and the click of Marcus's gun as he made sure yet again that it was not loaded (not for nothing had he been trained by his grandfather). It was even, although she did not much like her, to do with Aline's hat which was a dark velvet thing with a sweeping feather on it and above her tense acutely beautiful face looked romantic, and with the keen expectation shining in Cicely's eyes as she walked beside Tibor Rakassyi, and with Tibor's own dark eyes for that matter, and his neat rather too tight jacket and his beautiful leather boots, and with Sir Randolph's distinctive large-brimmed hat and his dog a shadow at his heels and with those fine broad-shouldered sportsmen whom she followed, and with their air of assurance, their common assumptions, their absolute authority. Are we really all so beautiful and brave, she thought, or do we just think we are?

She could have said that aloud to Lionel, who was walking beside her. Unlike her husband he would not have been shocked. Instead she turned on him a gaze of marvellous brilliance and said, 'We are lucky, aren't we? To have such weather I mean.'

*

They were to start on the outskirts of the woods, and work their way through them in successive drives. On the path by the river before they struck uphill to spread out on the edge of the first covert, Tom Harker in good humour smiled again as they passed a colony of rooks in a group of high elms (they were in the mixed woods now towards the beginning of the park).

'My first job,' he said. 'Scaring birds. Age of eight.'

He was walking beside Percy Maidment, the man from Lincolnshire, who did not answer.

'Rook pie,' Tom went on. 'You don't want too much of it. Ever eaten blackbirds? I remember my mother making blackbird pie at Christmas more than once.'

'Ah,' said Percy Maidment.

'Picking dead daffodils, that was my next job. A shilling a day, all over the garden and the park, thousands of them, after they was over.'

'You know that fellow Jarvis, then, you was talking to?' said Percy Maidment, as if it followed in some way.

'That's his name, is it? Never met him till today. From your part of the world, is he?'

'No. West of us someplace, he said. Seems an ignorant kind of man to me.'

'Would you say so?'

'Jealous. Grabs any old bird and says his man got it.'

'One of those, is he? You don't want to pay any attention to that. We don't count scores here, only the whole bag.'

'Him and me are counting all right. And they are, his man and mine. It's a close thing but we'll get them all right. Mine's a better man than his. Shoots better after lunch too. I've been with him long enough to know that. We're going to smash the other fellow this afternoon.'

Tom looked at the small man beside him in surprise, a reaction to which the other seemed oblivious, continuing only to look straight in front of him with an unsmiling pale intensity.

'You'd better watch out Sir Randolph doesn't catch you at it,' said Tom with a definite note of reproof in his own voice. 'He's what you might call a sportsman of the old school.'

'Bugger that,' said Percy Maidment.

The beaters having been sent off to the outskirts of the first covert, the shooters walked slowly towards their appointed positions along the ride between the trees.

'Minnie is so clever,' said Aline, who had decided to stand beside Sir Reuben Hergesheimer in the hope of annoying Charles Farquhar who would have been expecting her to stand with him. 'She knows exactly how to time things so as to go home and have a nice little rest and get herself driven back just in time to see the last drive.'

'She's coming for that then?'

'She and Ida are coming. It's only a little way from the road.'

'Then if you other ladies can stand the pace we shall have all of you as audience. We shall really have to do our best, shan't we?'

'Gilbert always does his best.'

'Of course. That's why he's the great expert he is.'

'I think always doing one's best is a bore.'

'I have never seen you do less than your best at your particular art.'

'My art?'

'The art of looking beautiful.'

'Oh that. That's a bore. And yet I suppose if one has acquired some sort of reputation – though goodness knows why, in my case – one feels one has to keep it up. It's all pride.'

'Quite.'

'And the spirit of competition. Are we proud and competitive, would you say?'

'Probably. Like racehorses. That's why I enjoy racing so much.'

'They're also a little mad, racehorses, I often think. If you look at their eyes when they're walking round the paddock there seems to be madness in them.'

'They're very highly bred. Proud, competitive and mad, those are aristocratic attributes.'

'Oh we're certainly arisotcratic,' said Aline gaily.

Sir Reuben smiled, enjoying the joke in anticipation with Minnie, who had once told him that Gilbert Hartlip had married Aline in order to 'dorer le blazon'. Her father was a Scottish industrialist, still living and in the meantime not sufficiently dazzled by his daughter's elevation to have been more than really rather mean with the marriage settlement.

But he had underestimated her.

She suddenly laughed and putting her arm though his said, 'Of course the truth is I'm no more of an aristocrat than you are.'

*

Lionel Stephens was to stand at the end of the line, in the Park just beyond the corner of the wood. Nodding in a friendly manner to Gilbert Hartlip who was to stand nearest to him on the ride and whose preoccupied air he failed to notice, he walked on slowly with Olivia. There was no hurry because the beaters could not be expected yet to have reached their starting point. He preceded Olivia over the stile so as to be able to turn back to help her. Glancing behind her along the ride he saw Gilbert deep in conversation with his loaders. Instead of merely holding out an arm, he put both hands on her waist as if to help her jump down from the stile. She hesitated.

'You were going to tell me something,' he said looking up at her. 'You said, as if . . .'

'As if what?'

'You didn't finish. I said we'd known each other before and you said it was as if . . .'

'Oh,' she said, smiling and hopping neatly down from the stile. 'As if . . .' He had not stepped backwards and still held his hands on her waist so that they were very close. She looked up into his face with an expression of unabashed and affectionate friendliness. 'As if you were my long-lost brother.'

'Brother!' He turned away sharply, put his hands in his pockets and walked a few steps with head bent along the fence bordering the wood.

Percy Maidment, who was waiting further out in the Park with the boy who had been assistant loader, raised his arm as if he thought Lionel might have failed to notice him.

Olivia, distressed, hesitated by the stile. Her first thought was, he must have had a sister who had died. How could she have been so clumsy?

He had stopped, apparently staring at a fencing post. She approached him.

'I am so sorry for what I said. I wouldn't for the world have said anything you wouldn't like. Will you forgive me?'

He raised his glance from the post to meet hers. Her eyes had tears in them. Unable to look away he said 'I love you terribly,' and saw her expression change from concern to astonishment.

'Sir, Mr Stephens, sir,' Percy Maidment was trying to attract his attention by a harsh whisper. Lionel raised his arm to show that he had understood. Distant whistles and tapping sounds showed that the beaters were approaching, though still with some way to go. Lionel began to walk slowly towards the place where he was meant to be standing.

'I've been so stupid,' she said.

He turned, waiting for her to catch up with him.

'No.'

'Yes, I have. I've been stupid beyond anything. I thought it was just that we liked each other, that we had things in common.'

'We do, we have.'

'But it was more than that. I didn't recognise it.'

125

'I shouldn't have said it. Don't let it mean that you change, that you avoid me.'

'It's wrong to avoid things. Or not recognise things.' Preoccupied by her effort to understand herself, she slipped her hand into his arm in her old companionable manner. He could not prevent himself from putting his other hand on hers.

'That was what it was,' she said slowly. 'All the time.'

'Yes, all the time.' His hand was crushing hers. She hardly noticed.

'That was what it was,' she repeated, dazzled by the light which was dawning on her. 'That is what it is. I love you too.'

The boy from the village standing behind Percy Maidment (it was one of Ellen's brothers) stared in amazement at these tremendous beings standing dazzling and dazzled before him, speaking in such a truly astonishing manner. There was no question of his not having heard them correctly; they were only a few feet away. In a muddled sort of way it just crossed his mind that they might be reciting their parts in a play, since he knew that sometimes when they had house parties at the Park they went in for amateur theatricals.

Percy Maidment was not interested in what anyone was saying. His only concern was to get the gun he was holding into Lionel's hands. The whistling and tapping, the cracking of branches and the odd shout, were nearer now. There was the first shout of 'over', the first shot from far along the line. Lionel took the gun mechanically, still looking at Olivia. 'Over on the right. Your bird, sir,' muttered Percy urgently.

Lionel swung and fired. The pheasant fell, upon which he was seized with a wild joy. The pheasants were breaking out fast. He could not keep from smiling. They were breaking out in two directions, over the ride and over the Park. He shot them, smiling. Two shots, a change of gun, two more shots; each shot brought down a bird. Percy trembled like a whippet straining to pursue a hare, everything concentrated on the reloading of the smoking barrels, the holding out of the gun exactly where the hands would reach for it. Lionel, his sense of glory endowing him with an extraordinary alertness, shot with complete carelessness and complete accuracy, Olivia beside him in what seemed to her a column of divine flame, hardly noticing the noise or the smell of cordite or the shouts and cries of the beaters or the continual thumps of birds falling dead on the grass all round her. She was absorbed in the wonder and amazement of her discovery, deaf to everything except the soundless shout of triumphant love.

Lionel's concentration was nearly all on the physical process in which he was involved, but he had just enough consciousness to spare to entertain the thought as regards the birds of a kind of constant 'Come on, come on,' and beyond that an awareness that the urgency of the thing was because of the need to get the shooting over and turn back to look into Olivia's eyes.

The slaughter slowed, and the shots became less frequent. Lionel picked off two late-comers trying to make a sideways dash out into the Park, then paused. One shot from further down the line, then silence. The beaters were out in the open, the dogs beginning their work. He handed his hot-barrelled gun to Percy Maidment and turned towards Olivia.

Percy, still trembling slightly as he began to relax, looked round at the grass thickly strewn with corpses. He exhaled slowly, with half a whistle, half a sigh.

'Glory be to God,' he said.

*

The guns gathered together to walk to the next stand.

'Tremendous, that last drive,' Bob Lilburn said to his host in congratulation.

'It was good today, wasn't it?' said Sir Randolph. 'Quite exciting.'

'A bit too exciting for some people,' said Gilbert Hartlip.

The three of them were walking together, a little apart from the others. Sir Randolph took Gilbert's remark to be a reference to the number of birds he had had to let go because of a superfluity of opportunities.

'I hope they weren't coming over all together at your end,' he said. 'I have sometimes put the guns two deep, but I don't think that would have been justified today, do you?'

'There was nothing wrong with the placing of the guns. It was the way some of them were shooting.'

'Really?'

'Lionel Stephens seems rather a jealous shot.'

'Lionel? I can't believe it. He's always the most sporting of shots.'

'Not this afternoon I'm afraid. I really think I shall have to have a word with him about it.'

'Very mildly, I do beg you, if you do. I'm quite sure it must have been a mistake, a very rare one.'

Gilbert had already diverged and begun to walk over towards Lionel and Olivia who were following the others, slightly apart from them but with now hardly an outward sign of their emotions.

Sir Randolph said to Bob Lilburn, 'I really can't understand what's happened to Gilbert. He seems very jumpy today.'

'If you ask me I think Aline's playing him up a bit.'

'Aline's been playing him up for years,' said Sir Randolph impatiently. 'It's never made him jumpy before.'

*

Daniel Glass walked with his father to the next covert.

'Did you see Mr Stephens at that last stand?' his father asked him.

Dan shook his head.

'I was too far over.'

'He was shooting like an angel.'

'The birds were coming out well.'

'As good a sport as you could wish for, that's what we're giving them. And they know it. I reckon we've got two of the best shots in England here today. And the others not much worse.'

'Tom Harker was the stop. He'll have got the best sight of it.'

'He's good Tom, damn him, not one of those that just walks along in a daze. He works, does Tom. I tell you what, next time I see either Mr Stephens or Lord Hartlip getting the best position I'll put you opposite so you can see some of the skill, right?'

'Thanks.'

Dan watched his father hurry on ahead to deploy his troops for the next advance. He was glad to see him so pleased with the way the day was going. Dan was pleased too – he liked the feeling of being part of a success, just as he liked the feeling of being part of a village that had been much the same for a long time and part of an Empire that he had been told at school and had found no difficulty in believing was the best there had ever been. At the same time he knew that he could never feel as secure in his assumptions as his father was. It was something to do with having one special thing. Most people didn't have one special thing, so it was easier for them to identify themselves with whatever they found around them, but if you did have a special thing you were a little set apart, a little more self-conscious; Dan had recently become increasingly aware of this, and he was not sure whether the awareness made him pleased or sorry. He had to be some kind of scientist. There was too much to be found out in that way for it to be anything less than a lifetime's work. And because every time he was working on something, however small and apparently simple, he always knew with certainty what observations mattered, what methods he ought to use, and what conclusions he might expect to come to, he knew perfectly well but without wanting to go into the matter or to put it into words that really it would be quite wrong of him to leave such work to other people. They could not be counted on to get it right. How he had arrived at this conclusion after no more than a few years of Naure Study with Mr Rudloe the schoolmaster and a few random conversations with such of his elders in the village who were interested in the habits of wild animals, or with Sir Randolph before and after reading such books as the latter could find for him on the beginnings of life or the structure of natural organisms, was perhaps mysterious, but that made it no less a fact. He was sure of what he had to do. The only question was whether he could do it alone.

He had had until recently the half thought out notion that he could go on as he was – that was to say as his father's assistant and perhaps eventual successor – and somehow at the same time make his observations and pursue his reading and eventually come out with some theory or piece of original research which he would then publish. Lately it had been becoming clear to him that this was hardly realistic and that he was condemning himself to being always an amateur. But to go into that wider world – of the true nature of which he had only the vaguest notion, except in so far as he knew it must be wider, and must hold out for him the hope of something which he wanted badly and was in some way ashamed of wanting but which was really only that recognition which every talented person wants – to go out into that world which Sir Randolph was offering him by saying he would pay for his further education, would mean to desert his father, and to desert him in a manner a good deal more fundamental than the mere leaving him to find another boy to take on as assistant gamekeeper. It was a dilemma Dan did not want to have to face, and tried to think about as little as possible; but as he tapped with his stick on the trunks of the trees and from time to time emitted his own particular form of call, a sort of mild whoop such as cowmen sometimes use to call up cattle, his mind was on the dilemma rather than on his immediate task.

It was Tom Harker's conversation with Charlie Pass and Albert Jarvis which had made him think of it. He disapproved of Tom, towards whom his sentiments were less tolerant even than his father's, and a great deal less so than Sir Randolph's. He was young and he thought that Tom was dishonest and a nuisance to his father and that was that. He also disliked being lectured by such a person on a subject about which he considered himself to know more, the habits of game – 'a lesson in life' as Tom called it – or on another subject on which he considered himself to be in no need of advice, the evils of drink. Those very characteristics which made Tom Harker in the eyes of Sir Randolph, and to a lesser extent even in those of Mr Glass, a 'personality', in Dan's view of things simply showed him up as a sanctimonious hypocrite. To hear him in conversation with the other two, whose contributions seemed to Tom as antiquated and inappropriate as the old pump on the village green, induced in Dan an uncharacteristic mood of impatience and frustration. He *must* get away. But then again, no one should make him hurt his father.

*

Ellen was in the attic bedroom which she shared with the kitchen maid, tying up her black laced boots. She had finished clearing away the lunch in the servants' hall and had two hours of free time before she needed to be back to change out of the blue and white gingham she wore in the mornings into her afternoon uniform of black dress and small white apron, in time to go round the bedrooms lighting the fires and drawing the curtains.

She put on her hat and coat and ran down the back stairs fastening her coat buttons as she went. John was walking along the back passage, on his way to smoke a cigarette in the boiler room.

'I'll come with you,' he said. 'Where are you going?'

She hurried past him.

'Nowhere in particular.'

'Wait, I'll come.'

'I can't wait. I've got to go alone.'

The back door banged. John walked on slowly. Perhaps his letter had been a mistake. She hadn't been very nice to him since she'd got it.

Ellen was running through the kitchen garden.

'Want some apples, Ellen? Take to your Mum?'

Bernard the garden boy, who had a big hollow behind his ear where he had had an operation for meningitis, was pushing a wheelbarrow along the mossy path between the apple trees.

'Apples! She's got more than she knows what to do with as it is.'

But she was kind to Bernard because of his being a bit funny, so she added. 'Thanks all the same, Bernard. Sorry I'm in a bit of a rush.'

She went through the door in the wall, closing it carefully behind her, and hurried on down the back drive towards the Park. She was making for the river. Osbert was not back and that presumably meant that he had not found the duck. She had promised to help him.

Osbert was generally liked in the servants' hall, except by Mr Rodgers who detested all children. Osbert was preferred to Lucy, who was considered spoilt; he had such a funny way of putting things, and sometimes seemed so lonely. Ida was considered rather a hard sort of mother, which she probably was. In spite of it Osbert found her wonderfully reassuring, because she was always the same, and because in some ways it was comforting not to be understood. It made his preoccupations seem unimportant and therefore no longer, as they sometimes were, overwhelming. He liked being alone, but Ellen thought that he should have friends, other boys with whom to wander round the woods, or fish, or make spears, or throw stones at squirrels, as her brothers had done when they were that age, walking to and from school. She thought he spent too much time learning Latin and ought to be outside more, getting roses in his cheeks. She remembered Mr Marcus at that age back from prep school and full of life. 'Master Osbert dreams too much,' she'd said more than once to Cicely. 'Waking or sleeping he's in a dream'. Cicely would say that he was all right, he was sharper than anyone thought, but Ellen had noticed that Cicely was just as protective towards Osbert as she was.

When Ellen reached the bridge and leaned over the wall she saw a pair of mallard below her in the river, just where she had seen a whole group of them the other day. But how could she tell whether this was the right duck? She looked round for Osbert but there was no sign of him.

'Duck?' she called tentatively.

They did not look up, paddling quite hard to stay in the same place in the water, turning a little in the current, and hearing presumably nothing but the rush of the water over the stones in the shallow rapids just above the pool where they loitered without apparent purpose, swinging on the current and paddling.

'Duck! Come on, duck!'

But this time she had called too loudly. The drake flew first, splashing the water as he took off, and the female immediately followed. They flew down river a few yards then landed near the bank and began dabbling among the weed. Deciding that she would never be able to recognise the duck on her own, let alone catch it, Ellen crossed the fence by the stile and began to walk quickly along the river path, looking for Osbert.

She knew the path well, because she often walked here with John. The association made her think of him, though with more perplexity than usual. She was perplexed because something seemed to have changed him, and since the French maid Hortense was the only identifiable threat she could see on her horizon she ascribed the change to Hortense, quite unjustifiably. Her first reaction to John's letter had been one of amazement, quickly followed by gratification. It was so romantic. She had been unable to resist telling Cicely about it while she was helping her to dress for riding, and Cicely had thought it tremendously romantic too. It was only after elevenses in the servants' hall, when to her own surprise she had found herself thinking that John's smile as he offered her a plate of biscuits was somehow rather sickly, that she began to feel sure about it. As the morning wore on she felt a slow disappointment developing: it was not right, the letter, the voice in it was not John's. She had to admit that the voice was not Hortense's either, unless Hortense had a secret voice for intimate occasions which was quite unlike her usual stage lady's-maid tones. She could not think whose the voice was, but she knew it was not John's, not just because of the vocabulary but because of the sentiments. She did not believe that John thought in that way about such things as Beauty and Truth, Love and Death. That was not to say that he did not think of them at all, only that he did not think of them like that.

Walking briskly along the path, keeping an eye on both river banks in case Osbert should have crossed to the other side, and with her skirt held firmly in both hands so that it should not brush against the damp grass or be caught in the occasional brambles, Ellen tried to make up her mind what it was that on consideration she found displeasing in the letter. She would have much preferred to go on thinking it wonderfully romantic, and was cross with herself for not being able to do so and cross with John for being the cause of her crossness.

'It's all so silly,' she said, tall and thin in her black hat and coat, hurrying along the river bank. She wanted to be able to tell him just to drop it, to be like he'd always been. A girl didn't want to be died for, all because of a lot of stuff about Beauty and Truth. No one could really think like that, it wasn't serious. It wasn't real.

'It's a lot of nonsense,' she said frowning with the effort to be honest. 'That's what it is, a lot of bloody nonsense.'

She seldom swore, tho' she heard other people do it often enough. Her mother would have been very angry if she had heard her. That was perhaps one reason why she now found herself wanting to cry, that and the intense annoyance she felt. Why couldn't John stay as he was, why wasn't life as romantic as his letter, why did she have to have this tiresome way of noticing when something was so much tripe?

She had crossed the water meadow and come to the edge of the wood. With a hand already on the stile which she would have to cross to follow the path through the wood, she saw Osbert ahead of her, and paused. He had not seen her. He was holding a long strand of bindweed, and passing it in a desultory way through his fingers, walking slowly from side to side of the path in the sun-dappled shadow of the beech trees. He was talking to himself in a disconnected drone. She held her breath, watching him as she would have watched a wild animal in such a place, only that a wild animal would not have aroused in her on its behalf such a feeling of extraordinary anxiety.

'Hullo!' He saw her and smiled. 'I haven't found the duck.'

'I've come to help you. There's a pair up here but I don't know if it's her.'

'I think I've seen them. It's not her. But we could have another look, in case.'

A distant volley of shots made them look at each other.

'That's right the other side of the woods,' said Ellen. 'They've got a long way to go yet.'

'We'd better hurry though.'

'We'll find her, don't you worry.'

She waited for him to cross the stile, then grasping her skirt again led the way back towards the river.

*

It was colder now. Though the sun was still shining there was not much warmth in it and the shadows were longer, the light more oblique than ever through the trees and on the Old Man's Beard which climbed to a great height over the hawthorn and hazel on the edge of the next plantation.

'I wish it was teatime,' said Cicely, turning up the velvet collar of her tweed coat.

'Already?' said Tibor. 'There's hours to go yet. Where are your sporting instincts?'

'In abeyance.'

'You can't be hungry, so soon after lunch. It's my company that bores you, I know. In that case I shall have to shoot myself and I don't want to do that at all. What an awful nuisance.'

'Please don't. It would be very inconsiderate.'

'Inconsiderate?'

'I should have the burden of your death on my conscience all the rest of my life, shouldn't I?'

'But I should be dead, which is worse I suppose.'

'It might be lovely. You might be in Heaven having a simply

marvellous time.'

'Now you are being very perverse. You know perfectly well that my idea of Heaven is being with you, and that I am having a simply marvellous time now this very minute.'

'Oh that's very nicely said. And very nice of you to say it. I'm so sorry to be so grumpy.'

'Will you tell me what the trouble was, if it wasn't me?'

He looked down at her face, not wanting to miss the happy expression which he knew a compliment usually induced in it.

She beamed at him, pushing her stray hair underneath her rather bulky hat with a gloved finger.

'The truth is,' she said confidingly, 'that though I love all my family very much, I sometimes feel that my mother doesn't want to recognise that I am grown-up.'

'Ah!'

'I suppose it often happens, but I do find it annoying when I can't even carry on a conversation with someone without her giving me reproving looks. Of course I say very silly things but then so does everyone really, don't they? And after all I manage perfectly well when she's not there. But even my grandmother thinks I laugh too loud.'

'It's better than not laughing at all. You should spend more time away from them, staying with your friends.'

'I do. But even then she sees the hostesses afterwards and asks how I've behaved.'

'But I don't suppose she spends much time in Vienna.'

'Vienna?'

'If you came to stay with me in Hungary, that would perhaps be beyond her sphere?'

'I doubt it. There'd be some fifth cousin by marriage who'd send her a report on me. But I don't really mind. There can't be anything very bad to say, except that I've spilt my soup or something. Will you really ask me to stay?'

'I shall ask my mother to write to you as soon as I go home.'

'How wonderful. I shall look forward to it tremendously. What sort of thing shall we do?'

'It will be quite boring. We see no one but relations. My mother doesn't consider anyone else worth speaking to. The house is always full of cousins and very old aunts.'

'I can't speak Hungarian.'

135

'Nobody does. We speak French. How is your French?'

'Très convenable, according to Mademoiselle.'

'Then you'll do very well. There'll be riding, hunting even, if you like – there are some good horses. If you hunt with me no one will be allowed to ride in front of you.'

'Why not?'

'Because you are my guest. Then there may be some partridge shooting.'

'Will there be a lot of that, do you think?' Cicely did not much enjoy shooting parties.

'Not necessarily. Some times we will drive about and visit other relations. They are all quite boring too, but some of them have beautiful houses and beautiful things in them which I can show you. And I can show you some of our churches and so on. And in the evening there will be musicians and we can dance. The ballroom is quite pretty, all surrounded by Venetian looking-glasses. I think you would like to waltz there.'

'I know I should. You won't forget, will you, when you get home?'

'No,' said Tibor seriously. 'I won't forget.'

It was time to stop talking because the beaters were approaching and the shooting would soon begin again, but Cicely was content to wait in silence, thinking about Hungary. What should she wear? She would take Ellen of course. Surely her mother would agree that she ought to have at least one new dress, for all that waltzing? She did hope she would not say she should make do with the dresses she already had, done up with the addition of a little lace here or a beaded trimming there, bought after hours of matching and choosing at Marshall and Snelgrove. Why not a proper dress for once, the sort Aline Hartlip would wear, from Worth or Fortuny? Thank goodness anyway she'd got her new hunting boots.

*

Lionel and Olivia were both beginning to feel the strain of concealment. They had exchanged banalities with the rest of the party as they walked to the next stand and had taken as long as possible over the short piece of grassy ride which they had to cross alone, having left Charlie Farquhar at his place with Aline by his side, to reach Lionel's appointed position and his waiting loaders. During that time and the few minutes after the shooting in which they strolled back towards the rest of the party, they had walked with Olivia's hand on Lionel's arm, but had only been able to agree how necessary it was to be alone together.

'We could say we had a headache and go home,' Lionel had suggested. 'Two headaches.'

'No one would believe us. Only Gilbert Hartlip has headaches.'

'Gilbert? Does he?'

'It's not generally known. For some reason he's ashamed of it. He gets them after shooting, Aline told me.'

'He's an odd chap. What did he mean by all that nonsense about my poaching? I'd have been furious if my mind hadn't been on other things. Stupid ass.'

'I suppose you were shooting awfully well. I should have congratulated you.'

'On that particular occasion I think I was probably poaching. But it's a thing I never usually do, and I apologised profusely. I thought he was fairly ungracious about it.'

'I thought he was very rude. You apologised handsomely and he went off looking as if he'd have preferred a stand-up fight.'

'Perhaps I was a bit airy about it. I couldn't think it mattered. There was something so much more important on my mind.'

Inevitably they had come closer to the others; there was no avoiding them. Olivia, suddenly feeling that perhaps they ought not to draw attention to themselves, went over to join Aline and Charles Farquhar, who were beginning to move off down the ride in the wake of Sir Randolph, Gilbert and Bob Lilburn.

Aline slipped an arm through hers.

'What a perfect day.'

'It's getting rather colder.'

'Not for you, my dear. It's no use sounding so sensible. Anyone's only got to look at your face.'

'Aline, I . . . Now tell me, why is Gilbert not in a good mood?'

Aline squeezed her arm.

'Don't try to change the subject. You know I am the soul of discretion.'

Lionel, less cautious than Olivia, came up to walk on her other side.

'That's what I mean,' murmured Aline; then as Olivia turned

to look at her in confused surprise, she squeezed her arm still tighter and whispered into her ear, 'Congrats, old thing!'

Bob Lilburn, happening at that moment to turn round, saw his wife in conversation with Aline Hartlip, and noticing on her face an expression of slightly appalled confusion and knowing that Aline's conversation could sometimes be on a level a little too worldly for Olivia's more delicate taste, paused, smiling benignly, and waited for them to catch up with him. Lionel dropped back to walk with Tommy Farmer and Marcus, who were trudging along behind in companionable silence. Bob took Lionel's place beside Olivia.

'How goes it?'

'Very well.'

'You'll have to get to like shooting you know, if you're going to take an interest when young Charlie starts.'

'Surely that won't be for a long time?'

'Only thirteen years or so. Stand with me this time, why not? D'you think old Stephens can spare you? Lionel!' he called over his shoulder, 'Can you spare my wife for this stand? I want to show her how ordinary men shoot.' He turned back to Olivia, taking Lionel's smiling consent for granted.

'Don't expect me to shoot how he's been shooting today. He's almost put Gilbert's nose out of joint for once, Aline, hasn't he?'

'Hush,' said Aline. 'It mustn't be said.'

'Very naughty of me. They're both superb. We're jolly lucky to be in the same party.'

Thirteen years, Olivia thought, where will I be in thirteen years?

*

Cornelius Cardew was tiring a little by the time the Nettleby woods came in sight. He had still some way to go before he reached them but the road was straight and though the stillness and chill of the air, and the bluish mist which lay in thin wisps between him and his destination, foreshadowed evening, he was not afraid of being too late. His design was to arrive at the very end of the day's shooting, to approach Sir Randolph in the most polite manner, and to ask whether he might call on him later to discuss with him one or two problems in which he felt sure they were both equally interested – not animal rights, no, no, that could be left for another day, after Sir Randolph had read the pamphlet – but matters concerned rather with the land, with country life, with the needs of the country districts. That was how he would put it, and if Sir Randolph, understandably tired after the day's disreputable activities, should say he was unable to see him until the next morning, well then the next morning it would have to be, even if it meant another night in that unspeakably uncomfortable inn. The chance of a sympathetic hearing, the possibility of a convert, should never be missed. Cornelius too often felt that he did nothing but preach to the converted – it was so difficult to find anyone else who would listen – and just at this moment, after his stimulating visit to the Cotswold Tolstoyans, his brain was humming with ideas and arguments such as no man of Sir Randolph's obvious sympathies and independence of view – unexpected as they were in one on the face of it so likely to have his opinions predetermined by his social position – could resist. All the same Cornelius hoped Sir Randolph would not make him wait until the next day. He hoped he would take him up to the house and offer him a cup of tea, not with the entire company, naturally, but quietly somewhere, in some small, book-lined study in front of a coal fire, where they could talk in peace.

He knew he was being optimistic, but he knew too that optimism sometimes had the effect of carrying all before it, and that that was why one had better let it have its head when one found it in oneself, for it was not to be relied on to stay. Too often the other thing took over and then life was not half so much fun, nothing but struggling to finish pamphlets that seemed to have lost their impetus, and finding nothing to say in answer to the fine philosophical points so frequently raised by his neighbour H. W. Briginshaw.

With his feet beginning to ache, and the vision of the book-lined study and the fire and the tea in his mind's eye, Cornelius walked steadily towards the woods.

*

Sir Randolph, walking on towards the next stand in ignorance of the approach of so determined a new friend, had preoccupations no less vague than Cornelius' but more worrying.

It had been a perfect day. Everything had gone according to

plan, there had been no unexpected difficulties, no disappointments. The weather was perfect, the game plentiful, the company congenial. At the least the company should have been congenial, but Gilbert Hartlip was in an odd mood, Lionel Stephens seemed to be making very little effort to soothe him, preferring to talk earnestly to Olivia Lilburn – a preference Sir Randolph understood but thought he should not make so obvious – Aline seemed to be whispering to someone whenever he saw her, a habit he considered obnoxious – surely some nanny or governess must have told her it was bad manners? – and Cicely was flirting much too openly with Tibor Rakassyi, which he knew would have annoyed Ida. He could not put it all down to the presence of women, because they had not been there in the morning, and even in the morning, though things had been better, there had been evidence of the spirit of rivalry which he so much disliked.

He walked over to the gamekeeper. 'Glass,' he said. 'Are your beaters all right, all in order? There was a bit of feeling, I thought, between Lord Hartlip's man and Mr Stephens' fellow. Did you notice that?'

'They're at daggers drawn, Sir Randolph. They seem to think it's a private competition. Trouble is Mr Stephens' score is higher just now as I understand it and the other chap's not used to that. I did have a word with them about it. They was practically at each other's throats.'

'I'll talk to Mr Stephens about it. I don't like that sort of thing.'

Glass nodded, preoccupied with the planning of the next drive. When everything went as it should, it was one of the more spectacular. The guns were positioned in the valley, near the river, facing the woods which sloped down towards them. In order to make the birds fly out all together at the last minute, it was necessary to have two lines of beaters, one standing at the top of the hill and the other walking up towards them. At a certain point the first line had to move forwards so that the birds, checked by the second line from running downhill, flew out high over the guns. The trouble with the particular manoeuvre was that each time it was done it had to be varied, according to the weather, the wind speed, Glass's estimate of the number of birds he wanted shot, for except on days like this one, when the object was to provide the maximum number of shots for the highly skilled shooters, it was sometimes an acceptable policy to combine reasonable sport with the saving of a good proportion of the game, to make sure there was a plentiful supply for the rest of the year as well as for the following breeding season.

All these considerations, well understood and many times discussed with Sir Randolph, weighed on Mr Glass's shoulders as he walked round from man to man of his beaters to remind them of the plan of campaign. He had the bent shoulders more usually associated with sedentary occupations but in fact often seen on men who walk most of the day. Like most of the keepers and some of the beaters he wore a bowler hat, but his was slightly higher in the crown than most, giving him an old-fashioned look. Though a healthy man he was no longer young.

'Here a minute, Dan,' he said, passing his son dawdling along with a couple of other boys of his age. 'Go over to Walter Weir and tell him to start taking his lot up to the top, will you?'

Dan nodded and walked off with his strong even stride. What was the good of a son, Mr Glass thought, if you couldn't use him as a messenger boy?

*

Bob Lilburn was a bigger man than Lionel Stephens. He seemed to Olivia, standing beside him as he waited for the birds to fly out, immobile and solid as an effigy, a great stone Crusader perhaps, raised from some mediaeval tomb, propped up and clothed in giant tweeds. Crusaders too perhaps were sometimes silly men. For all his physical splendour and outward show of large authority she felt she knew him now as simply that, a silly man, who cared for nothing but the social niceties and grew quite sweaty on his forehead at the thought of going down to dinner with the wrong sort of studs in his shirt. She would admit that knowledge to no one, as long as she lived, that was the one resolution she could make, standing there beside him. If there were others to be made, she wanted desperately not to have to make them yet. She was still feeling the shock of Aline's remark, of the spirit of complicity implied in it. After the heights on which she seemed to have been walking to have had to come down to that, to 'Congrats, old thing!'

*

Stretched comfortably on her bed, Minnie was borne along towards sleep by the calm procession of her afternoon thoughts as if she were some frescoed goddess floating on white clouds across a ceiling of cerulean blue. In her room there was no sound except the ticking of the French clock in its glass case on the mantelpiece and the occasional flutter of a tortoise-shell butterfly which, caught in a spider's web which the housemaids had failed to notice in the top corner of one of the windows, every now and then made a feeble effort to escape, then subsided semi-comatose in the late afternoon sunlight. From outside came the sound of the rooks in the elms, and the occasional soft cooing of a wood-pigeon.

Echoes of conversations, recent, to come, or imaginary, floated round her. She thought of vol-au-vents and consommé (the former had been better than usual at lunch, the latter, for this evening, could be looked forward to with confidence, for Mrs Bilston's Consommé à la Reine was one of the certainties of life); of Mrs Walker Kerr and the dullness of academic society (besides which, she and Sir Reuben Hergesheimer were both convinced that Mrs Walker Kerr had revoked at bridge the last time she came to dinner); but the girls were pretty – she liked a group of girls. There would be the two Miss Walker Kerrs and beautiful Grizel and dear hopeful Cicely – they would make a charming group. She meant to leave her aquamarine ring to Cicely, the one Randolph had given her for their Silver Wedding; it was the colour of Cicely's eyes. In the meantime she might wear it herself this evening, with the blue satin with the bodice of lace guipure (blue was Minnie's favourite colour). Galantine de Faisan aux Truffes . . . now why had she thought of that? They must have had it somewhere. Had she some recipe tucked away in a pocket or a glove, which she had asked for, for Mrs Bilston? It was so difficult to think of things to do with pheasants, and one had so many. One could do without the truffles probably, though Ida might ask John to bring some next time he came home via Paris. They did that sort of dish so beautifully at the Hôtel du Palais in Biarritz. One could never get English cooks to make things look pretty enough; they had no picture in their mind's eye, nothing to work towards. She could carry her blue fan, the one painted with the rather plump lady and gentleman sitting in front of blue willow trees beside a blue lake, with a naked amaretto (back view) hiding behind a sort of sheep-pen, bow in hand, and ivory struts inlaid with mother-of-pearl. Not that she needed a fan, but who should prevent her, it being her own house? The ones she loved most were ostrich feathers, but for that sort of thing it really did have to be a dance, with long white gloves. She had some Parma violet gloves, a colour she liked almost as much as blue . . . pearl buttons at the wrists . . . satin, sequins, every kind of finery . . . and then such a pretty silk nightie. She really ought to do some shopping . . . an evening jacket, sequinned, perhaps the tiniest frill of tulle round the high collar? . . . a simple little blouse, silk with lace panels at the sides . . . underclothes, new stays? . . . Parma violets again, with silk ribbons and laces . . . all silk, satin, muslin and no rags at all . . .

'Are you awake, Belle-Mère?' Ida's rather strident voice awoke her. 'We ought to be getting ready.' She was tapping at the door. Ida with her teeth and her integrity.

'Coming!' Minnie sang out sweetly, her musical voice itself a reproach to Ida's lack of charm.

What a bore to have to leave her comfortable bed, put on her brogues, her hat (those stupid hatpins!) her coat, her gloves, be driven a smile or two, stand in the now rapidly chilling air and watch a lot of silly birds being killed, as if one hadn't seen it all hundreds of times before; but never mind, it was a duty, and what was life, thought Minnie cheerfully, swinging her legs over the side of the bed and getting a little heavily to her feet, but one long round of duty?

*

'What's our score, Percy?'

Lionel was waiting by the wood with Percy Maidment and Ellen's brother Johnny. Olivia had gone to stand with her husband.

'92 pheasants, 3 hares, 2 woodcock,' said Percy, without reference to his notebook.

'Not too bad. How's everyone else doing, do you know?'

'Lord Hartlip has 88 pheasants, 2 hares, 1 woodcock, sir. No one else to touch the two of you.'

143

'You've been taking a pretty keen interest then?'

'Yes, sir.'

'Is Lord Hartlip keeping his score?'

'He is, sir. And his man is.'

'I see. Well, I don't mind, but it's not popular with our host, so keep quiet about it, will you?'

'Yes sir.'

Lionel turned to look in the direction from which the next batch of pheasants could be expected to appear, his back towards the loaders.

'How many more drives?' he said without looking round.

'Two, sir.'

Lionel stood in silence for some moments, his gun under his arm, its muzzle pointing downwards. The sounds of the beaters began to approach.

'I daresay we can manage to keep ahead of Lord Hartlip,' said Lionel quietly.

Percy smiled, delighted.

'Yes, sir. That's the spirit, sir.'

He had been within an inch of glory, Lionel felt. She had faced him with all her marvellous courage and truthfulness and said I love you.

The spirit of love possessed them, but the world had been all round them and they had not been able to possess each other. He had wanted – how could he not have done so? – the immediate triumph; they should have fallen to the ground among the red gold leaves like a lion and lioness; instead he had had to talk polite nonsense, to smile and fall back when her husband claimed his place by her side. The consummation must come, of that Lionel felt certain, but how and where and after what difficulties? And then to be told his man was causing feeling, would he restrain him, would he restrain himself as well, was no doubt meant, not shoot so well, not bother Gilbert Hartlip – but why? For form's sake. Form meant too much to people like Randolph Nettleby (of course in a quiet way until now he'd rather idolized the man, thought of him as someone to be admired and appreciated, listened to and emulated as much as anyone that he knew; but everything was different now, not because he was in love – that was nothing new – but because he was loved). Form was not enough; or rather it was too much, too restricting a framework

144

for the natural man. He was a better lover for Olivia than Bob Lilburn and a better shot than Gilbert Hartlip. It was impossible and unnecessary for him to conceal these things.

Another way of putting it might have been that if he was not to have Olivia now this very minute in his arms then at least he was going to thrash Gilbert Hartlip when it came to shooting.

*

Aline's thoughts, as she stood beside her husband – to stand once with one's husband, she felt, fulfilled one's obligations in that direction – were full of what she considered to be her discovery about Olivia.

Aline was known to her friends to have a kinder heart than mere acquaintances sometimes suspected. The congratulations she had offered to Olivia were genuinely meant. She hoped that she and Olivia might now become better friends, and if there was any way in which she could help to forward the intrigue between Olivia and Lionel she would be happy to give loyal and understanding support. Olivia's horrified apprehension of the spirit of complicity implied in Aline's friendliness was an accurate understanding. Aline felt that Olivia was now on her own level, but her feeling contained no malice and no triumph, she merely felt that now there need be no barriers between them.

Aline had had a strict upbringing. Her father had, as it was unkindly said, bought his way into Society for her sake; her looks and native wits had done the rest. She had made a good marriage, and on that basis had achieved a certain position as a London hostess. Her chief mentor in this last endeavour had been an older woman of impeccable taste and credentials, whose acolyte she had been for many years. In modelling herself on this great Edwardian hostess, Aline's only consideration had been to be as like her as possible, in voice, manner and dress, to learn from her where to be and when, who to know and who not to know, how to charm, how to lie, how to laugh. These lessons learnt she would have liked now to progress to another role, that of mistress to an important man.

She had married Gilbert Hartlip as a result of a straight deal between their parents, social position in exchange for money – a deal on which her father had to some extent reneged in that it had turned out he meant to make his daughter and son-in-law wait until his death for most of his money. Discreet infidelities seemed in order; her first, with a famous figure of the time, handsome, brilliant, no longer young, no longer quite so promising, had been a disillusioning experience. He had kept her waiting once when she had come to see him in his comfortable bachelor apartments, and she had seen on his desk, left lying around with such carelessness that she wondered afterwards whether he had meant her to read them, love letters from what seemed to be half the married women in London. When he had arrived at last and she had faced him with the letters, he had been savagely unkind. She had taken defeat quietly. He went everywhere and was thought much of. She had no alternative.

She knew that her present lover was not much of a catch, and had a feeling that in allowing herself to be swayed almost entirely by her own sensual desires she had been too self-indulgent. She ought to have had her eye more firmly on the prospects of advantage. She allowed herself to think of Charles Farquhar as a sin, which had its own appeal; but she was under no illusion that the thing could last.

When Gilbert had irritably accused her of disparaging Lionel Stephens because she was put out by his apparent immunity to her charm, he had been to some extent right. Aline would have liked Lionel Stephens to fall for her. He was a promising young man. It was generally thought that after a few more years at the Bar he would have made enough money to go into politics and that when he did so either party would be pleased to have him. An older woman to guide him at this stage, to entertain for him, intrigue for him, would be perfectly appropriate. Well, he had chosen Olivia and clearly it was love of the highest sort, such as would be suitable for someone of Olivia's qualities. Aline was generous in her recognition: all she wanted was to be allowed to be an intimate. Olivia had not so far been in the inner circle of Aline's acquaintances: she had been also – or so Aline considered – in a position, should she wish to do so, to look down on Aline from a moral point of view. Aline was quite clear in her mind that the way of life she had chosen was the right one for her talents, but she also knew that there was another way of life, one in which married ladies did not have lovers; and though generally speaking one could shrug that off by the thought of how incredibly dreary and middle class it was, it was difficult to apply that criticism to the lovely, well-born and admired Olivia Lilburn. But if Olivia were to stoop – if stoop it was – then it not only made a franker friendship between the two women possible by making Olivia more like Aline, but it was likely to help to quieten those odd prickings of conscience left behind by her really awfully boring childhood by making Aline more like Olivia.

It was therefore with genuine kindliness that she expressed to Gilbert the view that Lionel was wonderfully good-looking. After all, what was the point of the whole thing if they were not all wonderful people?

'I suppose he is really one of the best-looking people one knows.'

'Would you say so?' said Gilbert coldly.

'Bob Lilburn is very fine-looking of course but he is more massive. Lionel has such a sensitive face, don't you think? Like Phoebus Apollo turned fasting friar.'

'What?'

'George Meredith. In *The Egoist*, you know, the hero, I can't remember his name, the man she loves, not the egoist himself. He's supposed to have that rather ascetic look, although frightfully handsome and strong. He describes him as Phoebus Apollo turned fasting friar; I've always thought he sounded so attractive.'

'Can't think what it means.'

'You do sound cross.'

'I am cross. Your friend Lionel Stephens is being thoroughly annoying. For some unknown reason he's setting himself up in rivalry to me. He's trying to beat my score. I've already had to speak to him once about poaching.'

'And is he beating your score?'

'He's pretty near to doing so.'

'By how much?'

'Oh, the odd brace.'

'If it's only the odd brace, does it matter? Everyone knows you're a wonderful shot, and if every now and then someone gets the odd brace more than you, does it really matter?'

'That's not what you were saying last night.'

'I was in a bad mood last night.'

'It's bad form. He's younger than me. He should know better

than to set himself up in competition. Besides, Randolph doesn't like it.'

'That's just a fad of Randolph's. In plenty of places where one goes to shoot one's actually given a score card to fill in.'

'I know, but if one's host doesn't like it... He thinks it's a foreign habit, and ungentlemanly.'

'But you don't agree with him.'

'No, I don't, as it happens.'

'It's just one of his old-fashioned eccentricities. I shouldn't pay any attention to it. You've got two more drives. Why don't you beat him in those?'

'I can't shoot any more birds than I'm shooting already.'

'I expect you could if you tried. Poach a bit or something. Why not? It's more fun. I don't see why Lionel should have everything his own way.'

*

The October afternoon turned early towards evening, extending over the countryside a veil of mist so light as to be barely discernible, giving only an effect as if everything were to be seen through water, faintly opaque. The smoke from the village chimneys rose straight into the air, bluish-grey against the pinkish-grey of the sky. Cornelius turned away from the village, taking the road which led towards the woods, whose soft green or mouse-brown expanse, interspersed with autumn red and gold, lay now only a mile or so in front of him. A few yellowish leaves fell slowly onto the road from the almost bare branches of the elms which grew here and there along the hedgerows; a blackbird flew across his path with a loud alarm call, and a jay, flying higher, gave its own raucous warning. Cornelius rubbed his forehead irritably; in spite of the chill in the air, the midges were still biting. He heard the sound of shots from the wood and looked at his watch. It was a quarter to four and the light was still good. That would be likely to be the drive before the last one. His timing was perfect.

Minnie and Ida heard the shots too, sitting side by side in the back of the Daimler. They also congratulated themselves on the accuracy of their timing, but they did so inwardly and severally, each staring out of the window on her own side of the car. It was not unusual for Minnie and Ida to have nothing much to say to each other.

The lodgekeeper's wife and six-year-old daughter came out to open the gates for the car. The little girl struggled to push back the heavy wrought-iron gate, then stood flushed and self-important beside it. Minnie wound down her window and put her face close to the opening to say 'You're a great help to your mother, aren't you Lily? Well done!'

Lily went even redder in the face but managed a bobbed curtsey and a breathy, 'Yes, m'lady.'

'Dear little thing,' said Minnie leaning back in her seat and winding up the window. 'Such a pretty face. I do hope she doesn't take after poor Jessie.'

'What happened to poor Jessie?'

'Babies happened to poor Jessie. Babies and babies and babies. So naughty. She was the elder sister.'

'Married?'

'Oh dear me no. She wasn't old enough to be married. And then they got her a job in service somewhere near Gloucester. I gave her a wonderful reference but it was no good; it happened all over again – the son of the house I believe. Too dreadful – I don't quite know what happened after that, her parents washed their hands of her. I must ask her mother some time if she ever hears from her. I'd like to send her something, poor silly creature.'

'She sounds worse than silly,' said Ida.

'She was very naughty, yes. But such a dear little thing you know, to meet, you wouldn't have believed it really.'

'Butter wouldn't melt in her mouth, *I* know.' said Ida.

Minnie sighed. Ida was right, of course, but there was no need to be unpleasant about it. Feeling in the capacious pocket of her long full tweed skirt she abstracted a tiny leather note-pad with silver corners and a silver propelling pencil and in writing which was rather hard to read because of the movement of the car wrote 'Jessie (ask Mrs C. about).'

The Daimler proceeded with due dignity towards the river. As they approached the bridge, and the stile beside which they had seen Violet with Nanny that morning, Minnie asked, 'Did they find the duck?'

'I suppose so,' said Ida. 'I expect we should have heard if they hadn't.'

*

After the bridge, after the shallow rapids, after the quiet pool, the river ran in a series of bends before straightening out into the wider stretch which flowed past the boat-house. The bends had high banks with miniature cliffs of reddish earth, in places overgrown with thick stubby bushes and in places merging with a tangle of reeds and kingcups. Here and there a break in the bank allowed for a steep descent onto a foot or so of greyish sand, but mostly it was impossible to walk immediately beside the water. From the bank one could not see all of the river's edge below; the occasional loud splash which was probably a fish just could have been a duck which had dashed to take shelter in the reeds and remained there in concealment. To be quite sure it was better to walk along in the river. Osbert had wellington boots on and was wading slowly through the water with Ellen on the bank above him. Round each bend as they came to it something splashed – fish, moorhens, water voles – each time it might have been the duck. A wagtail flew ahead of them, stopping every now and then to perch on a stick or stone, bobbing its tail before flying off again low over the water with a sharp chinking call. Two dark rather stout little dippers flew away downriver. Once a kingfisher flashed ahead of them but Osbert did not see it; he was looking over towards the other bank, where a movement in the reeds turned out to be only another pair of moorhens.

Reaching a miniature bay he paused on the edge and looked up at Ellen.

'Just look at your trousers,' she said.

The water had come over the top of his boots and his tweed knickerbockers were wet.

'It's getting deep.'

They were not exactly disheartened. The river held so much life that their expectations were kept alive; there might be ducks round any bend. Besides, the activity, the sound of moving water, the soft sliding river in its continuous forward progress, made them feel something must be being achieved. It was hard to believe in an unchanging state of affairs beside such evidence of flux; something must be going to happen. Ellen noticed however that Osbert's face was beginning to have a certain transparent look which was familiar to her; he was getting tired.

'Here,' she said. 'Have an apple.'

She had put a few in her pocket after lunch without being seen. She rubbed one on her sleeve and held it out to him, a large red Worcester Pearmaine, a little wrinkled on the outside but still juicy. She sat down on the damp grass and bit into one herself.

In the still air the sound of shots carried easily. The volley heard by Cornelius Cardew on the road from the village and by Minnie and Ida in the Daimler as they waited for the lodge gates to be opened for them sounded very close. On the river bank Osbert and Ellen stopped eating and stared at one another, their apples in their hands. It seemed a long time before the sound of shooting thinned, then faded away.

Ellen found herself speaking in a whisper.

'It's not as near as it sounds.'

'It is.' Osbert's voice rose higher as he spoke. All day he had managed to submerge the thought; now it overwhelmed him. 'It is, Ellen. It is near. They're going to shoot her. They're going to shoot her, Ellen.'

Ellen twitched up her skirt and began quickly to unlace her boots. Her hands were shaking with anger. The tears which momentarily filled her eyes were tears of tremendous rage. How dared they? What right had they? All those men with guns after one poor little duck. She wrenched off her boots one by one, slipped down her stockings and stuffed them into the boots, threw her coat over them on the river bank, gathered up her skirt and stuffed it anyhow into her belt, and slid down the bank into the river. The water came over her white knees. She hitched her skirt over one arm and began to wade downstream. Osbert followed.

*

Glass walked along the line of dead pheasants, crooking two fingers round the neck of every tenth bird and pulling it forward to make re-counting easier.

'Five hundred and four,' he reported provisionally to Sir Randolph, before going on to count the hares, rabbits and woodcocks (and the jay shot as vermin by young Marcus).

'Well done.'

Glass knew that Sir Randolph's congratulations were for his organisation of the drive.

'I must say,' said Bob Lilburn strolling towards them. 'That last drive was superb.'

Sir Randolph pointed at Glass, as if accusingly.

'There's the man you should congratulate.'

'I certainly do. Superb.'

'Thank you, m'lord. It's a lovely lie of the land, that.'

'Superb. Famous. Justly famous.'

'This next one's often quite lively if we're lucky,' said Sir Randolph. 'I thought we might just wander over afterwards and take the duck if it would amuse you.'

'Rather. What a day you're giving us.'

Glass had already hurried over to marshall his men for the final drive. The guns were to stand in the water meadow outside the last plantation, where clumps of privet, holly and low spruce had been planted in groups beneath the taller trees to form natural corners into which the pheasants would run and from which they could gradually be flushed so as to be presented to the guns in succession.

'Now I want everyone to stop short of the last corner. I'll blow my whistle and Walter here will repeat it from the centre of the line. Four of us will go forward twenty or thirty yards to flush out the first batch. Everyone stands still when we stand still. Then you move forward, taking your cue from Walter and Tom. Then we do the same again three or four times till we get to the end. Everyone clear?'

Everyone was clear; most them had done it many times before. On most of their faces Glass could see a reflection of his own mood. They knew it had been a good day and the end of it was in sight; the evening's relaxation would have been earned. Everyone liked being a part, however small, of a success. He saw Dan grinning at him, aware of the sense of occasion. What better life for a boy, Glass thought; or for a man, when he grew to be a man? What was the point of taking him away from that, away from where he belonged, stuffing his head with needless facts, shutting him up in some laboratory somewhere? This was where he belonged, in these woods, within these few miles of ground, every inch of which was his known territory. Why move away? The foxes didn't move, the badgers didn't; the rabbits, squirrels, deer, owls, all of them, whether friend or foe in the professional sense, they stayed where they belonged. Dan should do the same. It was right and proper; the other was unnatural.

'Dan, you can go for stop this time, see the sport. On the outside, and mind you don't let anything through, not a single one. We're beating our best record today, we've got to keep it up. Right?'

*

Minnie and Ida walked side by side briskly along the river bank, substantial hats at sensible angles, capacious tweed skirts sweeping the muddy path, towards the scattered groups of people talking idly under the trees. The beaters had just moved off, the rest of the party was about to walk along to the water meadow for the last drive. Aline was the first to see them; she gave a short cry like a green parakeet.

'Minnie, you are the cleverest person. Every time I've been here you've arrived at exactly this moment.'

'If you're as lazy as I am and yet don't want to miss all the fun, you have to be methodical.'

Sir Randolph, who was still standing with Bob Lilburn, turned to greet them; he came over to take Minnie by the arm. He knew she didn't care for shooting, though no one could have guessed it from her animated face; he appreciated all the more the fact that she came. Bob Lilburn followed them with Ida as they set off towards the outskirts of the wood. Olivia, noticing that it would be natural now for Ida to stand beside Bob while he was shooting, dropped back and walked with Tommy Farmer and Marcus.

'So Marcus, you will soon finish school, I suppose. Will you go to University?'

'I may be going into the Army. It might be more fun. I want to travel and my father thinks he might be able to get me an ADC's post somewhere – perhaps in Canada, or else in India. I'd rather India myself.'

'Canada's good fun,' said Tommy. 'My elder brother was ADC to the Governor General for a bit and he had great fun. Lots of parties. In fact he married his daughter. George did, I mean. The Governor-General's daughter.'

'That's not what I want at all – parties and getting married! I want to explore the unmapped wild and all that sort of thing. A friend of my father's lives in Tibet, actually lives there – he's a famous botanist. I could go and see him when the Viceroy goes to Simla in the summer. And climb the Himalayas and go tiger-shooting.'

'I knew a man who lost an eye pig-sticking in India.'

'You are a wet blanket. I bet you know a man who died of fever on the Gold Coast.'

'I do actually. Funny you should mention that.'

Olivia walked beside them in silence, her head bent.

Before long Lionel came up to walk beside her, but as she did not turn her head or in any other way acknowledge his presence he did not speak. At the end of the wood there was a wicket gate leading into the meadow. Lionel held it open for Olivia, and said quietly as she passed through it, 'Will you stand with me?'

His place having been indicated to him by Sir Randolph, they walked there slowly.

'I never thought that when I fell in love it would be with the most beautiful woman in the world.'

He had been looking at her with some anxiety, trying to gauge her change of mood, and he spoke spontaneously, because her beauty had struck him anew. Her expression, which had been preoccupied, changed to one of genuine amusement.

'That's ridiculous!'

'Oh I am so glad to see you smiling again.'

'Lionel, I said something foolish a little while ago, something I shouldn't have said. Will you forget it?'

'I can't.'

'I should like you to.'

'I can't believe that.'

'It is true. I should like you to forget it.'

'That sort of thing isn't meant to be forgotten.'

'I think perhaps sometimes it is. Or if not forgotten exactly, then put aside.'

'Olivia, I cannot put you aside.'

'But some things are – impossible.'

'That is impossible.'

'The other,' she spoke with a low voice, 'is also imposible.'

They walked in silence, as slowly as they dared.

He said quietly, 'I think I could make it possible. I have thought about it.'

He had thought about his London flat, his discreet man-servant.

She shook her head.

They were approaching the waiting loaders.

'Is it something to do with your idea of duty?'

'I don't know.' Hr voice trembled, but she made an effort to achieve accuracy. 'I won't know until I get to Heaven whether it is duty or cowardice. I think it is a little to do with the fact that already sometimes I have to say to my son, be good, and already sometimes I wonder how I dare, on what possible grounds I dare to do it.'

'But Love is the most important thing in the world.'

'I used to think so too. I think I still do think so. Only I don't exactly know what Love is.'

'I know what it is. I can show you. I know I can show you.'

Olivia now felt completely faint. She would have liked to throw herself weeping on Lionel's breast. She was astonished as much by the strength of her own emotions as by anything else. Steadying herself with a hand on Lionel's arm, she managed the last few paces towards the loaders and turned with her back towards them to face the wood. Lionel covered her hand with his.

'I'll show you,' he said again.

'It will be so hard,' she murmured.

Hard to go on resisting Love, or hard to live under its rule? He did not know, but as the beaters approached and he still kept his hand over hers though Percy Maidment was already holding out his gun, he chose to think the latter. He would show her. Her happiness, marriage, child, reputation, none of it should suffer; only they must love each other.

*

Gilbert Hartlip looked towards Lionel Stephens. Olivia Lilburn was leaning on his arm, his head was bent towards her. Funny way to behave, Gilbert thought, hanging on to another man's wife like that when he ought to have been concentrating on his shooting. Those few minutes before the birds came over were important, in Gilbert's view. One ought to give oneself over to the feeling of anticipation; it sharpened one's perceptions, made one's reflexes quicker, when the time came. One ought to be at a white heat of excitement, kept concentrated by a ferocious control. This was what Gilbert believed and practised and it was perhaps the reason why shooting so often left him exhausted.

Seeing the direction of his glance, Albert Jarvis muttered, 'He's fifteen ahead of us now, sir.'

Gilbert knew it already. In these moments before the last drive he allowed himself to hate. At school he used to box, and his coach used to say to him, 'Hate him. If you want to win you've got to hate that boy's guts before you go into the ring.' In that spirit Gilbert Hartlip hated Lionel Stephens. He hated his looks, his youth, his skill, his broad shoulders, his kind eyes, the clean, well-shaped nails on his long fingers; he hated his love for Olivia, and his apparent success with her; he hated his urbanity and good manners; he hated his guts.

'All right, Jarvis.'

He held out his hand for his loaded gun.

Lionel stood motionless ten yards or so away, Olivia beside him, Percy Maidment and the boy alert behind them, Percy seeming hardly more than half the height of his master. Beyond them stood Sir Randolph in his wide-brimmed hat, with Minnie beside him leaning on a shooting stick, his two loaders behind, the dog Lorna at Charlie Pass's feet, her eyes fixed on the wood from which the pheasants would come; beyond again was the erect figure of Bob Lilburn, his hat at a slightly rakish angle, Ida beside him solid on her shooting stick, a long silver-fox fur loosely round her neck, his loaders behind him (the second of them quite a young boy whose cap and cartridge bag seemed both too big for him); then came Charles Farquhar in a rather larger-checked tweed than the others, Aline's figure beside him almost Carolean in outline, with her soft-brimmed velvet hat and its one sweeping feather; a springer spaniel waited behind them with the loaders.

All these, and the next little group, which was Tibor Rakassyi's, Cornelius Cardew could see as he slowly approached the wood across the water meadow, and stopped by a big willow tree which stood alone in the field. Opposite Tibor the line of the wood began to curve, and the other guns were concealed from Cornelius by the intervening trees. Leaning against the willow tree, Cornelius prepared to watch the shooting; this time he had no intention of disrupting it.

The light, though still good as to visibility, was now the light of evening; it was as if the gold in the scene had been lightly sponged away to give a less emphatic tone, and the sombre greenish-black reinforced; the figures were dark and the background a little misty. Cornelius had to admit to himself that it was a picturesque scene, in this curiously poetic light and stillness, and with the smell of autumn sharp in his nostrils. The element of ritual lent it a kind of solemnity; like so many rituals it required a sacrifice.

That the harvests may be good and the tribe increase, thought Cornelius. He was glad he had turned back.

*

The beaters approached, tapping on the tree-trunks, trampling through the undergrowth. The wood was full of men, and of creatures running. The men stopped; four walked forward, there were several shots. The longer line of beaters moved forward, more birds flew; the shooting now seemed uninterrupted. The noise of the beaters grew louder; the air was full of falling birds and gunfire, the smell of cordite, the sound of shot raining on the leaves, the thump of bodies on the ground.

'It will be so,' thought Lionel. 'It is destiny. She will be mine.'

Percy pressed the gun into his hands. Two high birds fell in quick succession.

'Should have been our bird,' muttered Albert Jarvis, thrusting the two cartridges he held ready between his fingers into the breach of the gun his boy had handed to him.

Gilbert held out his hand for the gun without moving his gaze from the oncoming birds and muttered through his teeth, 'Is he doing it again?'

'He is, m'lord.'

'Asking for it, isn't he?'

He pulled the trigger twice, held out his gun, received the other one. 'How was that?'

'That'll teach him, m'lord.'

The bird he had shot fell close to Olivia's feet.

'Fool,' muttered Lionel. 'What does he think he's doing?'

'Pay no attention, sir, I wouldn't.'

Percy's voice as he thrust the gun into Lionel's hands was so urgent in tone in spite of the reassuring nature of his actual words that it acted as a spur to Lionel. His next two shots brought down birds flying so high and fast that many good sportsmen would have missed one if not both. Dan Glass, pausing a moment in his perambulation up and down the length of the wood, stopped on the corner only a few feet away from Gilbert Hartlip and looked across towards Lionel in time to admire his skill. Gilbert was so close that Dan could see the expression on his face, which was one of concentrated hatred. Shocked, Dan wondered if he looked like that himself when he was shooting, but had hardly time to think about it before he was again lost in admiration of the exhibition of pure skill, this time from Gilbert himself. He turned back to walk once more up the side of the wood and felt the small shot scatter over his head and the dead leaves beneath his feet.

Further up the line of beaters in the wood, Dan's father was tramping solidly through a thicket of brambles laying about him with a stout stick as he went. 'Fast and furious,' he was thinking. 'Fast and furious it is now.' He was getting close to the line of guns. As he lifted his foot to crush the last spur of bramble he could look ahead and see beyond the trees the familiar figure of Sir Randolph with his gun raised. It was nearly over. Leaving the bramble thicket behind him he walked out onto the soft grass beneath the trees at the edge of the wood. Birds were still flying out but most of them had already gone. The shooting was beginning to die down. As he stepped out of the trees he did not see the woodcock which flew out low and fast at the end of the wood, or the controlled swing of the whole of Gilbert Hartlip's body as his gun followed it, but he heard the sound which succeeded the shot, the extraordinarily penetrating sound of a man screaming.

Glass stood still. He looked towards Sir Randolph, who, having lowered his gun and instinctively unloaded it, stood in the same petrified position as he did. Both men took several hasty steps forward, then stopped at the same moment. There was silence – everyone seemed to be standing still – then the sound of people moving through the wood and a shout passed along the line of beaters towards Glass 'The stop. The stop's been shot.'

Glass broke into a run. He caught up with Sir Randolph as the latter threw his gun towards Charlie Pass, saying, 'Stay there, will you?' Charlie caught the gun and stayed where he stood. Sir Randolph and Mr Glass ran along beside the wood together.

'Tell them to keep back,' said Sir Randolph.

'Keep back,' said Glass, as they passed Walter Weir pushing his way out of the bushes. 'Tell them to keep back, Walter.'

The men were coming out of the wood in twos and threes. Walter Weir held out an arm. 'Keep back. Don't crowd.'

Some were already gathered in a small group at the edge of the wood looking down. Gilbert Hartlip was with them. As Glass and Sir Randolph approached Dan, who had been on his knees, stood up and turned towards them. He was pale and seemed to his father to be covered in blood.

'What happened?' Glass seized his blood-soaked sleeve. 'Are you all right?'

Dan looked down.

'It's Tom.'

Glass saw that there was a figure lying on the grass and that Sir Randolph was already kneeling beside it.

'I thought 'twas you. You was stop, wasn't you?'

'There were two of us. Tom Harker said one wasn't enough. We were crossing each other, going up and down.'

Glass nodded. He was very white and breathing heavily. Dan looked away.

Tom Harker was lying on his side, with both hands over his face. Blood was pouring through his fingers.

'My eyes,' he said in a loud voice. 'Don't want to lose my eyes.'

'Just turn over a little onto your back and let's have a look.'

Sir Randolph took a clean white handkerchief out of his coat pocket, then took off his coat and rolled it into a pillow. 'Let's just take your hands away for a moment. That's the way.'

He held Tom Harker's bloody hands in his and looked into his face. The shot had caught him on the left side of his face which was bleeding copiously; his eye was closed. It was impossible to tell the extent of the injury without cleaning the wounds. Sir Randolph folded the handkerchief, placed it over the injured side of the face and put Tom's left hand over it.

'Hold that and we'll get you home. Who's the fastest runner here?'

'I am, Sir Randolph.'

'Go and get Doctor West as fast as you can.'

Dan was off across the field at once. Glass looked after him in a bewildered way as if he were still not quite able to take in what had happened, and saw a vaguely familiar figure which had been standing by a tree move forward to speak to the boy.

'Can one help at all?' asked Cornelius Cardew.

'I don't think so, sir. I'm going for the doctor.'

Cornelius hesitantly approached the group round the prostrate Tom Harker. He heard Tom speak in a loud trembling voice.

'If my time's come I'll go, but I don't want to be a blind man.'

'Of course not, Tom. Don't worry. Doctor West will be here soon.'

Sir Randolph looked up at the men standing round, and caught sight of Gilbert Hartlip. His glance rested on his face, his expression bleak; then he very slightly shook his head. Gilbert's expression of aloof though solemn calm did not change.

Sir Randolph raised himself onto one knee and looked round for Glass.

'Tell the men what's happened, will you, and ask them to go home. Then you'd better tell everyone else to do the same. There's no point in their waiting around. We don't want a crowd. Tell them everything's under control and the best thing they can do is go home. Get a message to Patten to bring the car for Lady Nettleby. And then he'd better bring it down again in case Doctor West wants the use of it. And get a few men to make a litter, will you, something to carry him on if necessary?'

Galvanized by the need for action, Glass hurried about to relay these instructions. Walter Weir produced a flask from his pocket and silently handed it to Sir Randolph, who still kneeling said, 'Take a drink of this, Tom,' and held it to Tom's lips. Tom turned away his head so that the brownish liquid ran down his cheek and mingled with the red blood.

'Never in my life the worse for drink. No man can say that against me. I have never in my life been the worse for drink.'

'Of course you haven't, Tom, we all know that. This is medicinal.'

160

Tom turned his head back and allowed Sir Randolph to hold the flask to his lips.

'We'll get you home as soon as possible.' Sir Randolph stood up. 'Or hospital.' He had suddenly remembered Tom's home, and that it was more like a badger's than a man's, and that the old witch his mother had been dead a few years now. 'Whatever Doctor West thinks.'

'My own bed would be a better place for me to die in. I'm not partial to hospitals.'

'We're not going to let you die yet,' said Sir Randolph, but his face remained serious.

He stood beside Tom as if guarding him, looking over the field in the direction from which Doctor West might be expected to come. Gilbert Hartlip, giving as if fastidiously a wide berth to Tom's feet, came round to Sir Randolph and approaching him on the side furthest from Tom said quietly, 'Awful thing to happen.'

'Yes.'

'It was a woodcock. I'd no chance of getting it unless I'd swung fast. Of course I'd no idea the man was so close.'

Sir Randolph did not speak.

Olivia had approached and stood between two of the beaters, looking down at Tom. Lionel stood behind her. Minnie was to be seen walking towards them across the field with Ida and Bob Lilburn. Beside and behind them the beaters in their pale smocks grouped and regrouped as they moved slowly away in obedience to Glass's command. From one of the groups came a loud laugh, quickly hushed; someone on being told that Tom Harker had been shot had thought it funny, a question of a fright or a flesh wound, a pellet in a leg maybe, and had had to be shut up and told it had got him in the face.

Sir Randolph shifted his weight from one foot to the other irritably.

'Where's this doctor?'

Cornelius had approached in a tentative sideways sort of way and now looked down at Tom, and at the blood which having already soaked through the handkerchief was now covering with fresh scarlet the hand which held it there. Cornelius felt the immediate onset of violent indigestion. He looked across at Sir Randolph standing guard in his wide-brimmed hat, white shirt, tweed waistcoat and watch-chain – his coat was still under Tom's head – and at Gilbert Hartlip expressionless beside him, and next to them the two beaters who still stood and stared at Tom, and between them Olivia, in piteous contemplation of this or some other tragedy, behind her Lionel, beyond her the long-skirted, hatted and furred figures of Minnie and Ida escorted by Lord Lilburn; and the slowness with which those who moved did so and the stillness with which the others stood, and the gathering dusk which brought tones of violet to the shadows, and the intermittent golden leaves which slowly fell through the still air, all reinforced the ceremonial aspect he had noticed before.

'Oh!' he started, as if there were something he must tell them; but stopped, twisting his fingers ('Don't writhe,' Ada had said to him more than once. 'Your platform manner would be far better if you didn't writhe so much.') No one looked at him.

Gilbert was saying to Sir Randolph, in the same quiet voice as before, 'I'm most awfully sorry, naturally.'

Sir Randolph moved irritably again. He did not want to speak to Gilbert. Particularly he did not want to speak to him in front of other people. At the same time he was very angry; not only did all transgressions against the rules of safety in shooting make him angry, but one glance at the wound had told him that the shot which made it had been fired from far too close to have been anything but the shot of a fool or a madman. Since he knew that Gilbert was not the first he must believe him to have been however temporarily the second.

'I'll make it all right with him,' Gilbert was saying. 'Financially, I mean.'

Sir Randolph gave a short exasperated groan; then said in a low voice, 'You were not shooting like a gentleman, Gilbert.'

'Oh,' gasped Cornelius again, clasping and unclasping his hands more furiously than ever, and moving from one foot to the other in an ecstasy of embarrassment, excitement, horror and apprehension of revelation. 'If only I could make you see how utterly absurd you all are!'

They looked at him; all the faces turned towards him with expressions varying from total aloofness to mild enquiry. Cornelius stared back, aghast at his own bad taste.

'I cannot think that a helpful observation,' said Sir Randolph eventually.

'No,' said Cornelius, wringing his hands and retreating step by step across the grass. 'No, it is not helpful.'

*

Aline had been standing with Charles Farquhar. They had heard the scream but not at full pitch because they had been screened by the trees; however, it had been perfectly clear that it was a human cry.

'Oh dear,' Aline had said at once in her coolest voice. 'Gilbert has over-reached himself.'

She meant it as a joke. She had not accompanied her husband on shooting parties for so many years without coming to know that on the rare occasions when there was an accident (and never in her experience had this gone beyond a harmless flesh wound and a scare), it was not Gilbert who was responsible. More than once when she had asked him why he had let some opportunity slip he had told her that he never shot unless he could see further than where his bullet might fall if he missed – 'A good shot is a safe shot' – so that when she spoke she did not mean it. Even so it struck Charles as rather a heartless remark – after all, some poor fool had probably thought his hour had come – and when, following slowly in the direction which Ida and Bob Lilburn had taken towards the scene of the accident, they had been met by Glass and had realised it was true, he was deeply shocked. He thought it not at all the sort of thing a woman should say about her husband, even to her lover, and even if it was true.

'Is the fellow badly hurt?' he asked.

'It caught him in the face, sir. Doctor West has been sent for.'

'Blinded,' said Aline seriously, as Glass, touching his hat, hurried on his way. 'Expensive.'

Charles Farquhar wondered how he had failed to be offended by her lack of taste before. This was the sort of thing, he thought, which showed people up.

'Most unfortunate,' he said. 'I suppose we'd better be getting back to the house if we can't do anything.'

Aline looked round to see what everyone else was doing.

'Are they not going to shoot the duck then?' she asked vaguely.

'My dear Aline, when a man has been shot in the face ... It's not as if he'd just been peppered you know.'

As Aline looked at him, taking in the fact that she had some need to redeem herself, she was distracted by the appearance from the wood behind him of two unexpected figures.

'Oh,' she cried, seizing the opportunity to display the warmth of feeling he seemed to think she lacked. 'The poor creature. They've shot it already.'

Osbert and Ellen had been by the river while the shooting was going on and were making their way by the shortest possible route back to the place where Ellen had left her boots. They had not expected to run straight into the shooting party; and indeed would not have done so but for the unexpected delay, for if things had gone according to plan everyone would by now have moved on to the lake where it was customary to shoot the duck.

They stopped in some embarrassment but were unable immediately to think of any way round to their destination.

'We'll just have to run for it,' said Ellen.

Her skirt was still tucked untidily into her belt, her long white bony legs were bare and her hair, most of which had escaped from the pins which had once held it in a bun under her flat black felt hat, hung straggling over her shoulders. She was unable to walk fast because her feet were bare and Osbert, pale with exhaustion beside her, was impeded not only by the fact that the insides of his boots were very wet but because clasped in his arms, her head limp on his shoulder, was his duck.

Aline hurried towards them.

'My poor child,' she said tenderly. 'We'll get you another.'

They stared at her, wet, uncomprehending and alarmed. Charles Farquhar who had followed Aline now stood looking down at Osbert, who, reminded of the earlier drawing-room threat whose jocularity he had quite failed to see, tightened his grip on the duck and stared back. The head which lay on his shoulder, its greenish-grey beak touching his thin neck, did not move, but the lower eyelid on the side exposed to view slid suddenly downwards, exposing one bright black eye.

'D'you mean to say it's alive?' asked Aline sharply.

'Of course it's alive. It's tired, that's all.'

Charles Farquhar gave a short laugh; at which the duck

raised her head and began to tremble.

'We'd better go,' said Osbert, setting off in his squelching boots across the field.

'You ought to get dry,' Aline called after him, her concern now rather half-hearted.

'I'll see to it, m'lady,' said Ellen breathlessly, skipping over the cowpats with her bare feet.

'Who on earth is she?' said Charles Farquhar.

'God knows,' said Aline, disheartened.

*

Cicely, having been told by Glass what had happened and that her grandfather wanted everybody to go home, was about to do so when she caught sight of Osbert and Ellen in their hasty and bedraggled progress across the field. She called to them to stop.

'Are you all right? What happened?'

'We found the duck. It's just that we got a bit wet. Ellen came to help me.'

'You'd better hurry home and change before anyone else sees you.'

'Why is everyone waiting about? Has something happened?'

'Someone's been hurt. One of the beaters. Not your brother, Ellen; it's Tom Harker.'

Osbert had never particularly liked Tom Harker; it had always seemed impossible to walk down to the village, or to go into the Post Office for some acid drops or call at the Vicarage with a note or some extra Latin construe for Mr Fortescue, without meeting him walking with his long stride and his stick and his red handkerchief knotted round his neck and his thin collie dog.

'Oh!' he said, suddenly aghast. 'Who will look after his dog if he's dead?'

'He's not dead.'

'Well, if he has to go to hospital then?'

'Someone will, I'm sure. I'll remind them. Go on, Osbert, do go home. I'll go and find someone and make sure they look after the dog.'

'Promise.'

'I promise. Go on, run!'

Ellen took him by the arm and led him away, and the two of them continued their encumbered progress across the field. Cicely turned back towards the group standing at the edge of the wood.

'It would be better to go home,' said Tibor, who had followed her.

'I said I would tell someone about the dog.'

'We can send a message about the dog later.'

'I said I would. I think I'd better. Don't you bother; you go on home.'

'Of course I won't go on home. Why don't you wait here and I will give the message to one of the keepers?'

'It's too cold to stand about.'

She had started walking and Tibor followed her reluctantly. The shoot having been called off, he would have preferred to go home; besides, he thought Sir Randolph might not be pleased to see his granddaughter disobeying his instructions and approaching a scene which for all Tibor knew might be unpleasant. In his view it would have been better to have let the wounded man be looked after by one or two of his own kind and to have carried on with the day's sport. Accidents would happen, and the fact that it appeared that this had been an unlucky one in that the victim had been hit in a vulnerable spot did not alter the nature of the thing. A beater had been hit, that was all; it was not unknown.

As they approached the group standing round the prostrate Tom they were met by Minnie, Ida and Bob Lilburn, who were walking towards them.

'We are all to go home,' said Ida firmly. 'Come along, Cicely.'

'Yes, I will come. I must give a message to Glass and then I'll come at once.'

Ida looked displeased and as if she might insist.

Minnie put her gloved hand over Cicely's arm and said, 'It is most unfortunate, my dear. The poor man is badly hurt and your grandfather is very angry. It seems that someone took a shot they should not have taken. But still it is not for us to judge these things. The best thing we can do is to go home and be very calm.'

'May I just give my message quietly? It was a promise.'

'Of course, my dear. But then come home. It is the best way in

166

which we can help your grandfather.' Minnie patted Cicely's arm and continued on her way, contriving to sweep Ida along with her before she could protest. Bob Lilburn followed them looking magisterial and grave. He had indicated to Olivia that he expected her to accompany him and he could not understand why she lingered, showing what he considered to be a morbid interest in the unfortunate event; but Lionel Stephens was with her and would no doubt bring her along in due course.

Cicely looked round for Glass and saw him standing near Tom Harker's feet; it was as if Sir Randolph stood guard at his head and Glass at his feet. Cicely approached slowly.

'Is it getting dark?' said Tom loudly.

'Yes, it is beginning to get dark,' said Sir Randolph.

'No wind though, not a breath of wind.' Tom's voice rose and fell as though he were feverish, but since his conversational manner had always tended towards the histrionic, no one quite knew how to interpret the symptom. Sir Randolph continually looked in the direction from which he expected Doctor West. Tom's thoughts seemed to be rambling.

'A dark night, a dry wind and you'll get rabbits. No wind, no rabbits, I've always said. My old mother used to say, if you'd take a drink now and then, if you'd go down the Pub a bit more, Tom Harker, she'd say, you might never been a poacher. But I say I'd rather be a poacher than a drunkard. I'm a rough man, an ignorant man, but I never in my life been the worse for drink. Take a bit of game is one thing, wait for a hare in the roots towards dark, it's natural justice that is. The poor man's pot has got to be filled.'

'Come on now, Tom,' said Glass heartily. 'Remember who you're talking to.'

'I remember, I remember. Is it getting dark?'

'It's not very dark yet, Tom,' said Sir Randolph.

'It's dark to me. It's getting dark to me. It's my belief sir, the bullet has penetrated the brain, I feel it so. To lose the sight of an eye is one thing, but I feel it has penetrated the brain.'

'We shan't have long to wait. Doctor West must be here soon.'

'It has penetrated the brain. I shall be called home. It grows dark. A prayer, I beg you, sir at the last. You and I sir, we may not be always on the same side of things, you are a gentleman and I have always been a poor man but we share one thing sir, we share a God. Say a prayer for me, sir, before I go.'

'Now Tom for Heavens sake, man...' Sir Randolph, momentarily divided between laughter and embarrassment, looked down at the half-concealed face beneath him. The blood was still seeping out of the handkerchief between the fingers. He looked again for the doctor. There was only the unwanted wavering figure of the animal rights fanatic.

'Send someone to get more water from the river,' he said to Glass. 'And someone to run after Lady Nettleby and ask her to send Patten down with some ice from the house directly. Where can Doctor West have got to?'

'Maybe he was out,' said Glass. 'Mrs Page is expecting again any day. But his housekeeper would know. Dan will find him.'

'Too late, too late,' intoned Tom. Then he gave a tremendous groan.

Cicely hovered on the edge of the group, frightened by Tom's voice but determined to deliver her message to Glass. She was also shocked by an apprehension which in fact was a misunderstanding: as she had approached the group round Tom she had intercepted a look between Olivia and Lionel which had expressed such unutterable and infinite sadness that she had immediately assumed that it must have been Lionel who had fired the shot which had hit Tom. She had not spoken to either of them, but as they turned and began to walk very slowly side by side across the field towards the road which led back to the house she looked after them with sympathy; she thought she had never felt anything so deeply as whatever it was they were feeling.

*

'I could have prevented it,' said Lionel eventually.

They had reached the road and were walking towards the lodge gates. It was the first time either had spoken since they had left the little group gathered round Tom Harker by the side of the wood.

'No,' said Olivia.

'If I had refused to join in that absurd rivalry which had somehow started up between us, if I had simply missed a few birds on purpose... I have never shot so competitively as I did today. I don't usually shoot like that. I'm not so keen. I don't

168

bother. I shoot to enjoy myself.'

'That was all you were doing today.'

'No, I was trying to get a better score than Gilbert. God knows why.'

'He provoked you.'

'That's no excuse. I was not as insane as he was but I was a little insane.'

'It was to do with what we were talking about.'

'No.'

'Yes. We were talking about something that was impossible as if it were possible and it was because you were mad in that way that you were mad in the other. We were not thinking clearly. We were not feeling clearly.'

'I can't accept that. Perhaps because I was preoccupied in thinking about us I didn't give enough thought to what I was allowing to happen with Gilbert. That's the most I will allow.'

'We were allowing ourselves to think extravagances. We were not testing them against reality.'

'It was not an extravagance. It was true.'

'It was a dream.'

'I will always dream it.'

'But we have to live in the real world, a world with other people in it, not a dream world, with only us.'

He felt an extraordinary heaviness of heart. It was not that he was going to give up, so much as that he foresaw he might not succeed.

As they approached the lodge gates he said doggedly, 'But it is true that we love each other?'

'Yes, it is true that we love each other.'

'Then I shan't say another word.'

He took her arm in his and they walked the whole length of the drive in silence, between the elms which from time to time let fall a yellowed leaf from their almost bare branches, and past the clumps of beeches and the view towards the lake, and between the fences of post and rail and through the gate beside the cattle grid, and past the black horned sheep grazing concentratedly on the short smooth turf in front of the ha-ha which divided the park from the garden.

*

Glass was talking to Walter Weir, holding out to him his own hard hat (his balding head clean and exposed – it was seldom uncovered) and telling him to take it to the river with any others he could find that would serve the purpose and fill them with water. Cicely noticed two men carrying guns and cartridge bags hovering undecidedly behind him as if they wondered whether they too should fetch water. Percy Maidment and Albert Jarvis had not spoken to each other since the accident and neither was anxious to meet the other's eye.

'You'd best go on home if you don't mind,' Glass said to them. 'Sir Randolph wants everyone to go on home.'

They nodded and set off across the field, but being both puzzled as to what to think about the outcome of a contest into which they had thrown themselves with such passion, they felt no wish to enter into conversation. Percy gradually fell behind. Albert strode on ahead, the more solid of the two. Percy, an undersized wisp of a man, followed in dejection; the day was ruined, as far as he was concerned. His man had won, had beaten the champion; but who was going to remember that now?

'I know it's not really important,' Cicely said to Glass. 'But I promised Osbert I would ask you to make sure someone looked after Tom's dog.'

Glass looked at her blankly for a moment; he had still not recovered from his shock. Having changed Dan's position and told him to act as stop, and then to have heard that the stop had been shot, and then to have discovered that by some extraordinary miracle Tom Harker had decided on his own initiative (and in fact quite rightly) that there ought to be two stops, and had thereby put himself as it were in Dan's place and received the wound which might have been thought to have been intended by Providence for Dan – all this had shaken him deeply. Nevertheless when he did understand what Cicely was saying, he smiled at her.

'I'll see to it myself. Tell Master Osbert not to worry, I'll go down there just as soon as we've got Tom seen to. I'll get her up to my place, in the kennels with the other dogs, she'll be all right there.'

Cicely's thanks were interrupted by a much louder groan from Tom, a sort of quavering bellow, fading to a descending

170

scale of 'Oh, oh, oh!'

Sir Randolph knelt beside him and put his hand on his shoulder.

'Come on Tom, it can't be long before the doctor comes. I'm sorry you've had this wait. We're getting some ice to stop the bleeding. Here, where's that flask again?'

The flask was handed down to him, a worn leather one which had seen much service in the pocket and at the lips of Walter Weir, a faithful follower of the alcoholic faith; but it was held in a hand too white and well manicured to be Walter's. Sir Randolph did not look up. Why did Gilbert Hartlip not go home? There was nothing he could do except embarrass everybody. He would be told soon enough whether or not his victim died; there was no need to hang about to see for himself.

Tom swallowed a mouthful of spirit, then turned his head away.

'Alcohol never interested me,' he said. 'I seen too much of what it can do to a man.' His speech was increasingly slurred; the left side of his jaw was shattered and was beginning to stiffen. 'A smoke I like. A smoke and a chat is a sociable thing. I seen too many men brought low by drink or gambling.'

Glass, to whom this theme of Tom's was familiar, said from his position near Tom's feet, 'Stay quiet, Tom, I would. Relax, that's what you want to do. Don't try to talk.'

'Not talk?' Tom's voice rose. 'Not talk, he says. I've all eternity not to talk, haven't I?'

Sir Randolph had taken a cigarette case from his waistcoat pocket, and now lit a cigarette and held it to Tom's lips, at the same time raising Tom's right hand so that he could hold it himself. Tom inhaled deeply.

'Ah, that's tobacco, that is. Turkish, I shouldn't wonder.'

'Yes, it's Turkish.'

'That's fine tobacco, that is. If I'm to go that's a fine last smoke. It gives me some strength to replace what I feel draining out of me. Draining out of me it is, sir. Give me a prayer, sir. Don't deny me that. It's your way to pray – 'tis you that orders up the prayers in Church, the Vicar only prays what prayers you tell him to, even I know that that hardly crosses the doorstep of the Church from year to year. Say a prayer, sir; I'll say Amen.'

'If that's what you want, Tom.' Sir Randolph put his hand on

Tom's shoulder, cleared his throat and repeated last Sunday's Collect at high speed – in fact, such was his embarrassment, he more or less gabbled it.

'Oh almighty and most merciful God of thy bountiful goodness keep us we beseech thee from all things that may hurt us, that we being ready both in body and soul may cheerfully accomplish those things that thou wouldest have done through Jesus Christ Our Lord, Amen.'

'Amen!' echoed Tom loudly. 'Amen, I say. Amen! Amen!'

He rolled his head from side to side, puffing at the cigarette that he still held in his right hand. The movement was obviously extremely painful and caused him to groan as loudly as before, but at the same time his excitement seemed to increase. 'Don't stop, sir, I beg you. More prayers, more prayers.'

Sir Randolph looked desperately over the field towards the gate through which Doctor West might be expected to come.

'We could say the Lord's Prayer together,' he said, and began, 'Our Father which Art in Heaven. . . .'

'Our Father . . .' Tom seemed to seize on the words with a kind of greed, although as he repeated the prayer phrase by phrase after Sir Randolph his words ran into each other, becoming increasingly blurred, a difficulty he tried to make up for by increasing the volume.

Cicely was standing a few feet away, having resisted Tibor's efforts to persuade her to leave after giving her message to Glass. She felt the scene infinitely distressing but could not bring herself to leave it, determined only not to draw attention to herself by sobbing aloud. Cornelius, looking at her across the prostrate Tom and the kneeling Sir Randolph, across the other silent watchers, across Sir Randolph's quiet voice and its terrible loud echo, would have liked to walk round to speak to her, stand beside her, lead her away, but felt frozen by his own helplessness and by the curious sensation he had as if he were watching the whole scene reflected in a mirror or through a window he could not open.

As they reached the end of the prayer and the laborious indistinct Amens continued, Sir Randolph covered both of Tom's hands with his. The cigarette had dropped so he held the right hand on Tom's chest and the other over the blood-soaked handkerchief and said, 'Now say after me, Into Thy hands O

Lord . . .'

'Thy hands O Lord . . .'

'I commend my Spirit.'

'Commend my spirit . . .'

There was a merciful silence. He lay still. Sir Randolph, leaning over him holding his hands, looked again towards the gate and said quietly, 'It's all right, Tom, here's Doctor West.'

Dan was leading the way, running; the Doctor following, bag in hand. And then Tom Harker suddenly sat upright, startling Sir Randolph who steadied him by putting his arms round him, shouted at the top of his voice though with the same indistinctness as before, 'God save the British Empire!' and fell back against Sir Randolph, covering with crimson the encircling white shirt sleeves.

'Oh God,' said Cornelius, as if to say, now look what they've done.

He felt overwhelmingly that apart from himself, the helpless spectator, they were all in it together, the big men in tweeds, the smaller men in smocks, the sorrowing girl, the bleeding victim. What the ritual was that had required the sacrifice he could not exactly say, only that he was outside it, condemned by something in himself, some cowardice, some over-cerebration, only to watch, to comment, scold, diagnose, analyse, but not to cure; the cure could not come from a non-participant, from someone who was not part of the game, for how could a mere spectator be expected to be listened to when he wanted to tell the players not just that they were using the wrong rules but that they were playing the wrong game?

Sir Randolph gently lowered Tom onto his former pillow. The faces turned to the doctor, who approached, and knelt, and put his ear to Tom's chest and looked at Sir Randolph and shook his head.

*

Cicely walked rapidly across the field. She had turned away just as Doctor West knelt down. Tibor followed her.

She seemed to him a frail figure, walking so determinedly in front of him, both hands holding her skirt as she crossed the long damp grass towards the gate which led on to the road. Poor little creature, he thought, she should never have been allowed to see that. He caught up with her, and taking one of her small gloved hands in his tucked it into his arm.

'I am so sorry. I should have insisted that you came away.'

'Why?' She was pale but not tearful.

'Such a scene is not suitable for a young girl.'

'As a matter of fact,' said Cicely, speaking rather distinctly. 'There is nothing that is not suitable for a young girl.'

'Nothing?'

'Nothing. Not even murder.'

'Ah, come now. This was an accident.'

'Accidental murder then.'

They walked a little way in silence. This was not quite the mood Tibor had expected.

'Unfortunately it does sometimes happen,' he said.

'It has never happened here.'

'No? Well then, you have been fortunate. I have known it elsewhere, I assure you. Of course it's more often a case of wounding.'

'Grandfather will never forgive Lord Hartlip.'

'It could have happened to anyone. It was very bad luck.'

She continued to walk rather fast in silence. It appeared that she was angry, rather than shocked or distressed as he had anticipated.

'Come, Cicely,' he said in expiation. 'He was only a peasant.'

There was another silence. She gave a long trembling sigh. Then she said softly, 'Yes, he was only a peasant. But we all knew him, you see.'

Tibor felt that he had not been adequate to the occasion, but if he could not gauge her mood how could he meet it? He had expected tears and had been ready with a strong supporting arm and a monogrammed handkerchief; now, puzzled, he would have liked to change the subject altogether but felt it was a little soon after the event. They continued their silent progress until, reaching the gate which led onto the road, he held it open for her and said, looking at her a little pathetically, 'Why don't we talk, just quite quietly, about how you will come and visit me in Hungary?'

She paused, one hand on the gate, and then she sighed again, and then she looked him full in the face with a bright, eloquent, warm, inexplicable gaze, and said, 'Oh I think I shall never visit you in Hungary.'

*

There was another shooting party at Nettleby, of course. The late November shoot, already organised, duly took place. The guests were different, the birds were plentiful, the weather though much colder was dry and bright. No one enjoyed it as much as usual; even for those who had not been there when it happened the shadow of the accident fell over the day. For the rest of the season Sir Randolph went out only with a few neighbours, or with Harry Stamp and his grandson Marcus. By the time the next season came round a bigger shooting party had begun, in Flanders.

By that time too a small notice had appeared in the Court Circular of the Times: 'Lord and Lady Hartlip have taken up residence in Kenya and their permanent address in future will be . . .'

There had been an inquest and a verdict of accidental death and an expression of sympathy from the Coroner for the unfortunate sportsman whose skill was well known and who had certainly not deserved this stroke of bad luck. (The Coroner, in other words, simply grovelled to Lord Hartlip, but no one seemed to think this odd, or even deserving of comment.) The Hartlips continued their lives as before; only the trouble was that in their small world the news very quickly circulated that the accident had not in fact been bad luck, and that Gilbert had been shooting dangerously. He's losing his skill, they said, and can't accept it; it's making him a dangerous shot; he's not the great sportsman he used to be; one finds oneself reluctant, they said, to go on asking him to shoot.

Aline, quick to sense the direction of opinion, gave a series of dinner parties. She tempted her guests with musicians, with Russian Grand Dukes, famous beauties, Society painters, great newspaper proprietors, Sir Reuben Hergesheimer and high-class bridge. Invitations to shoot failed to follow. Aline was confident that all they had to do was to sit it out, but Gilbert was too proud for that. He had spent several months in East Africa, big-game shooting, and had taken a particular liking to Nairobi and the White Highlands. He sold his estates in England and bought a farm near Nanyuki. Aline, at first horrified, soon settled down. She took up rifle shooting herself, and carried on a discreet affair with the ne'er-do-well scion of a noble family who had been sent to Kenya to redeem himself. At least, she felt, one was out of the way of that ghastly War.

*

Violet and Osbert went down with Nanny to see Tom Harker's dog.

She had been taken to the kennels next to the gamekeeper's cottage. Dan Glass let her out to see the children and she came creeping towards them with her sheepdog's subservient crawl, wagging her tail and smiling so that she made herself sneeze.

Violet crouched down to stroke her.

'Isn't she sweet?'

The dog, who did not know Violet and was not used to being petted, snarled and gave a quick snap very close to Violet's face. Violet fell over backwards, but quickly picked herself up. She had gone very red but did not cry because she did not want Dan to think she was a baby.

'If you want them to be kind,' said Dan, 'you have to start being kind to them when they're very young.'

Violet nodded, and consented to go with him to see whether the hens had laid any eggs; but the episode stayed in her mind as a thoroughly unsatisfactory one, of which she felt obscurely ashamed.

Dan was to move quite soon to lodgings in Oxford. His father had been to see Sir Randolph soon after the shooting accident, and had told him that after all he would like on behalf of Dan to accept Sir Randolph's offer. Sir Randolph had been pleased, and because he knew how hard Glass had taken that episode (as if it reflected in some way upon his management of the shoot) he guessed that it had something to do with his change of heart, but feeling that it was no concern of his did not ask further.

Glass felt that God had spoken. He, the father, had told his son to stand in the place where it was written that someone should die, and God had substituted another man so that the son should be spared. It was clear then that God had something particular in mind for the son, and Glass could not persuade himself that that something was that he should be a gamekeeper like his father before him. With a heavy heart therefore he submitted himself to God's purpose and going to Sir Randolph said, Take him. Since everybody else considered it a great opportunity for the boy and a cause for rejoicing he kept his sorrow and forboding to himself.

*

Olivia and Lionel corresponded regularly until the second year of the War. They wrote about the books they had been reading and the importance of friendship, and other things of that kind. They also wrote with tender concern about each other's hopes and fears, and about the pain of separation. Lionel was killed in October 1915 at the battle of Loos. Olivia's letters were found among his possessions and sent in due course to his mother, who read them with displeasure. For some years she had hoped her son would marry and she resolved now to hate for ever this woman who had evidently stood in the way and so deprived her of the grandchildren who might have consoled her for the loss of her son. Grief wore down her resolution and made her more charitable: eventually she wrote to Olivia, sending her the letters, and later they met.

The letters gave Mrs Stephens no clear indication as to whether or not her son had ever had what she would have called une affaire à outrance with the beautiful Lady Lilburn; all she knew was that the woman who had written so often and so tenderly to her son had cared for him and more than that had known him, for though she saw only one side of the correspondence, it reflected the son she knew and not a stranger. Neither woman was particularly disposed towards intimate confidences, but they had in common their concern to keep his memory alive. Mrs Stephens saw no point in struggling to maintain an estate without an heir; after the War she sold it to a school and took a lease on the dower house of the Lilburn estate. Over the years she and Olivia developed the kind of relationship they might have had had they been mother and daughter-in-law, sometimes critical, occasionally exasperated, generally affectionate.

'Old Mrs Stephens is a terrific asset,' Bob Lilburn said. 'She's so sharp she makes me yell with laugher.'

Bob continued to have his own particular splendour, survived the War with gallantry, sat on committees with dignity, never lost his increasingly old-fashioned concern with good form. He became a bit of a philanderer in a gentlemanly kind of way, was to be seen escorting charming Society ladies here or there, to the opera or to the races, while Olivia's interests came to be more and more in the country. As the years went on she became rather solid in appearance and her husband often wished she would do something about her clothes; nevertheless even when she was quite old young people who were told she had once been beautiful would say, But she still is. She was fond of her husband. The disillusionment consequent upon unfulfilled expectations faded, along with the desolation of Lionel's loss. The sound of Bob's car, arriving back from London, his step in the hall, his voice calling for her, never failed to lighten her heart, make her smile, ask the news; she was a deeply domesticated wife. If their four children were each in their different ways more open to adventure, more developed in sympathy and imagination, more likely to have – as Olivia had once thought of Lionel – 'nothing they were not prepared to consider', than might have been expected from the offspring of such a conventional father – that was because Olivia had, quite consciously and with the unspoken connivance of Mrs Stephens, dedicated them to the memory of the man whose character she considered to have been, if not quite perfect, even so more or less what God must have had in mind when it first occurred to him to make Man. In one of his letters Lionel had written to her, 'You wrote something about me which was not true, something which made me out to be a better thing altogether than I am. So much so that then the strange thought crossed my mind that if you have illusions perhaps I have them too, and perhaps you are less perfect than I think you. And when I had stopped scolding myself for the incredible baseness of that idea, I thought anyway, anyway, my dearest and most adored Olivia, while we can, for as long as we can, oh let us believe . . .' She never ceased to do so.

*

In the dark December of 1913 Cornelius Cardew decided to become a monk.

The aftermath of the sense of despair which had overtaken him as he witnessed Tom Harker's last moments – a despair which seemed to become more metaphysical the more he thought about it – had been a period of fierce thinking in which, walking steadily through mile upon mile of Surrey woods and fields he faced the fact that he had lost faith in the power of reason. Reason could not halt the rush of victor and victim into the abyss, socialist planning could not regulate the human heartbeat, the lessons of love were too harsh to be learnt without the ferocious discipline of faith.

When he tried to explain some of this to Ada she thought him mad. She saw no sign in the world around her of the Apocalypse he seemed to anticipate, and as he was extremely vague as to the form he expected it to take, whether war or revolution, and if war whether between nations, classes, or sexes, and if revolution whether of the workers, the intellectuals, or even the beasts of the field, she thought it likely that he was deranged, and consulted their trusted friend and neighbour the philosopher H.W. Brigginshaw. He after some consideration came to the conclusion that Cornelius was suffering from mania, and after further consideration that the mania was religious. He therefore put it to him that the logical course of action was to enter a monastery.

It is not easy for a man approaching late middle-age to be accepted as a novice monk. The abbots whom Cornelius visited, while convinced of his fervour, doubted his capacity to withstand the physical hardships of a novice's life. It was only when Cornelius, about to write to the Abbot of a monastery which incorporated a boys' public school, recognized the name as that of a former schoolfellow and so reminded him in his letter of the rigours of their early years and pointed out that no novitiate could be harsher than that one, that he found someone disposed to look sympathetically on his aspirations.

He entered into his new life with enthusiasm. Arrangements were put in train for the dissolution of his marriage. (About this time H. W. Brigginshaw unexpectedly left the Hindhead district and moved to Hampstead; later on Ada married a vegetarian from Cheam). Cornelius did not really achieve happiness in his new vocation until, it being one of the duties of the Order he had joined to provide a parish priest for the small congregation of Catholics in that part of Somerset where the monastery was situated, he was given this function, and finding himself in circumstances which suited his gregarious nature better than the more solitary life he had been leading within the monastery walls, he became more cheerful and even grew quite fat. He had the good fortune to find as the newly arrived local landowner a millionaire who had made great profit from the manufacture of armaments during the War and was now suffering from a troubled conscience. In no time Cornelius had interested him in any number of schemes. What with arranging interdenominational oecuminical conferences (to the alarm of his superiors and indeed of the authorities of all the Churches involved) and supporting the Peace Pledge, the Anti-Vivisection Society and Major Douglas's Movement for Social Credit, Cornelius managed not only to relieve his patron of the burden of inordinate wealth, but to provide for himself in his declining years the happiness which comes from total conviction as to the usefulness of one's work.

*

Cicely had been right; she never went to Hungary. It seemed to her that she had taken all the fine frivolities, the fur-lined sledges racing over the snow-covered plain, the waltz in the glass-walled ballroom, the wolf-hunt, the pinnacled castles, the sweeping curtsey to the Emperor himself, and heaped them like a great bundle of white flowers onto poor Tom Harker's grave. She could not prevent herself from thinking sometimes that it had been rather a wonderful thing to have done.

She was a nurse all through the war; so was Grizel Warburton, so were the Walker Kerr girls. There was a time, after Marcus was killed on the Somme, when Cicely felt she would never have a frivolous thought again as long as she lived; but she underestimated her own resilience.

'The girls in their uniforms have learnt to glide along the passages like nuns,' Sir Randolph wrote in his Game Book (the house had been turned into a Convalescent Home). 'But the laughter that often follows their progress through the wards isn't quite the same – or at least one rather hopes it isn't quite the same – as that which would follow a cortège of Holy Sisters.'

The giant fist that took the young men of that generation in its grasp somehow allowed Dan Glass to slip through its fingers. He survived the War. He even, to his father's surprise, survived being educated. He continued his scientific studies and became a great man in his profession. He still walked often in the woods with his father, delighting him as he had always done by his acute observation of natural phenomena and by his sweet simplicity of heart.

Sir Randolph lived to a great age. Minnie died in the influenza epidemic which followed the Armistice in 1918. When he had recovered from his grief he was glad she had not lived to see the post-War decline of civilization. Although he felt himself now too old to be able quite to make out what were the assumptions, orthodoxies, hypocrisies, even events, of the new age, he was certain that they embodied changes for the worse, a sort of mass loss of memory, and the replacement of the common understandings of a civilised society by the destructive egotism of a barbaric one. He had not yet found himself obliged to take to the hills, but he did consider that he was living after the end of the Age of Humanism; and for such a situation a quiet style of life seemed appropriate. Since it was anyway the one he had always preferred, his old age was not unhappy.

Sometimes in his study, looking at the picture over the fireplace of the mysterious rider on the impatient horse and the infinite blue distance, he thought of all the young men who had died and all the endeavours which had failed, and of the cruel wastefulness of a spendthrift Nature. More than once at such moments it was Osbert, arrived unexpectedly from goodness knew where, who dispelled such thoughts with his own extraordinary gaiety; but the story of Osbert (who took to Art) belongs to the story of the Twenties, a period of which Sir Randolph, despite his deep affection for his grandson, entirely disapproved.

FOR THE BEST IN PAPERBACKS, LOOK FOR THE 🐧

In every corner of the world, on every subject under the sun, Penguin represents quality and variety – the very best in publishing today.

For complete information about books available from Penguin – including Pelicans, Puffins, Peregrines and Penguin Classics – and how to order them, write to us at the appropriate address below. Please note that for copyright reasons the selection of books varies from country to country.

In the United Kingdom: For a complete list of books available from Penguin in the U.K., please write to *Dept E.P., Penguin Books Ltd, Harmondsworth, Middlesex, UB7 0DA*

In the United States: For a complete list of books available from Penguin in the U.S., please write to *Dept BA, Penguin, 299 Murray Hill Parkway, East Rutherford, New Jersey 07073*

In Canada: For a complete list of books available from Penguin in Canada, please write to *Penguin Books Canada Ltd, 2801 John Street, Markham, Ontario L3R 1B4*

In Australia: For a complete list of books available from Penguin in Australia, please write to the *Marketing Department, Penguin Books Australia Ltd, P.O. Box 257, Ringwood, Victoria 3134*

In New Zealand: For a complete list of books available from Penguin in New Zealand, please write to the *Marketing Department, Penguin Books (NZ) Ltd, Private Bag, Takapuna, Auckland 9*

In India: For a complete list of books available from Penguin, please write to *Penguin Overseas Ltd, 706 Eros Apartments, 56 Nehru Place, New Delhi, 110019*

In Holland: For a complete list of books available from Penguin in Holland, please write to *Penguin Books Nederland B.V., Postbus 195, NL–1380AD Weesp, Netherlands*

In Germany: For a complete list of books available from Penguin, please write to *Penguin Books Ltd, Friedrichstrasse 10 – 12, D–6000 Frankfurt Main 1, Federal Republic of Germany*

In Spain: For a complete list of books available from Penguin in Spain, please write to *Longman Penguin España, Calle San Nicolas 15, E–28013 Madrid, Spain*

Also by Isabel Colegate in Penguins

STATUES IN A GARDEN

The passion, the politics – and the folly – of that glittering, decadent era ...

As the long, golden days slipped by, the Weston household prepared for the wedding, serenely unaware that something was being destroyed. Then Philip, the insouciant, restless nephew, loses his uncle a small fortune on the Stock Exchange – but Aylmer Weston, a member of Asquith's cabinet, is too preoccupied with the Irish question to acknowledge this threat to his ordered, privileged life. Driven by a private fury, Philip goes further – and precipitates a tragedy.

'A subtle and graceful novel ... Miss Colegate is beautifully precise and invests that sticky feverish time with just the right mixture of doomed fun, melancholy and faintly lascivious despair' – *Observer*

'She writes so gracefully and with such skill that her "private fable" acquires a truly fabulous quality' – *The Times Literary Supplement*

and .

The Orlando Trilogy comprising *Orlando King*, *Orlando at the Brazen Threshold*, and *Agatha*.

FOR THE BEST IN PAPERBACKS, LOOK FOR THE 🐧

A CHOICE OF PENGUIN FICTION

Trade Wind   M. M. Kaye

An enthralling blend of history, adventure and romance from the author of the bestselling *The Far Pavilions*

The Ghost Writer   Philip Roth

Philip Roth's celebrated novel about a young writer who meets and falls in love with Anne Frank in New England – or so he thinks. 'Brilliant, witty and extremely elegant' – *Guardian*

Small World   David Lodge

Shortlisted for the 1984 Booker Prize, *Small World* brings back Philip Swallow and Maurice Zapp for a jet-propelled journey into hilarity. 'The most brilliant and also the funniest novel that he has written' – *London Review of Books*

Village Christmas   'Miss Read'

The village of Fairacre finds its peace disrupted by the arrival in its midst of the noisy, cheerful Emery family – and only the advent of a Christmas baby brings things back to normal. 'A sheer joy' – *Glasgow Evening Times*

Treasures of Time   Penelope Lively

Beautifully written, acutely observed, and filled with Penelope Lively's sharp but compassionate wit, *Treasures of Time* explores the relationship between the lives we live and the lives we think we live.

Absolute Beginners   Colin MacInnes

The first 'teenage' novel, the classic of youth and disenchantment, *Absolute Beginners* is part of MacInnes's famous London trilogy – and now a brilliant film. 'MacInnes caught it first – and best' – *Harpers and Queen*

FOR THE BEST IN PAPERBACKS, LOOK FOR THE 🐧

A CHOICE OF PENGUIN FICTION

Money   Martin Amis

Savage, audacious and demonically witty – a story of urban excess. 'Terribly, terminally funny: laughter in the dark, if ever I heard it' – *Guardian*

Lolita   Vladimir Nabokov

Shot through with Nabokov's mercurial wit, quicksilver prose and intoxicating sensuality, *Lolita* is one of the world's great love stories. 'A great book' – Dorothy Parker

Dinner at the Homesick Restaurant   Anne Tyler

Through every family run memories which bind them together – in spite of everything. 'She is a witch. Witty, civilized, curious, with her radar ears and her quill pen dipped on one page in acid and on the next in orange liqueur . . . a wonderful writer' – John Leonard in *The New York Times*

Glitz   Elmore Leonard

Underneath the Boardwalk, a lot of insects creep. But the creepiest of all was Teddy. 'After finishing *Glitz*, I went out to the bookstore and bought everything else of Elmore Leonard I could find' – Stephen King

The Battle of Pollocks Crossing   J. L. Carr

Nominated for the Booker McConnell Prize, this is a moving, comic masterpiece. 'Wayward, ambiguous, eccentric . . . a fascinatingly outlandish novel' – *Guardian*

The Dreams of an Average Man   Dyan Sheldon

Tony Rivera is lost. Sandy Grossman Rivera is leaving. And Maggie Kelly is giving up. In the steamy streets of summertime Manhattan, the refugees of the sixties generation wonder what went wrong. 'Satire, dramatic irony and feminist fun . . . lively, forceful and funny' – *Listener*

FOR THE BEST IN PAPERBACKS, LOOK FOR THE 🐧

A CHOICE OF PENGUIN FICTION

Bliss   Jill Tweedie

When beautiful Lady Clare La Fontaine marries for money, she enters a glittering world of luxury and corruption and discovers the darker side of sexual politics in Jill Tweedie's blockbusting, bestselling novel. 'Huge, vital and passionately written' – *Cosmopolitan*

Fair Stood the Wind for France   H. E. Bates

It was France, and wartime – and not the moment to fall in love. 'Perhaps the finest novel of the war . . . a lovely book which makes the heart beat with pride' – *Daily Telegraph*

The Flight from the Enchanter   Iris Murdoch

A group of people have elected ambiguous and fascinating Mischa Fox to be their god. And thus begins the battle between sturdy common sense and dangerous enchantment. Elegant, sparkling and unputdownable, this is Iris Murdoch at her best.

Very Good, Jeeves!   P. G. Wodehouse

When Bertie Wooster lands in the soup, only the 'infinite sagacity' of Jeeves can pull him out. 'A riot . . . There are eleven tales in this volume and each is the best' – *Observer*

To Have and To Hold   Deborah Moggach

Viv was giving her sister, Ann, the best present she could think of – a baby. How Viv, Ann and their husbands cope with this extraordinary situation is the subject of this tender, triumphant and utterly absorbing story. Now a powerful TV drama.

A Dark and Distant Shore   Reay Tannahill

Vilia is the unforgettable heroine, Kinveil Castle is her destiny, in this full-blooded saga spanning a century of Victoriana, empire, hatred and love affairs. 'A marvellous blend of *Gone with the Wind* and *The Thorn Birds*' – *Daily Mirror*